Uprooted

A Canadian War Story

Also by Lynne Reid Banks

The Adventures of King Midas
Alice-by-Accident
Angela and Diabola
Bad Cat, Good Cat
The Dungeon
The Fairy Rebel
The Farthest-away Mountain
Harry the Poisonous Centipede
Harry the Poisonous Centipede's Big Adventure
Harry the Poisonous Centipede Goes to Sea
I, Houdini
The Magic Hare
Maura's Angel
Stealing Stacey
Tiger, Tiger

The Indian in the Cupboard
Return of the Indian
Secret of the Indian
The Mystery of the Cupboard
Key to the Indian

Young Adult Fiction

One More River
Broken Bridge
My Darling Villain
The Writing on the Wall
Melusine, A Mystery

Lynne Reid Banks

Uprooted

A Canadian War Story

HarperCollins *Children's Books*

First published in Great Britain by HarperCollins *Children's Books* 2014
HarperCollins *Children's Books* is a division of HarperCollins*Publishers* Ltd,
77–85 Fulham Palace Road, Hammersmith, London W6 8JB

Visit us on the web at
www.harpercollins.co.uk

1

Uprooted: A Canadian War Story
Text © Lynne Reid Banks 2014

Lynne Reid Banks asserts the moral right to be identified as
the author of this work.

Text from 'The Spirit' by Will Eisner on page 96 © Warner Bros.

ISBN: 978-0-00-813235-4

Typeset in Bembo by Palimpsest Book Production Limited,
Falkirk, Stirlingshire

Printed and bound in the United States of
America by RR Donnelley

To Glady who read and liked it first.
To 'Cameron' who wouldn't read it at all!
And in memory of 'Alex' – Pat Reid Banks, my mother.

Prologue

O ur families travelled to Liverpool from London, where I lived, and Cheltenham, where Cameron lived, to see us off.

My mother and father, two aunties, an uncle – even Grampy, our mothers' father, made the journey, although Grampy was old and not well, but he *would* come. And Shott, his dog. He wouldn't leave Shott behind in case he got bombed.

Travelling by train was crowded and very uncomfortable in wartime, with all the soldiers and people being moved around the country on war work. But Shott was popular. Grampy had to stop the soldiers feeding him. I'd never liked him much – he sometimes growled and even snapped – but now, for some reason, I wanted him on my knee. I stroked and stroked his curly fur and for once he let me. He was quivering. Dogs sense things. And there was a lot to sense. The whole carriage was crackling with feelings.

Cameron kept looking at Shott, but he didn't touch him. I didn't always know what Cameron was thinking because he kept his feelings shut in. But I knew then – he was thinking of Bubbles, his dog. The 'Bulgarian bulldog'. Leaving Bubbles must have been awful. Not as bad as leaving both his parents, but awful just the same.

I kept my eyes down a lot of the way. I didn't want to look at my beautiful daddy, grim-faced, holding my mother's hand. Hardly talking. Or at my Auntie Millie, Cameron's mother, keeping Cameron close to her. Uncle Jack, reading a medical journal. And Grampy. He only spoke to Shott. I think he was struggling not to cry. My mother was his favourite, and she was going away.

Mummy didn't say much, either, except to ask me every now and then if I was all right, if I wanted anything. Only the aunts chatted, brightly, trying to keep up our spirits. Auntie Millie, who was the liveliest of us all and could always cheer us up, had her work cut out this time. Mummy, Cameron and I were going to get on a ship and sail far away. Who knew when, if ever, we'd all be together again?

I didn't know how I felt. I think I just didn't know how to feel. There was too much feeling all around me. If I thought anything on that long train journey, it was, *I wish this was over. I wish we could be on the ship.* Did I not mind leaving Daddy, leaving the aunts, leaving England? I couldn't get to grips with that. I had Mummy. I had Cameron — though not then; he just sat by the window watching England go by. Auntie's arm was round his shoulders but once I saw him twitch as if he simply wanted to be left alone.

At Liverpool docks, I remember standing there with them all around us. The ship's great side — grey, dotted with portholes — loomed up beside us. The gangway was ready and the loudspeakers were telling us to go on board. Grampy clasped me to his little round stomach.

"Be a good girl, Lindy," he said. "Help your dear mother. Keep your eyes and your mind open. New things are frightening at first but sometimes they turn out better than the old. And don't worry about us!" He held me away and smiled through his tears. Then he boomed, "I always wanted to go to Canada! Wonderful country! It'll be a great adventure!"

I saw over Grampy's shoulder Cameron's parents hugging him. And Daddy holding Mummy tight. Then Daddy held me tight. His moustache scratched my cheek and it was wet. Daddy crying? Never. I'd never seen him cry. It must be the rain… I held him round the waist… Then somehow we'd left them and were on the ship, standing against the rail, waving and waving. Shott was barking up at us, shrill little goodbye yaps. Then the ship's hooter drowned out every other sound, the saddest note I'd ever heard.

Chapter One

The Voyage

The sea journey, Liverpool to Montreal, took five days. It was summer, 1940 – the first summer of World War Two – but the ocean didn't seem to know it was summer. It didn't want us on it. It pitched our ship, the *Duchess of Atholl*, from end to end and from side to side, and then in a sort of swirl, like a spoon stirring, which was the worst.

When you're seasick you can't think about anything else. Nine times on the first day out of Liverpool I threw up – twice over the rail, three times in the washbasin in our cabin, three times on the deck before I could reach the rail, and once at dinner in the dining room in front of everybody.

I shouldn't have gone to dinner of course. Cameron didn't, but then he was on hunger strike. He wouldn't leave our cabin or eat anything we brought him from the dining room to tempt him. He didn't eat a thing for two days. *What doesn't go in, can't come out,* as Mummy used to say, so he wasn't sick even once. I tried to coax him out by telling him about the life-drills.

"But you have to! Everyone has to do lifeboat drill!"

"Leave me alone."

"But what if the ship sinks?"

"I don't care if it does!"

By the time he decided to come out of our cabin and out of his strike, the worst was over. The ocean had calmed down. Even I wasn't being sick any more, and I was able to show him around Our Ship.

It was a big ship, with two funnels and three decks. It had a large lounge and two dining rooms with tables and chairs fixed to the floor. Not much else was fixed. If your glass of water started to slide, you had to drop your knife, quick, and grab it.

I told Cameron about the boat-drills again. When a siren blew, we had to take our lifebelts and go to our stations. Everyone on board knew where their station was. Ours was on the port side – the left – near the back of the ship. I showed Cameron our lifeboat, swinging overhead.

"How do you think we'll get into it?" I asked. I'd been worried about this, being a bit plump and not very athletic.

"They'll bring it down level with the deck then they'll open the rail – here. See? There's a gate – and we'll have to jump in."

I didn't speak. I didn't think I could jump that far. Especially the way the ship could rock... Perhaps a sailor would lift me in. I wondered if Mummy would be able to jump. If she couldn't, I wouldn't let the sailor lift me in without her. I could imagine the lifeboat dropping down into the sea with Cameron in it and Mummy and me still on the sinking ship. Only I knew Mummy wouldn't be parted from Cameron.

Cameron shared Mummy's and my cabin, but he nearly hadn't. Mummy made it happen. On the first day, when we'd pulled out of Liverpool Harbour, an officer showed us to a cabin for two down on the lowest deck. Mummy took one look through the narrow doorway, at the tiny room with an upper and lower bunk and no window, and said, "I'm very sorry, officer, but there must be some mistake."

"No mistake, madam." He looked at his clipboard. "Hanks – that's the name, isn't it? You and your little girl are in here."

"No," said Mummy, politely but firmly. "There are three of us. Where is my nephew to sleep?"

"Male passengers over the age of eleven have to sleep in all-male cabins."

"My nephew is sleeping with me. I am responsible for him. How can I be, if he's somewhere else?"

"I'm sorry, madam—"

"Please don't be sorry. Just give me another cabin with three berths in it. In any case I can't sleep down here, in such a tiny space. I suffer from claustrophobia."

This was true. When she was little, Mummy had been playing hide-and-seek with her sisters at a party. She'd hidden in a wardrobe in an upstairs room. The door had stuck. She'd shouted and hammered on the door for what felt like hours and finally she panicked and banged so hard the wardrobe fell over, and since then she'd been terribly afraid of being shut in small spaces.

She wasn't panicking now, but she was an actress. She made a sort of mad gleam come into her eye and did a funny twitchy thing she could do with her face. One of my favourite stories was how, when she was on tour with a play, she would sit on the train and do twitches whenever someone who wasn't one of the actors tried to come into their carriage.

It had worked then, and it worked now.

The officer took one horrified look at the twitchings and said, "Oh. Well, that's different. I'll see what I can do."

And before long we were led upstairs (up the *companionway*) to a higher level and shown a cabin for four with a porthole. We could see the sea through it, and although we were told we mustn't open it, it was much better than being in the dark, stuffy cabin downstairs, where we would have been "battened under the hatches", as Mummy said later.

"Have we got this whole cabin to ourselves?" I asked. "The spare bunk too?"

"Yes," she said. "It's for the suitcases."

"You are clever, Auntie," said Cameron in a strange, flat voice. He went and lay on one of the bottom bunks, took his favourite book, *England, Their England*, out of his backpack, and began to read.

"Absurd," Mummy muttered. "Off somewhere in a cabin full of men! Imagine what your mother would say to me!"

I saw Cameron bite hard on his lips.

What must it be like, not to have your mother with you? To have left her behind to be bombed? I wondered.

I squeezed his hand, but he took it away from me to turn a page. Cameron never liked you to see him showing any weakness.

Now, standing on the deck, I showed him how the great propellers or 'screws' churned up the water into a boiling white froth, leaving a spreading trail across the sea behind us. I loved to stand on the lowest deck where I was closest to this seething mass of white water. Cameron stood beside me for a while, gazing back the way we'd come. He looked so stricken I thought he might go on hunger strike again.

But then he went off by himself. He wasn't satisfied with just seeing the parts of the ship that any passenger could see. Before the third day was over, he'd made friends with one of the crew and managed to get down into the engine room. He emerged from the hatchway looking happier than I'd seen him look for a long time. Also dirtier.

"You should see the engines!" he said. "Huge. Fires roaring away in great tunnels. The way they have to work to keep them going! They let me throw a chunk of coal in. I threw it like a cricket ball."

I felt happier than I'd felt so far too. Cameron – my Cameron – was back.

The captain had heard about my marathon sick day. At dinner on that third evening, he was moving among the dining tables saying a few words to some of the passengers, and he stopped next to ours.

"Are you the little girl who was sick *nine times* on our first day out?" he asked with a smile.

I said I was, feeling ashamed of being 'feak and weeble', as Daddy would have called it.

"Well, I think that's a ship's record," he said. "I'll put it in the log! Are you feeling better now? How's your little Derby Kelly?"

"My what?" I mumbled.

"Derby Kelly – belly," he said, patting his through his uniform, and everyone at the table (there were eight altogether) laughed, especially one woman, who said, "How do you know Cockney rhyming slang, Captain?"

"By being born within the sound of Bow Bells," he said. Some of the others looked surprised. "They have to take all sorts in wartime," the Captain said with a faint smile.

I asked Mummy later what he meant.

"Being born within the sound of the bells of Bow Church is supposed to be the mark of a true Londoner," she said. "But Cockneys usually talk working class. That's why that woman was surprised. Because working-class men don't often get to be captains."

"And what's rhyming slang?"

"Oh, that's fun," she said. "Now let me see. Apples and pears are stairs. Frog and toad is a road. Barnet Fair is hair. Rub-a-dub-dub is a –?" She looked at us, expectantly.

My mind was a blank, but Cameron said, "A pub?"

"Yes!" said Mummy.

"What's 'war'?" Cameron asked with a frown.

"I don't know. 'Beastly bore', perhaps… You'd better ask the captain."

So I decided to do that. After all, he had spoken to me, and after dinner several people who'd been at tables near us stopped me and said, "Aren't you the lucky girl, being singled out by the captain!" I thought we were practically friends.

So the next morning (the fourth day of our voyage, by which time I was feeling as if I'd been on the ship for a large part of my life) I waited around at the foot of the bridge. Cameron had told me that if the engine room was the stomach of the ship, the bridge was its brain. There was a sailor at the bottom of the steps leading to it and when I asked if I could see the captain, he said, "Sorry, miss, he's busy steering the ship just now."

"I only want to ask him something."

"You and half the people on board!" he said.

"I want to ask him," I persisted, "what's rhyming slang for 'war'."

"Bless you," he said. "You don't need to trouble the captain for that. I can tell you! It's 'buckets of gore'. Or 'buckets' for short. And ain't it the bleeding truth!"

I knew 'bleeding' was a bad swear word. *Naughty little curse words — bother, dash and blow — lead you on to worse words, and take you down below!* Nanny used to say. I just said, "Thank you," and ran to find Cameron to tell him. But he was already in the middle of a group of boys and I knew I should keep clear. When boys get together they don't want girls hanging around.

That night, tucked into our bunks before Mummy came to join us (she liked to walk around the deck on her own before she went to sleep) I dared to ask Cameron why he'd gone on strike.

"Why do you think, Lind?" he said. He sounded impatient.

"Because they made you leave England?"

"England. Parents. School. Friends. The war. Everything."

"Do you mind leaving the war?"

"*Of course*," he said, as if I was being stupid.

"But there'll be bombs. Maybe Hitler will come," I said.

"And do you want to be safe in Canada if that happens?"

Yes, I do, I thought. But he made me feel that was wrong. "We're too young to help," I mumbled.

"I'll miss everything," he said. And he suddenly raised his voice. "And I'll miss Bubbles most of all. He's old. When I get back he'll probably be—" He turned his back on me. "Leave me alone. I want to go to sleep."

★

On our last day, the fifth, it suddenly got very cold. We hadn't expected to need our new 'Canadian winter' clothes until – well, until it was the Canadian winter. But now, if we wanted to go out on deck, we needed them.

Before we left England, Mummy had bought a lot of clothes with clothes coupons we'd saved up, with other members of the family contributing. We'd bought woollen jerseys and thick skirts and warm stockings and undies, and heavy winter coats, gloves, scarves and caps. Cameron's mother had bought him winter clothes too. Now we needed them if we didn't want to be stuck 'below' for the whole day. And where were they? Not in our cabin. They were down in the hold, in our big cases, completely out of our reach.

But Cameron and I weren't going to be beaten. We just piled on everything we had with us, in layers, and each wrapped a blanket over our heads and around us, covering our hands. Then up we went.

As we opened the door on to the deck, a blast of freezing cold air nearly knocked us over backwards. But we soon recovered and scrambled out, nearly tripping over the ledge, staring. Straight in front of us – instead of empty ocean – we saw what looked like a huge blue mountain.

"Oh, look! An iceberg!" breathed Mummy.

It wasn't only blue, of course – it was mainly white,

with some greeny bits. It gleamed like an enormous lump of sugar that glittered and flashed in the sun. Hundreds of other passengers had come up on deck – dressed in strange clothes like us – and stood against the rail, staring and whispering to each other.

Why are they whispering? I wondered. It just seemed you had to, it was so awesome. I didn't know that word then. But it's the only one that fits.

As we stood there, watching this magnificent thing seeming to move past us, Mummy said, "That's the most beautiful sight I've ever seen!"

A man was standing beside her. There weren't many men on the ship; it was mostly women and children. But this man turned his head and said, "Madam, you are so wrong! It's not beautiful at all. It's a menace – a threat to our ship! Don't you know what happened to the great, unsinkable *Titanic*? One of those deadly things tore the guts out of it."

For once my mother had nothing to say. But I did. I said, "It's still beautiful! Even dangerous things can be beautiful."

"What, for instance?" this man asked. "Guns? Bombs? You think they're beautiful, I suppose!"

"Tigers," I said. "And my mother's right. That iceberg *is* beautiful. And it won't hurt us either, because we've passed it."

He turned away from us. Mummy put her arm round me and hugged me to her side. She hugged Cameron too, and he let her. We watched the iceberg get smaller behind us until it was just a blue peak on the horizon.

"Why was that man so nasty?" I asked.

"He's scared," she said. "A lot of people are scared."

"You're not!"

She hugged me closer and didn't answer.

What I'm going to tell now, I didn't know about until long afterwards. The third night at sea when we were halfway through the voyage, Mummy couldn't sleep. She didn't know what it was going to be like where we were going, and she'd never been away from Daddy since they were married. And besides, she felt shut in. She wanted desperately to open the porthole but she knew she couldn't. So she got dressed and went up on deck.

She walked about for a bit, and then stood at the rail. She was quite alone. It seemed everyone else on the ship was asleep, yet it kept moving steadily through the water. She felt much better outside than she had in the cabin. She kept breathing deeply and looking at the millions of stars shining overhead like a canopy embroidered with diamonds…

Just as she was thinking that she might be able to sleep, she saw something. The starlight shone on a straight path – a trail of whitish bubbles coming towards our ship like an arrow. I wouldn't have known what it was, but Mummy knew. It was a torpedo.

She was so frightened she couldn't move, let alone cry out. She could only watch in horror and fear as that arrow of deadly bubbles came quickly nearer and nearer… Our ship steamed on, unknowing, and just as she thought the torpedo *must* hit us, it sped under the back of the ship and off across the sea.

It had just missed us.

Mummy slumped over the rail. She hadn't been seasick at all so far, even in the rough early days. But now she threw up into the sea.

As she straightened up, looking out across the water in dread, expecting to see a second torpedo, she got another sort of shock. A hand fell on her shoulder.

"What are you doing here, madam? You must get below at once!" said a man's urgent voice.

It was one of the officers. She turned to him and gasped, "Did you see it? Did you see it? It nearly hit us! It—"

The man took her by the shoulders. "What's your name?" he asked, peering at her through the darkness.

"Mrs – Hanks—"

"Mrs Hanks," he said, very quietly and strongly, "I want you to go back to your cabin straight away. You mustn't come on deck at night. And whatever you *thought* you saw, please… say nothing to anyone. I want you to give me your word you'll say nothing."

Mummy just nodded. Shaking all over, she went down the steps and found our cabin and didn't say a word about it until long, long after we got safely to where we were going.

A month later a ship carrying evacuees was torpedoed and sunk. She didn't tell us about that, either. She'd always been very upfront about the war, and hadn't tried to shield me from it, but this was too close. When I think what she must have gone through every night — maybe every day too — after that till we reached Montreal, never showing her fear, I feel very proud of her.

Chapter Two

Montreal

Of course, we'd been told about where we were going, but I must say it didn't mean a lot, at least not to me. Cameron, who was a brain-box, probably did a bit of research, which may have been part of why he didn't want to go.

Great-uncle Arthur O'Flaherty lived in a place with a very funny name – Saskatoon, Saskatchewan, which was somewhere called the prairies in the middle of Canada. On the boat, whenever we'd told people where we were going, they either looked blank or said, "That's pretty far west." This made me feel we were going into some strange lonely place far from civilisation.

I knew that our uncle was quite old, and lived alone

in a small flat, on a pension, so he couldn't have us to live with him. So when my family wrote to him to ask his help, he'd found a middle-aged couple called Gordon and Luti Laine, who offered to receive us as 'war guests'. Mummy had told me that Canadians are usually very polite and nobody wanted to hurt our feelings by calling us evacuees so 'war guests' was what people like us were called.

Great-uncle Arthur turned out to be one of the kindest, gentlest, most generous men in the world. Good all the way through. But the trouble with really, thoroughly good people is, they often can't seem to realise that not everyone is as good as themselves.

We docked at Montreal in the evening. As we sailed into the harbour, we could see a tall, pointed hill with a cross on the top, all lit up; it was our first glimpse of the city.

Mummy sat on a bollard at the docks, after we collected all our big luggage. She took her wallet out of her handbag – which never left her – and counted our money. She'd changed it from pounds to Canadian dollars on the ship, and it looked a lot more – she got five dollars for every pound. But we'd spent a lot on the ship.

Daddy had had a talk to me before we left. He usually left serious talks to Mummy, but this time it was *about* her, so he did it.

"We're not a rich family," he said, "but you've never gone short. Now, when you and Mummy are in Canada, she won't have any money of her own."

"Why not? Can't you send us some?"

"No. Wars are so expensive. The government wants women and children to go abroad to be safe, but still they don't want money to go out of the country. They're not going to let me give you more than ten pounds apiece. With Cameron's ten pounds, that's thirty altogether. Not very much. Just about enough, if you're careful, to get to where you're going. After that, you'll have to depend on other people. Strangers.

"And that's going to be very hard on Mummy," Daddy went on. "Having to ask every time she wants something. Please, Lindy, be a very good girl and try to understand and not ask for too much. You're not greedy, I know that. But it will be hard on you too."

Mummy counted out the money we had left and took us to the hotel nearest to the docks for the night. It was pretty scruffy, but Mummy said, "Our train for the prairies leaves early in the morning. We have to sleep somewhere, and this place at least is cheap."

Cameron and I were hungry. We left our small mountain of suitcases in our three-bed room and went out into the shining, thronging streets of the city.

There were lights everywhere. England had been blacked out for months and months before we left, and it's hard to describe how wonderful it was to see all these lights blazing – street lamps, office blocks with all their windows lit up, colourful advertisements, car headlights… The whole city was like a Christmas tree. Even Cameron, who, I knew, was determined not to like *anything* in Canada, couldn't help twisting his head in all directions, drinking in all those lovely lights.

Another thing that was different from England was that the streets were full of people. In London people didn't go out at night much because without lights it was so dark you could fall over things. Here, there were crowds, all with loud voices – mostly French ones, which astonished me – and lit-up, cheerful faces. Nothing could have showed more clearly that we'd left the war behind. No one here was afraid of Hitler's armies or his bombs.

The man at the hotel desk had told us about a restaurant a short walk away. We headed there, through the bright night, not talking because it was all so strange and we were suddenly very tired. Mummy held our hands. We were still wearing our ship clothes, which were rather crumpled and grubby after five days at sea, but Mummy had dug out a mac for each of us to cover up the worst.

We reached the restaurant and stepped inside. There

was an orchestra playing. The place was crowded with lively people eating their dinners, all talking and laughing and clinking their knives and forks. But as they noticed us standing in the doorway, a silence spread out across the room.

Then the orchestra stopped what it was playing, and struck up 'There'll Always Be an England'.

Everyone stopped eating. Some people started singing the song. Several men began to stand up, and then sat down again. Every eye in the restaurant was fixed on us. It was as if we were standing in a spotlight.

They obviously saw that we were fresh off the boat from England. 'There'll Always Be an England' was the pop song of the moment and they played it for us. I thought they were being nice, but for Mummy, it was a horrible ordeal. She felt stared-at, exposed, humiliated – the poor refugee from war-torn London, an object of pity. She stood it for the whole length of the song, as if she was being punished somehow, and then she took our hands again and turned and fled.

I don't remember where or what we ate that night. Our first hamburger, probably, or our first hot dog. All I remember was seeing Mummy crying her eyes out for the first time since we left England.

Chapter Three

On the Train

The next morning we got up early and took two taxis to the railway station with us and all our luggage. Mummy didn't want to spend money for taxis – she kept watching the meter – but there was no other way.

She told us that the train journey to Saskatoon would take three days. This gave us an idea of how big Canada was – the longest train trip I'd ever taken was three hours, to Newcastle-upon-Tyne to visit my old nanny.

"Your fathers paid for our tickets before we left England," Mummy explained. "So we shouldn't have to spend any money till we get there. The ship was expensive – luckily there's not much to buy on a train!"

In the taxi I asked, "What will the Laines be like?"

"I think, very nice. We got a letter from them saying how much they're looking forward to having children in their home."

"Haven't they got any?"

"No."

Cameron frowned, and said, "I suppose we'll have to be very quiet and well-mannered then."

"Yes, you will," said Mummy. "And who knows for how long? It's not like a visit. We'll be living there. It'll be their house and we'll have to stick to their rules, whatever they are."

"Sounds like lots of fun," muttered Cameron.

We settled on to the train, as we had on the ship, but of course with far, far less space. We had two double seats, facing, with a folding table, to ourselves. Most of our luggage was taken away to be put in the luggage van. We just had the suitcases we'd had in the cabin.

"Won't I be glad when we can have proper baths and I can get all our clothes washed!" Mummy said.

Mummy was the cleanest person in the world and it was hard for her to put the same clothes on day after day. She'd washed our undies and socks out every night on the ship, but on the train she couldn't.

And the train wasn't very clean, I must say. It was a

steam train, which meant a lot of smoke blowing back from the engine. Even though the windows didn't open, everything soon felt gritty.

The locomotive let out a long hiss and sounded its whistle. As soon as it began to move, Cameron and I jumped up and started to explore.

We could run up and down the aisle between the seats, although Mummy said we should walk, and not disturb other passengers. There were a lot of children besides us on the train with their families, but I don't think any of them were evacuees – they looked too clean and tidy. I somehow knew we wouldn't make friends with any of them. We were set apart.

We went as far towards the engine as we could go, and then the other way, towards the last coach. We passed through a dining car where the stewards were laying the tables for lunch, which cheered us up. Beyond that, past the kitchen coach with its white-coated chefs and lovely smells and another three carriages, we found it – our happy heaven! It was called the Observation Car.

First there was a carriage with a bar in it. People were sitting around with drinks and snacks and newspapers. We sort of sneaked past them, because we could see that at the far end – the very back of the train – there was an open place. When we got out there, we stood on the rocking, swaying, racketty boards, and stared around us in amazement. It was just like the back of a small ship! A half-moon space with a curved rail around it and a roof over it, but open sides. We could hear the clacketty-clack of the wheels racing over the rails, smell the smoke from the engine far away at the front of the train, and breathe the Canadian air. How different from English air, somehow!

"You could easily just fall off the back of the train," I said, leaning over, staring at the rails streaming out behind us.

"Only if you were extremely stupid," said Cameron, backing up his point with, "'Better drowned than duffers. If not duffers, won't drown.'" This was from *Swallows and Amazons*, which, before he found *England, Their England*, had been one of his favourite books.

There was nobody out there but us. We sat on the fixed seats and watched the outer suburbs of Montreal flash past, and then the countryside – wide, lots of lakes and trees, empty of people – everything utterly new and exciting. But also scary – it looked so wild. I could feel my heart beating in time to the wheels: *Clicketty-clack! Clicketty-clack! You're going so far you may never go back!*

"Aren't you liking any of it?" I asked Cameron at last.

"No. Yes. I don't know," Cameron said, scowling out at the wild scenery. "I wonder if there's hunting here."

After a while, Mummy came to find us.

"Isn't it *big*," she said.

I could tell she liked the wide open spaces. Nothing claustrophobic about this.

She sat with us for a while and smoked a cigarette. Her smoke streamed away with the rest of the smoke. Mummy smoked an awful lot – she always had, but she'd cut down since we left home, to save money.

At last Cameron said, "Isn't it nearly time for lunch?"

We worked our way back to the dining car and sat down at a table nicely laid with clean linen and cutlery and glasses. After the ship, the rocking of the train merely jingled the glasses against the knives and forks.

We were just looking at the menu, which was full of strange but interesting things, when the waiter came along and asked Mummy for our tickets.

She brought them out of her handbag and gave them to him. He looked at them for a long time and I felt a sudden prickle of unease. Something was wrong.

"I am very sorry, ma'am," he said. "These tickets only entitle you to ride the train to Saskatoon. They don't give you any meals."

Mummy looked at him in disbelief.

"No meals?" she said. "But my husband bought us first-class tickets from Canadian Pacific Railways in London!"

"These are standard-class tickets, ma'am. They don't include meals."

"So what are we to do?" Mummy asked with a shrill note in her voice.

"There's a snack bar in the observation car," he said, looking very uncomfortable. "You can get sandwiches, peanuts, candy bars, that sort of thing. And soft drinks. And tea," he added, as if that made up for everything.

"For *three days*?" Mummy cried.

People were looking at us now, and I became aware of how we must look – travel-worn and shabby. I was suddenly so hungry I felt tears come into my eyes. I looked at Cameron. He was just laying the menu down in a very *final* kind of way, as if he were saying, *Well, this is just what I was expecting. Complete disaster.*

"Of course," said the waiter, "if you care to pay a supplement on your tickets, to make them first class—"

Mummy stood up, and urged us to our feet.

"I can't," she said, as quietly as she could. "We left England with ten pounds each, of which I have less than half left. Let's just hope Canadian Pacific Railways does very cheap sandwiches."

She herded us into the aisle and back towards our seats, under the eyes of everybody in the dining car.

"Mummy, what happened? Didn't Daddy buy the right tickets?" I asked.

"I don't know," Mummy said. "I'm sure he meant to. There's been a mistake, that's all."

"So now we live on sandwiches and 'candy bars' for three whole days," said Cameron. "What's a 'candy bar' anyway? Is it like Brighton rock? I *hate* Brighton rock!"

"We'll soon find out," Mummy said grimly.

We went back to the observation car and Mummy bought us a ham sandwich each, and lemonade. The sandwich had mustard in it, but for once I was good and didn't grumble. I could see Mummy was in an awful state about the tickets – she hardly ate anything. I had to make her take bites from my sandwich. She told me smoking means you don't have much appetite but I didn't really believe her.

Candy bars turned out to be scrumptious, though. We got one each. Mummy said, "I'm sorry, darlings." We looked at the shelves behind the bar. They were laden with delicious food – no rationing here! But now we had money rationing.

Cameron, for once, couldn't hold back. "Could we have some peanuts, Auntie? They can't cost much," he said.

"Oh, why not!" said Mummy. She bought us a bag to share, and lit another cigarette.

We went back to our seats and Cameron and I played hangman for a while. Suddenly a man came and sat on the spare seat next to Cameron. He was tall and a bit grey-haired with a tanned face.

"Excuse me," he said. "May I talk to you?"

Mummy, who'd been powdering her nose with her little swansdown puff, snapped her compact shut and said, "Yes?" rather too sharply for good manners.

"I couldn't help hearing about your trouble – I was at the next table," he said.

I felt Mummy stiffen. I didn't know what was coming, but she did, and she was going to hate it.

"You're from the Old Country," he said.

I would soon learn that a lot of Canadians call England 'the Old Country'. "Well, I've got folks there. I'm very worried about them, with all this talk of invasion and all. I want to help them, and I can't. So I thought, maybe I could help you instead."

Mummy just sat there. Nobody spoke. Cameron and I stopped playing our game to listen. We needed some help. Was Mummy going to say no? I knew she wanted to. She was very proud. I remembered Daddy's talk.

"I couldn't take money from you," she said. "It's kind of you. I just couldn't."

"No? Well, could you allow me to invite you and the kids to dine with me in the dining car this evening?"

Mummy bent her head. Then she lifted it again and looked this kind man in the face.

"Yes," she said in a strangled voice. "I could. Thank you."

"Thank *you*," he said. "I think we should eat early, don't you? So the kids can get an early night. They begin making the berths up at around seven, and the first sitting for dinner is at seven too. They ring a bell. I'll come by for you."

He stood up to leave. "My name's Hank, by the way."

"Mine happens to be Mrs Hanks," said Mummy. She couldn't help smiling.

Cameron and I looked at each other. We pulled gleeful faces.

Hank paid for our meals from then on – two and sometimes three a day. Mummy tried to cut down on meals, and for herself I think she'd rather have starved, but she couldn't starve us or keep us on sandwiches (and lemonade called Seven-Up) for three long days. Even with the odd peanut.

By the time we got back from the dining car that first night, the night conductors had miraculously transformed the seats into beds. Each person had either an upper or a lower berth. To climb into the upper berths there was a ladder. Of course Cameron and I both wanted an upper berth but only he got one. I was in a lower berth and so was Mummy.

Once you were in your berth, you could draw thick

green curtains across and fasten them together from the inside, so you were in your own little room. On the first night I thought this was the best thing in the whole train.

But for Mummy it was a nightmare. Her claustrophobia kicked in.

"I don't know how I can stand this," she said to me in a tight, desperate voice. Then she was ashamed of worrying me, and said, "Never mind, darling. I'll manage somehow."

I got undressed in my berth. I loved being in it. I realised it was better to have a lower berth because I had a window. I could open the blind and watch the dark scenery going by. The rocking of the train and the rumble of the wheels soon put me to sleep.

When I woke up in the middle of the night, I climbed out into the empty, half-lit aisle, and looked into Mummy's berth. She wasn't there! Where could she be? She'd said "I'll manage", but how could she? She couldn't even sit up all night in her seat because our seats weren't there any more – they'd been turned into berths.

I pattered down the aisle in my bare feet. By instinct I headed towards the back of the train. Everyone was asleep behind their curtains. I opened the doors between the coaches and skipped through the swaying, accordion-y connectors, holding tight to the rail.

Suddenly I felt the train slowing down and when I was just in the middle of one of these tricky in-between bits, it stopped altogether. Not sharply enough to wake anyone; it just came to a standstill, with a lot of hissing.

I hurried on to the last coach – the observation coach. This would be where Mummy would head for – where she could sit outside and not feel shut in. I was absolutely sure of it.

A few men were there, having a late-night drink at the bar. Not bothering about them seeing me in my nightie I ran past them, through the carriage to the open bit at the back. I knew Mummy would be there – I just knew it. But I was wrong.

I stood on the platform, staring round. We'd stopped, not in the middle of all that emptiness as I'd thought, but in a little town. All the buildings were low and apart from a few lonely street lamps, it was almost as dark as London. There was just a wooden platform with a sign and a name that I couldn't read. The train stood, hissing and kind of chuntering – an impatient noise. A noise that said, *I'm not staying here long.*

I stood there, clutching the rail, staring into the dimness. A man came on to the platform behind me.

"Are you looking for your mom?" he said.

It was the first time I'd heard that word. But I nodded.

"She was here. And she didn't come back through the bar. She must've got off the train."

Got off the train? That was impossible. The train would soon leave. Had she – no! But if not? – run away?

I wanted to shout for her. *Mummy! Mummy! Come back!* But the man was there and I couldn't. I couldn't let him think I had thought for one split second that she would leave us.

"Are you cold?" the man asked.

It was very warm, for night-time, but I was shivering.

He took off his jacket and wrapped it round me. "Tell you what. You sit out here and I'll bring you a Coke while you wait for her."

The 'Coke' tasted not of coal as I expected, but of mouthwash. I hated it. I clutched the bottle tightly, because just standing there thinking the train was going to start forward, leaving her behind, was unbearable. I stared out into the half-lit station and my whole inside clenched up. I was barely breathing. The man sat on one of the seats.

"Coke OK?"

I forced myself to nod, my eyes straining in the darkness.

"Where you folks headed?"

"Saskatoon."

"That's mighty far west. You got family there?"

"Mummy's—" My voice stopped coming out.

"You from the Old Country?"

I tried to swallow. There was no spit. I took a sip of the sickly sweet stuff from the bumpy bottle to moisten my mouth. "Yes."

"I guess they're being pretty brave over there," he said. "And you folks are brave, too, coming to a strange country. Where's your pop?"

"My – what?"

"Your dad."

"He couldn't come."

"He's in the forces?"

"No. He's too old. He's a doctor."

"So your mom's doing this on her own." He shook his head. "She's one brave lady." He stood up suddenly. "And here she comes."

I looked where he was looking – at the end of the platform. It was true! She came out of the darkness at the far end, into the light. There was a man with her, one of the conductors. I recognised him.

When Mummy saw me leaning out over the rail, she broke into a run. In another minute I was in her arms. I hugged her as if I'd never let go.

"Lindy – my darling – what are you doing up?"

The conductor was waving a flag. The train hissed

once more and started to move. Both the men disappeared. It was just me and Mummy on the swaying back of the train, with the breeze blowing as we picked up speed.

"Mummy – Mummy – where were you? I thought you'd run away!"

"Oh, my God, you didn't!" she said.

She sat down and took me on her knee. I'd never loved her so much, or had such a feeling of relief.

"I was sitting out here," she said. "I'd run out of cigarettes. I'm afraid I was crying. I felt so lonely and scared. And that very sweet man came out and sat with me and I told him – about Daddy and how I didn't know what we were going to find in Saskatoon – and when the train stopped at that little town, to take on water, he took me for a cup of tea to the tiniest café you ever saw… It was all made of logs… He even bought me some cigarettes – look, they're called Black Cat! I knew the train couldn't leave without him. I never dreamed… Oh, my poor little poppet, you must have been so frightened!"

She slept the rest of the night in my berth, tops to tails, with the blind up on the window so the moon could shine in.

Hank was travelling alone, and at meals we talked. He lived in Calgary, which was even further west than we were going. We asked him what it would be like, in Saskatoon.

"When you get to your host's house," he told us, "the first thing he'll ask you is, 'Do you ride horseback?'"

"Well, we do," said Cameron eagerly.

"Y'see, out west, the folks want to keep some of the old pioneering ways. They don't want to get soft and citified, even if they're not ranchers and trappers any more. So, they eat regular meals, like those spoilt easterners, except for one, and that's breakfast. For breakfast they keep up the old traditions."

"What do you mean?"

"I mean, they go out and catch their own breakfasts."

Cameron's mouth fell open.

"You mean, they go hunting, on horseback?"

"Sure do. Can you shoot?"

"No."

He sucked in his lips. "Gotta learn to shoot. You start with a BB gun. Course, you can't shoot anything big with those, but you can get a few gophers."

"What's a gopher?" Cameron and I asked at once.

"You don't have gophers in England? They're little critters about this big – " He held his hands about eight inches apart – "They live on the prairie, in holes. Millions of 'em. You shoot a couple, fry 'em up – makes a dandy meal on toast. Of course you gotta skin 'em and gut 'em first."

Mummy had her nose in her hands. I looked at her. Then back at Hank. He looked completely serious.

"What about girls? Do they have to shoot gophers too?"

"Well, no, girls are let off shootin' if they don't like it. But they do have to ride out on the prairie, and then they can catch their breakfast another way."

"How?"

"I'll tell you. You make a loop in a long piece of string, and put it around a gopher hole. Then you wait. When he puts his head up, you jerk the loop tight round his neck, and there's your breakfast."

I made a face.

"Of course," Hank went on, "if you got a soft heart and don't wanna eat him, you can have him for a pet."

I thought of my pet rabbit, Moley, left behind. "How do I catch him?"

"Gophers are crazy about condensed milk."

Mummy gave a stifled snort.

"So what you do is, you take your tin of condensed milk. You punch two holes in it, top and bottom, and then you use that same length of string with the loop in it to drag the tin across the prairie. The gopher comes along and starts licking up the milk, and by the time the tin's empty, he's a-layin' there on his back with his belly full of his favourite food, and you can ride back and pick him up, and he's yours. For life."

I listened, entranced. I could see it all! My own pet gopher!

"I'll eat cereal for breakfast!" I exclaimed.

Mummy couldn't contain herself. She bent over her knees and exploded.

"And what about me?" she managed to choke out. "I can't ride and I can't shoot and I refuse to strangle little things to death."

Hank seemed to think about this. "Well, maybe on account of you're all fresh from the Old Country they may let you off and give you bacon and waffles for a few days, till you settle in. But I'm sure relieved you kids can ride horseback, because maybe they won't, and you'll have to go out and shoot something to eat on the first morning. Enough for your mom as well."

"I could do it. I bet I could," said Cameron. "I've hunted foxes and got the brush. I was in at the kill. I got blooded!"

So then he explained very seriously to Hank about fox hunting and Hank said, "You mean they smear fox blood on the kids' faces and give 'em the fox's tail? Are you telling me a tall story, by any chance?"

★

The last part of the train journey got us seriously worried. The windows were now so dirty that if we wanted to see out properly we had to sit on the observation platform. The interesting countryside we'd seen earlier, changed. It was no longer full of lakes and hills, pine forests sprinkled with little towns and the occasional log cabin, not to mention exciting wildlife – Cameron had seen an eagle, and I'd seen a huge thing with strange antlers that Hank told us was a moose. Now the landscape was flat. No trees. No lakes or rivers. Just flat, flat, flat land under a swaying sea of yellow wheat. There were few signs of life. Only some farms, miles apart – hours apart.

"What are those things?" Cameron asked Hank, who was sitting with us pretty much full-time now.

"Grain elevators," said Hank. "When the wheat's harvested they bring it to the railheads and store it in those big square towers. Then they load it on to the trains to take it all over Canada."

"But aren't there any towns – proper towns?"

"Sure there are. Saskatoon is a big town. Population forty-odd thousand."

"That's not big," said Cameron. "London's got millions of people."

"Ah well, I'm not saying it's a big city. Though that's what they call it. The Hub City of the Prairies."

"How old is it?" Mummy asked.

"Not old. Maybe sixty, eighty years. Might still be some old-timers living there who remember when it was nothing but an Indian settlement."

I pricked up my ears. "Indians? Real Red Indians?"

Hank looked a bit uncomfortable. "Well you know, they aren't red, and they're not Indians. We Anglos call them that, because we made a mistake when we first got here, thinking we'd arrived in India! But if you ever meet one, you don't want to say, 'Gee, are you an Indian?'"

"So what should we call them?" Cameron asked.

"By their tribe, maybe. Around Saskatchewan, it's Cree. And other tribes. But mostly Cree."

"Where are they? Can we see them?"

"They're all on reserves now."

Later, when I got Cameron alone, I said, "Wouldn't it be fun if we really had to ride across the prairie and we met some Crees!"

"What if they were Apaches? Or Navajos? There are hundreds of different tribes. There must be a generic name for them if we can't call them Indians."

Cameron and his lovely long words! Generic. I got it. Something for all of them, instead of Indians. But for the moment I forgot about them, whatever they were called.

"Look at it," he said. "It's all wheat. How could we ride through that? It's weird."

If 'weird' means strange, unknown, utterly different, then he was right about where we were going. Or, as Hank taught us to say, "He sure slobbered a bibful."

Chapter Four

We Arrive

We reached Saskatoon at six o'clock in the morning. Mummy woke us early, when there was hardly any light coming through the window of my berth – just enough to see the endless wheat fields rushing by. She took us along to the cramped, smelly washroom at the end of the carriage and produced some clothes she'd been saving for us to make a good impression when we arrived. My frock was very creased but at least it was clean. Cameron wore his school blazer, even though it had been getting hotter every day.

"Shall I wear a tie?" he asked.

"I don't know… We should have asked Hank," said Mummy.

She was putting make-up on. She hadn't worn much on the journey, just lipstick and some powder, but now she put on eye shadow and mascara, and earrings. I thought she looked beautiful, and actress-y.

She wore a very pretty dress I hadn't seen before, and stockings, and shoes with a bit of a heel. She wrapped her lovely blonde hair in a sort of turban. She looked like at home when she was going out for lunch. We bundled all the rest of our things into our suitcases as the train rocked the last few miles to our destination.

We stood near the exit door. Mummy smoked. She said, "I remember feeling just like this before I went on stage on a first night to play a big part."

I'd once acted a big part in a school play – a queen. I suddenly remembered standing in the wings in my red dress with my hair down my back, with such a sudden terror of forgetting my lines that I nearly ran away. Yes. It was like that now.

Only Cameron seemed completely calm. "I wonder if they'll come to meet us in a horse and buggy," he said.

Just as the whistle blew for Saskatoon, Hank turned up. He must have got up early to say goodbye.

"You've been quite wonderful," said Mummy. "A lifesaver."

He shook hands with her, but she suddenly kissed his cheek. She had to stand on tiptoe.

"You're welcome," said Hank.

We'd never heard that phrase before. Mummy stared at him.

"What a very nice thing to say," she said.

"Here's my address in Calgary," he said, giving Mummy a card. "Let me know if you need anything. Be good kids for your mom, now." He shook Cameron's hand and gave me a hug. "Go git them gophers!" he said. "Oh! I forgot to tell you – you want some pocket money, the government pays a bounty for every tail!"

The train pulled into the station. Right opposite where we stood, hung the sign that read 'SASKATOON'.

"Is that an Indian name?" my clever cousin asked.

"Yep," said Hank. "It's the name of a berry. And 'Canada' is an Indian word too. It means 'Big village'."

Mummy and I were hanging out of the doorway, looking up and down the platform. There were lots of people waiting. But suddenly Mummy said, "There they are. Look. Those three down there, the white-haired man and the man and woman. Bet you."

The train hissed to a stop and people started forward to get on or to greet people. 'Our three' were staring anxiously at the doorways. Mummy stepped out, waved, and called quite loudly, "Uncle Arthur!"

The older man turned quickly. Then, with the help of a walking stick, he came hurrying towards us, his face alight.

I didn't know him at all, only that he was Mummy's uncle, that he lived alone, that he was a retired bookkeeper. That he'd taken the trouble to find us some people to live with. But when I saw his face for the first time, warm with welcome as he strode towards us, I knew at once that I would love him.

He clasped Mummy in his arms, his stick falling to the ground. Cameron jumped down and scooped it up. We stood beside them, waiting. I happened to look up and saw Hank in the train doorway. He lifted our suitcases down and Cameron took them one by one. He looked at Mummy with a funny, soft look, and gave us a tiny wave. Then he disappeared, and we were smothered in a mass hug from Uncle Arthur, who smelled of pipe tobacco and welcome.

There was a lot of bustle all around us, but I felt someone close behind me. I turned, and faced a stranger with dark hair and glasses and a beaming smile.

"I know who *you* are! You're Lindy!" he exclaimed. "I'm Gordon! I'm your new Poppa, the guy you're coming to live with! Gee, this is great! Can I give you a li'l hug?"

I let him. *He* smelled strange. It was a smell I knew, but it was out of place here. Then he turned and a woman with hair too white for her face came forward rather shyly.

"This is Luti, my wife. Mrs Laine – Momma! – meet our little girl! And *this*—" he almost pulled Cameron forward with a hand on his shoulder, "this must be *Cameron*!" He wrung Cameron's hand, pumping it up and down. "Gee whizz, you're such a big boy, I didn't expect – I thought you'd be about this size!" He put his hand about a foot from the ground.

Luti said softly, "Don't be silly, Gordon." She gave me a quick kiss on the cheek. "Welcome to Saskatoon, Lindy."

Mummy had turned towards us, still holding Uncle Arthur's hand. There were introductions and more handshakes.

Mummy said, "We must go and see to our big luggage."

"Oh, don't worry about that!" Gordon said heartily. "They'll have it off the train by now. Our railways are wonderful! Don't you folks just love Canada? C'mon kids, let's go find your bags!"

I noticed Cameron had peeled off his heavy school blazer. It was sweaty hot at seven in the morning.

Uncle Arthur called a taxi for him and Mummy and some of the luggage. Cameron and I drove to our new home in the Laines' car. Cameron, who knew all about cars, hissed to me in the back seat that it was a Hillman Minx. He sounded surprised. Later he explained, "I thought they'd be rich." Hillman Minxes weren't, it seemed, what rich folks bought, at least not in England.

Gordon chatted the whole way.

"It's gonna be so great to have kids around the place, huh, Mrs Laine? I mean Momma? I can't wait to get started being a poppa! Look, kids, there's our river! Bet you didn't expect it to be so big, huh?"

We hadn't expected it to be, at all. It was certainly the most exciting thing we'd seen for twenty-four hours of prairie. It was wide and had waves and steep banks, and rushed under the big bridge we were crossing.

"The city of bridges! That's what we call Saskatoon! This one's called Broadway Bridge. You'll soon be criss-crossing it on the streetcar, to get downtown to the movies, I bet! We've got five movie theatres! Waddaya think of that? Almost like London, eh?"

"Of course it's not like London," said Luti in her quiet little voice.

"Only kidding," said Gordon.

The car pulled up in a curved street with some pleasant-looking houses on each side. The house where we were going to live had a lawn that came down to the pavement, and as soon as we opened the car door, a dog came rushing to meet us. I could *feel* Cameron's mood changing. He just couldn't help himself.

"Here comes Spajer to say hi to you!" said Gordon.

Spajer was a golden cocker spaniel with long, silky ears. He jumped all over us. He was a lovely dog and Cameron couldn't resist patting him, but I sensed he felt a bit disloyal to Bubbles.

"Is Spajer an Indian name?" asked Cameron.

Gordon *roared* with laughter, but Luti said, "We had another dog before him called Jasper."

"Oh, I see! An anagram," said Cameron.

Both the Laines stared at him.

"Smart boy," said Gordon, sounding surprised.

Mummy and Uncle Arthur arrived and there was a kerfuffle as we got the luggage into the house. There suddenly seemed to be an awful lot of it, and Gordon made a joke about "You folks planning to stay awhile?" which I don't think any of us got.

Mummy was very quiet and tense and stuck close to Uncle Arthur. He kept his arm around her whenever he could. I knew they'd never met before, but already they seemed to love each other. I know now that Mummy felt close to him because he was family and everybody else in this whole city was a stranger.

The house was pretty, though not like an English house – very new-looking with lots of windows and polished wooden floors and modern furniture, all clean and shiny. There were gardens on three sides. The curved street was wide and not too busy, with trees and front gardens without fences. We all wanted to see our bedrooms and I wanted to have a bath – Mummy kept sort of picking at her dress where it was sticking to her – but Gordon wanted to talk.

"You kids'll soon learn the neighbourhood," he said. "See that li'l park across the street? You can go there by yourselves and play and find pals. In the winter they turn the whole park into a skating rink. Bet you can't ice skate!"

We agreed we couldn't.

"I just can't wait to teach you! Bet you've never seen snow like we get here! Two, three feet at a time! That's not counting the drifts!" He held his hand right over his head to show how deep the 'drifts' got.

Snow higher than a man? Cameron gave me a look. He was thinking what I was – we could make forts and tunnels, crawl in and play amazing adventure games. From then on I started looking forward to winter. And not just because of the heat now, which was the worst I'd ever felt.

Luti excused herself and went into the kitchen while Gordon offered us drinks – Coke for us (ugh! – but at least it was cold) and iced water for Mummy and Uncle Arthur, after they'd both refused 'a li'l snifter'. I didn't know what that was, but then Gordon opened a shiny cupboard in the corner and brought out some bottles. Mummy looked amazed to be offered alcohol so early in the day, but Gordon had one. It didn't look so 'li'l' to me.

Gordon stopped talking to sip his whiskey and we just sat there on the chintz armchairs. There was a long, difficult silence. Finally Uncle Arthur said, "You know, I think my folks might like to see their rooms and maybe clean up before breakfast."

"*Luti!*" Gordon called. She came almost running in. "What are you thinking of, honey? Take these folks up to their rooms, huh? I'll bring the bags up."

"But I've just put the bacon on," she said.

Cameron and I looked at each other. We'd suddenly remembered Hank's tale.

"So we don't have to ride out on the prairie to shoot our breakfasts?" Cameron said.

"Whaaaat?" Gordon shouted.

Luti gaped at us, her blue eyes staring.

Their faces! We suddenly realised we'd been had!

Cameron and I laughed until we choked. We couldn't stop. Mummy had to calm us down.

"*Please* can we go to our rooms?" she begged.

Uncle Arthur left us. At the door, he said, "I don't like 'Uncle Arthur'. Sounds Victorian. Why don't you call me O'F?" Then he kissed us all goodbye.

Mummy seemed to cling to him. Luti led us upstairs

and showed us our rooms. One for Mummy and me with two single beds and a dressing table with a frill round it. The window overlooked the back garden. I went to look out, and noticed something funny. The window had netting on it, like our meat safe at home.

"We have screens on the doors too," Luti said, following my gaze. "The bugs get in anyhow. We say our mosquitoes are as big as cockroaches and the cockroaches are as big as gophers."

"What are the gophers as big as?"

"Beavers, I guess!" she laughed. "Tell me if I've forgotten anything you need." She stared at Mummy for a moment. "You're real pretty," she said suddenly. "Everyone's going to love you."

I decided I liked Luti. I liked her saying Mummy was pretty. Although she wasn't pretty. She was beautiful. Even tired out and stressed and with her make-up sweated off.

Cameron had a smaller room. He looked round it bleakly, but then he saw it had a desk with lots of drawers, and a bookcase with some books in it.

"In her letter, your mom told me you like to read, Cameron," Luti said. "I chose some books for you. I hope you like them."

"Thank you very much," said Cameron, sounding really grateful.

"We only have one bathroom," she went on, "so it

may get a bit crowded. But for today it's all yours. I'll delay breakfast. Come down when you're ready."

Mummy went first. She said she was desperate to get clean and asked us to wait, which we did, in Cameron's room. He started off by going through the books Luti had bought, but then there was a scratching at the door, and Spajer joined us, and after that no reading got done. I think Spajer decided round about then that he was at least half Cameron's dog.

Mummy came out of the bathroom at last, in a dressing gown, smelling lovely.

"Bubble bath. That Luti," she said to me quietly, "has thought of lots of little kind things." Then she said one of her favourite phrases, "The little more, and how much it is. The little less, and what worlds away!"

Cameron went next. I watched Mummy start doing her face.

"Gordon talks a lot, doesn't he?" I asked.

"Lindy."

"What?"

"Shut the door." I did. "Listen, darling. I want you to remember something. We're going to owe these people a lot. They're going to have to pay for everything – everything we need, everything we eat, and everything we do that costs money. I want you to *be aware* that this is their house, and that they're *here*. Don't say or do *anything* that might offend them." She took the towel off her head and began to comb out her long blonde hair. "I'll say one other thing. We're ambassadors for England. People will be watching us. They'll judge England by how we behave. Do you understand, my poppet?"

"Yes. But he does talk a lot, doesn't he?"

"Yes. I hear Cameron coming out... Go and have your bath and I'll come in and wash your hair for you."

That first Canadian bath, after the three-inches-of-hot-water ones we'd been rationed to at home, was unforgettable. So deep, so hot, so full of bubbles! I felt as if I was washing off the grime of a coal mine, and then I felt like a movie star. As I lay chest-deep while Mummy washed my hair, I forgot all about the journey, the war, the strangeness. I just wallowed.

"Maybe it'll be all right – Canada. Saskatoon. The Laines," I said.

Mummy just made lots of lather and said nothing.

Chapter Five

Freedom

We had three weeks of freedom to explore and find our feet before we had to start Canadian school, but I was too excited by everything around us to think much about that. Cameron, though, as usual, was better at thinking ahead. He asked Luti questions about school and then told me the answers.

"It'll be just an ordinary local school," Cameron told me. "They call them public schools here – the opposite of public schools in England. I don't think they have private schools here where you have to pay." He fiddled with his shoelace and then said, "It's boys and girls."

I'd never been to anything but an all-girls school.

"Do you think that'll be weird?" I asked Cameron, nervously.

"They'll probably think *we're* weird," he replied.

Luti had a 'daily' – a Swedish woman who came in to clean and who gave us a foretaste of how interesting we were. She didn't really talk to us (she couldn't speak much English) but she stared at us as if we'd fallen off the moon.

That, though, wasn't as bad as the visitors. They'd started coming on the first day. We'd hardly begun to unpack after breakfast when the doorbell rang, and after that it didn't stop ringing. It seemed all the Laines' friends wanted to meet us. Well – have a good look at us, anyway.

For the first week it was like one long party. Most of these strangers probably meant to be kind and welcoming, but Mummy still got the heebie-jeebies. She felt she had to be 'on show' to the visitors, and be a good ambassador, but she got more and more stressed. Twice I came home from playing out and found her crying (quietly) in our room.

"I feel like a fish in a bowl," she whispered, blowing her nose. "A performing fish." She reached for her Black Cats. She always whispered whenever we were talking privately, even with the door closed. "And the way they *drink*! At all hours! They tease me because I won't knock back the whiskey like they do. They're calling me Ice-water Alex! If I drank like they do, I'd fall flat on my face!"

"Does Luti drink a lot?" I asked.

"No. But Gordon drinks enough for both of them." She muttered this out of the side of her mouth, but I heard it.

Gordon wasn't around much, because he worked all day as a lawyer and had an office downtown. He had 'KC' after his name, which stood for King's Councillor, and which in England you didn't get to be until you were an important – and rich – lawyer. Gordon and Luti weren't rich. Cameron had been quite right about the Hillman Minx. Gordon was just an ordinary small-town lawyer after all. But it was quite a while before we realised this. The Laines were determined to show us and all their friends – and maybe even themselves – that they *could* afford to have war guests. Mummy hardly ever had to ask them for money at first. Gordon thrust wads of dollars into her hand every Saturday but she always gave them back, taking only what she needed for little things for us, and for her Black Cats.

All the grown-ups I knew smoked. Mummy tried to cut down, but it was very hard for her. She needed her 'coffin nails' as she called them. Of course I hated her calling them that but Mummy knew smoking was bad for you and she told me I must never start.

"My lungs are so full of tar by now they're like black sponges," she said.

"But then why do you do it?"

"Because I can't stop. Which is why you must never start."

Mummy was invited to a lot of people's homes. She didn't want to go, but she felt she had to. Luckily Cameron and I weren't included so till school started in September, we were free a lot of the time. Free in a way we'd never been before. And we made the most of it.

At first we just wandered about in the little park near the house. Spajer tagged along, hoping for a walk or a game of ball, when Luti agreed to let him out – she was terrified he'd get lost or be run over, but he stuck close to Cameron, and Cameron took good care of him.

"Bubbles is half-spaniel," he reminded me. "We only call him a Bulgarian bulldog to make him sound like a thoroughbred."

There were lots of other kids, and other dogs, around the neighbourhood. They stared at us too – we didn't dress like them; Cameron in his short grey flannel trousers and me in my English dresses. But they were a friendly lot and we soon started hanging out with them.

It was girls with girls and boys with boys, mixed school or not. So while I was learning ball games like 'One, two, three allairy' and skipping games and sometimes being invited to play in my new friends' 'back yards' (as they called their gardens), some of the boys were showing Cameron what they called 'the ropes'.

The railway ran past the back of our house. Of course, we'd heard the trains go by, but there was a big screen of fir trees that stopped us seeing much of them.

Cameron came home one day and told me casually that the best game was throwing things at the engine drivers.

"What!" I almost screamed. "Are you mad? What do you *mean*?"

"Wait till it's time for the next train, I'll show you. The railway's great fun. Only we'll leave Spaje behind, because he's not very train-wise."

In the late afternoon, he found me in the park and beckoned. I left the other girls and followed him round by the end of the street to the railway crossing. We crossed over then followed the tracks a little way back towards the house.

He took out a one-cent coin and laid it on the track.

"What's that for?"

"You'll see. Now, collect tin cans."

I looked around but only found two. He did too.

"That's enough. It's all you'll have time for," he said. "There's a train due soon. Put your ear to the rail and you can feel it coming."

"I'm not putting my head on the line! That's dangerous!"

"Oh, don't be babyish! You can see it coming for miles. It's just fun to feel the rail vibrate."

Very reluctantly I knelt down on one of the wooden sleeper beams and put my ear to the cold rail, next to the cent, lying there waiting for its fate.

"Don't knock the cent off!" Cameron shouted.

After a bit I felt a trembling, and at the same time I heard a sort of humming sound. I leapt to my feet and ran away from the line. Cameron was there with a tin can in each hand. Far away down the line I could see the smoke puffing out above the trees.

"What do we do?"

"When the train goes by, you throw them at the engine driver in his cab," he said.

We'd been up to mischief before in our lives. But this? "What if you hit him? You could hurt him!"

"Oh, you never hit them, they're going too fast. It's good throwing if you get it anywhere near the cab."

Now we could hear the train coming. Its whistle was

blowing and next moment it came into sight, round the bend. The great locomotive, spilling out smoke, came chuffing and grunting and whistling towards us. Just as the open part, where the driver and the fireman were standing, flashed past my eyes, Cameron shouted "*Now!*" and threw his tin cans swiftly one after the other like cricket balls.

They hit the fire-box and bounced off harmlessly, but one of the men shook his fist out of the cab at us, and then turned back, and made the whistle shriek, as if broadcasting our badness. Even though I never got around to even picking my tin cans up, let alone throwing them, I felt the shame of it.

We stood there. Cameron was panting and grinning. He looked as excited as if he'd been throwing tin cans at Hitler. When the whole long, long train – a goods train – had gone past, he rushed to the line, bent down, and picked up the coin.

"Look!"

He showed it to me. It was thin and flat and its dull copper colour had changed to silvery brightness. I touched it with one finger. It was *warm*.

"Here, you have it. Don't go telling Auntie," Cameron said.

I took the only bribe of my life – a train-flattened one-cent coin.

"I won't if you promise not to do that again," I said.

"Goody-goody," he muttered, not for the first time.

On the way home, he recited, in a thoughtful, matter-of-fact voice:

> "The boy stood on the railway line,
> The train was coming fast.
> The boy stepped off the railway line,
> The train went whizzing past.
> The boy stood on the railway line,
> The engine gave a squeal.
> The driver took an oily rag
> And wiped him off the wheel."

At the weekend Gordon 'did things' with us. He called himself our Poppa, as in "Poppa's gonna take his kids out tomorrow and show them the sights!" Mummy was expected to come too. Luti mostly stayed home, or sometimes went out to play bridge. Her bridge club was very important to her. She tried to take Mummy but she said she was such a bad player she'd only spoil the game.

We didn't always go on these trips by car because Gordon wanted us to learn how to ride the streetcars. These ran on rails down the middle of main streets, with a sort of arm on the roof that reached up to electrified wires overhead. They rocked and swayed and made a loud clanging noise. There were two sorts: the big ones that took us across the bridge into downtown, where the hotels, movie theatres and restaurants were; and the local ones that were smaller and were known as puddle-jumpers.

Apart from the movie theatres, downtown didn't mean much to us, except for one hotel, the Bessborough. It was rather grand, with pointed turrets, and it stood in a large park on the west bank. There, Gordon liked to take 'his family' for Sunday lunch in the smart restaurant that overlooked the river. O'F sometimes came too. We loved seeing him but we didn't very often, because Mummy said he preferred seeing us on our own.

Gordon seemed to know a lot of people, and the meal would always be interrupted by him jumping to his feet, waving and beckoning to these acquaintances, who would come over and be introduced to us. I could see how much this embarrassed Mummy. Luti had asked her to dress up for these outings and the men always looked admiringly at her.

"Gordie loves showing you off," Luti had said. "He thinks you're beautiful. He loves your hair. Could you leave your turban off, do you think?"

After lunch, Cameron and I would play in the park for a bit while the grown-ups sat on a bench talking.

The river fascinated us, not just because it was so wide and sort of wild-looking but because these lunchtimes were the only chance we had to play near it. Mummy had forbidden us to go to the riverbank by ourselves. The bank on our east side was untamed – steep and thick with undergrowth. She was always afraid we'd fall in and be swept away by the strong current. Cameron muttered his favourite *Swallows and Amazons* quote – "Better drowned than duffers" – a lot but it didn't make any difference.

It was especially hard for him because all the other boys went down there.

"That's where they go sledding and tobogganing in the winter," he said. "I hope Auntie's got over her terrors by then. There aren't any other hills to sled down."

But he did go out on to the prairie with the others (riding on the crossbar of a friend's bike) to catch gophers. He caught three, with the string-loop, and cut their tails off (when they were dead) to send in for the bounty. It was ten cents per tail. He used the thirty cents to buy Mummy some sweets.

"Candies," I said.

"*Sweets*," he said.

I was picking up lots of Canadian words that he refused to use.

Chapter Six

School

On our first day at school, Gordon took the morning off. He wanted to be the one to take us.

The school was quite far away. The puddle-jumper would have taken us most of the way but Gordon said we shouldn't use it. "All the kids here walk to school. I bet that's something new for you, isn't it?"

Cameron said nothing. I'd noticed he often kept a dignified silence when Gordon said something that hinted at Canada being somehow better than England. But I said, "At my first school, I always walked, even when I was only seven. By myself." I wasn't going to let Gordon think we were sissies or something.

When I first saw Buena Vista Public School, I stopped

dead in the gateway and couldn't make my legs move for a minute. Gordon tugged my hand.

"Aw, c'mon, Lindy! It's only a big ol' school! Bet you never went to such an impressive one, though!"

True enough. My earliest school had been in an ordinary house. My boarding school had been a low building surrounded by fields and woods. This looked like a castle out of *Grimm's Fairy Tales*.

Cameron was striding ahead. He wasn't going to let Gordon tug him along. I freed my hand and made myself walk across the front yard and up the wide stone steps; there were, after all, dozens of children and some grown-ups all around me.

Gordon took us to the head teacher's office. On the door was printed the word 'PRINCIPAL'. I remembered my first day at my convent boarding school and half expected there to be a nun inside, but it was just an ordinary woman. She stood up from her desk and came to shake hands with us.

"I'm Mrs Jameson," she said. "I'm very glad you've come to our school. We're very excited to welcome you."

Excited? Cameron flicked me a look. He didn't like 'excited', but I did. As much as he hated to be the centre of attention, I loved it.

"Cameron will be in 7A," she said, "and Lindy in 6B.

Your classmates are expecting you. Come with me now – I'll introduce you."

Gordon tagged along, but at the door to the first classroom, the principal turned to him politely and said, "Mr Laine, I think it would be better if you left the introductions to me."

Gordon looked disappointed. But he said he'd pick us up after school.

I don't remember what happened with Cameron. But I remember very well being led into my class, 6B. There were about twenty-five children of my age, all sitting in double desks facing a huge blackboard. There were big windows along one wall, and the others were a mass of colour, which turned out to be maps and charts and pictures. When Mrs Jameson and I came in, everybody stood up and every face turned to us.

"Class, this is Lindy Hanks. She's our war guest from London, England. Will you please give her a real Buena Vista welcome?"

To my amazement, everybody not only clapped, but cheered. I remembered the restaurant and 'There'll Always Be an England'. Well, at least they wouldn't start singing that!

The teacher, who was young and pretty with shiny black hair and lipstick, came over to me, and the principal left.

"Hello, Lindy. I'm Miss Bubniuk. Now, where shall we put you? Who'd like to have Lindy share their desk?"

Three girls sitting alone threw their hands up. Miss Bubniuk led me to one of them.

"This is Marylou, she'll be your desk partner."

Marylou was one of the girls I already knew from the little park.

"Oh, good, Lindy!" she said, so excitedly I thought she was going to hug me. She patted the seat beside her and actually did put her arm around me when I sat down. All the others kept their faces turned towards me until Miss Bubniuk clapped her hands for attention.

The time till lunch passed in a whirl of enthusiasm. You'd have thought I was a princess come among them, the way they treated me. At break, which they called 'recess', Marylou and the other girls from the park showed me off as if I were their proudest possession. My celebrity went to my head a bit so that by lunchtime I *felt* like a princess. I swaggered over to Cameron, who was sitting alone in a corner of the playground.

"These kids are really swell!" I enthused.

"Don't say 'kids'," he said. "And *don't* say 'swell'. It's beastly slang."

Cameron could be very scathing sometimes. But this time he couldn't squash me. I loved the new words.

Luti had packed sandwiches for us. We opened them up together. Peanut butter and jelly – a whole new taste experience, right up there with waffles and maple syrup, corn on the cob streaming with butter, and pork spare ribs cooked with brown sugar, one of Luti's specialities. I loved the food in Canada. Cameron didn't, or pretended not to. He said none of it was a patch on roast beef and fish and chips.

"This is ridiculous," he muttered as we sat on a wall, eating our sandwiches.

"What is?"

"The lessons. They're so incredibly easy. We did the maths they're doing ages ago. They don't know the first thing about British history. We were up to the Industrial Revolution at home. They've never heard of it here. It's all about Canada. And the book we're reading in class is for babies."

I hadn't found the lessons particularly easy, just strange. Miss Bubniuk was much less strict than the nuns and there was far more shouting out the answers and whispering. I saw two boys throwing rubbers at each other when she was writing on the board. I thought it was more fun than the convent, but so different I hadn't thought to compare what we were actually learning. It was new, that was the long and short of it. Everything was, and that stopped me comparing it with England.

I said, "I guess we just have to get used to it."

Cameron glared at me. "You *suppose*. You don't 'guess'."

"That's how they talk here."

"Well, it's not how *I* talk. If you start putting on a Canadian accent I won't talk to you *at all*."

I wasn't having that. "Can't I even say 'recess' instead of 'break'?" I teased.

Just then some of the girls from my class called me to come and play a ball-bouncing game. I stuffed the last bit of sandwich into my mouth and left Cameron sitting there alone. I didn't even stop to wonder why the 'kids' in 7A hadn't made a prince out of him.

I soon found out, though. Cameron's teacher having come to the same realisation as my cousin – that he was a good year ahead of his classmates – suggested he move straight to the local high school. So before I'd even got completely used to the way to school, letting him lead the way, I had to manage on my own. Cameron was now a student at Nutana Collegiate. There he joined a class called 9A. The high school was, I learnt, streamed – A students (the best) in A, Bs in B and so on. Cameron was the A-est student you could imagine, although he was nearly two years younger than the others in his year group.

I was secretly hoping that this age difference would mean that he'd fall back a bit on me, as the others in his class would be too old for him. But that wasn't what happened. Cameron didn't care whether people liked him or not, so of course they all wanted him to like them and he became something of a prince to them, which lasted long after I'd stopped being a princess and gone back to being just a girl who 'talked funny', like calling her mother Mummy instead of Mom.

After I stopped being special, I wasn't invited to play after school much and I didn't seem to have any real friends. I complained to Mummy that there must be something wrong with me.

"You're different, that's all. They'll get used to you."

"Should I start talking like them? Would you mind if I called you Mom?"

"I would absolutely hate it. I'd rather you called me Alex. But anyway there's no point in putting something on that isn't you. Be yourself and see what happens."

Nothing did for a couple of weeks. Then Willie happened.

One thing that we all did together – apart from playing with Spajer and taking him for walks – was go to the movies.

This involved a streetcar ride into Downtown, where the movie theatres were. We were all sitting in the stalls at the Capitol, the grandest, one Saturday afternoon, and I noticed another girl with plaits like mine, only red, sitting next to me with her mother. She didn't go to Buena Vista or I'd have seen her. She was wearing trousers and a khaki top like a battledress.

The double bill – two films – was always accompanied by a cartoon, trailers and a newsreel, and on this afternoon started with the newsreel. The famous Pathé theme music was blaring but I was eyeing this girl next to me and not paying a lot of attention, when suddenly I heard Mummy give a little gasp, and Cameron, who was on the other side of me, leant forward and gripped the seat in front.

I looked quickly at the screen. It seemed to have burst into black-and-white flames – there was fire all over it. People were running. There were hosepipes spraying the fire but they were obviously not going to put it out – it was far too big. Suddenly, the blazing building fell down.

The commentator was saying in a very excited voice, "This is London, under a rain of German bombs."

The bombing that hadn't begun before we left, but that Daddy always said would happen, was happening now. In London. Where I lived. Where home was. Where Daddy was – and Grampy and Auntie Bee and my little cousin Ray.

I sat there, frozen. Everyone in the cinema seemed frozen. And after we'd watched London burning, on came a Donald Duck cartoon.

Cameron stood up, breathing hard. He fought his way along the row of people, and out through the doors at the back. Mummy stood up and followed him.

"Stay here, it's all right," she said as she pushed past my knees.

The girl sitting next to me was watching this. She heard Mummy's voice. She leant towards me and whispered, "Are you English?"

I nodded, my eyes still on the screen, now full of colour and silly ducks making quacking noises.

"Me too!" And suddenly she squeezed my hand hard. "Filthy stinking Germans!" she said, right out loud.

"Sssssh, Willie!" hissed her mother.

Cameron and Mummy didn't come back. During the trailers I went out after them. Cameron was standing on the pavement shouting at Mummy.

"I want to go home! *I want to go home!* I won't stay here! We have to get back!"

Mummy was trying to calm him. "I want to go home too, Cam, but we can't—"

But he wouldn't listen or let her touch him. He turned and half ran up Second Avenue, blindly – he was going the wrong way. I started to run after him, but Mummy stopped me.

"Leave him. He'll come back when he's ready."

I looked at her. Her face was white.

"Do you want to go back and see the film?" she asked in a strangled voice.

"No – yes – I don't know. Do you?"

She shook her head, staring after Cameron.

"Is – is it all over London?" I managed to ask.

"No." She seemed to come back to herself. She focused on me. "No, darling, no. Of course not. London's huge. They can't bomb all of it. It's just the City and… some other places… They won't bomb the suburbs. Our house is quite safe, I'm sure. And Grampy's. They won't bomb – Redcliffe Square."

Redcliffe Square – Grampy's house – was where she'd grown up. I saw she was going to cry.

I said quickly, "We'd better go back in to the movie. We can't go home without Cameron."

So we went back in and watched, I think it was *The Wizard of Oz*. It must have been, because I've never been able to watch it since without feeling a sort of trembling in my throat.

Mummy had a serious talk with both of us that night.

"I know this is hard," she said. "Specially for you, Cameron. But what we have to keep in mind – what I keep in mind, whenever it gets too hard for me – is that this is our war work. It may not seem like it, but it is. It's my job to look after you and keep you safe, because you're England's future. And it's your job to get through the war and come home safe, when the time comes, with… well, with honour. We can't fight. But we can get through this as best we possibly can, so we can go home at the end of it and know that we did our job of being here as well as we could."

"So we can say that 'This was our finest hour'," said Cameron, quoting one of Winston Churchill's speeches.

I couldn't tell if he was being sarcastic or not.

Chapter Seven

Willie and the Crescent Club

Willie's full name was Willametta Lord. She had red hair and freckles and was a tomboy. Her father was in the British army, and she and her little brother and mother were like us – evacuees. They also lived with a Canadian family, the Warrens, and Willie went to a school out near the Exhibition Grounds, where poorer people lived. They'd been here for six months longer than us.

After we met at the movie, our mothers became friends – 'natch', as Willie would say. We began to meet after school – not in each other's houses, but in the park or at Pinder's, our nearest drugstore. The mothers would sit in a booth and drink tea, talking and smoking, while

Willie and I would look at the movie magazines, or sit at the counter and drink milkshakes and talk movie stars and dream of marshmallow sundaes or banana splits.

Both our mothers had no money. Both our mothers were lonely, and worried sick about the war and people at home. Both of them – though we weren't supposed to know about this – were having problems with the families we lived with.

"You're lucky to live with a rich family," Willie said.

"I don't think they're especially rich. They drive a Hillman Minx."

"Ours don't have a car. They both work in a garage."

Willie told me her mum had got a big shock when they arrived and found out that the family lived in a very small house in a poor district 'on the wrong side of the tracks'.

"Why did they invite you, then?" I asked.

"They're rellies of Dad's. They wanted to save us from Hitler," said Willie. "I don't think they'd thought about it properly. They never told us they're quite poor. Mum hates to take money from them. She hates it. She thinks they can hardly afford to feed us. And she's sick with worry about Dad. He's overseas. We haven't heard from him for three months."

To take her mind off this, I told her about the Canadian soldiers who'd been camped in the woods below my convent boarding school, and how my friend Sue and I had a club – just us two – and used to waylay them and make them do forfeits. Willie thought this was 'fantabulous'.

"I wish we could have a club like yours here. I love its name! The League of the Deadly Nightshade – how did you ever think of that?"

"Nightshade berries are the most poisonous you can find."

"Great! I love it! But nobody'd be allowed to join if it had a name like that!"

"We could call it the Crescent Club."

"I don't live in a posh crescent! Anyway, it sounds a bit tame after Deadly Nightshade…"

Next time we met, she'd changed her mind. "Okay, let's have a club. I'll be the recruiting officer."

Willie recruited like mad. After three days the Crescent Club had its first meeting, with a whole six members. In addition to the two of us, three were from Willie's school and the other was a girl called Patricia, from the little park gang. (Well, I recruited her.)

I thought we'd just have a meeting, but Willie had decided there should be a test you had to take in order to join. This sounded a bit like the Camel Club at the convent – a big girls' club, where you had to be able to ride a bike – so I didn't think much about it until she told us what the test was: we had to go on to the *riverbank* and jump off a sort of cliff, grab an overhanging branch and swing down to the river's edge, like Tarzan.

There was a silence when she announced this, but it didn't last long. All the others said they'd do it. All except me.

"Mummy won't let me go down on the riverbank," I said.

Willie looked at me as if I'd said I wasn't allowed to go to the lavatory. "But everybody plays by the river!" she exclaimed.

I bit my lip and said nothing.

"Your cousin goes," said Patricia.

I was shocked. "He does not!"

"Yeah, he does. He went last night with my brother Bob and all the gang. They had a weenie roast."

I couldn't believe my ears. "They *make fires* down there?"

"Sure. Weenie roasts are the best fun."

I got up from where we were all sitting on the grass in the park and ran home. Cameron was in his bedroom doing homework. When I burst in, he at once looked up, put his finger to his lips and said, "Widdiya, woddiya."

This was our secret code. It meant, *Keep your voice down*. I closed the door.

"Patricia Douglas says you went down on the riverbank with her brother."

"Oh," said Cameron after a moment. "She does, does she?" He went back to his homework.

"Well, did you?"

"So what?"

"But we're not allowed."

"It's not dangerous. It's just woods and steep bits, and a bit of beach. Nothing can possibly happen."

"*But Mummy said we mustn't!*"

"Auntie must think there are bears. Do shut up and go away. I'm trying to work."

"I'll tell on you!"

He gave me his basilisk look. He didn't do this often but when he did, I quailed.

"You'd better not," he said very quietly.

We both knew I wouldn't – we never tattled on each other. I felt torn. The trouble was, I hated to do anything I couldn't tell Mummy. I wasn't what you'd call the rebel type.

Downstairs, the doorbell rang. It was Willie. She'd followed me. Her freckled face was a furious red.

"You and I started the club," she said the minute I opened the door. "You can't chicken out. You're *English*!"

I wasn't sure what she meant by that but I got the general idea.

★

The next day the six of us trooped down to the river.

The prairie around Saskatoon wasn't only fields of wheat, after all. Lots of it was dusty flat land – no trees or bushes, just sort of rough grass. Lots of gopher holes. Nothing green. Of course, the gardens and parks were green and had trees. But that wasn't *countryside*. The riverbank was, and after the little park, the polite back yards and the manicured park around the Bessborough Hotel, going down there was like going into a wonderful wild jungle.

The moment I followed Willie across the road next to the river – the road that had always marked the border of Mummy's 'no-go area' – I felt a tingle of guilt. But then I thought, *Cameron's been down here. If he can, why shouldn't I?*

There were no paths, just tracks, beaten down by kids and dogs. There were trees and bushes and beyond them you could see the river racing by, glinting in the sun. Strange, beautiful and thrilling. An unexplored world.

Willie led us, walking single file, to the place she'd chosen. The 'cliff' was about six feet high – a place where the bank had broken down, with a pile of sandy soil at the bottom. At the top was a little ledge to stand on, and across the open space was an overhanging tree branch, just the right size to grip. But it was quite a long way away from the ledge – you had to make a dive into space to grab it, and swing yourself down.

Willie did it first. She gave Tarzan's cry, launched herself forward and grabbed the branch, swinging down and landing beyond the pile of sand. She threw herself so strongly that when she landed she slid on her bottom nearly as far as the narrow beach before she could stop herself.

My heart practically failed me. *I could never do that*, I thought. I could imagine missing the branch and just diving down face first. I could *always* imagine the worst that could happen. That's why I was such a scaredy-cat about physical things. (Forget scaredy-cat – try coward.)

Patricia made a face at me. She was scared too. But in the pause after Willie jumped, she suddenly took her place on the ledge, and as the branch stopped swaying she threw herself out and grabbed it, then down she went.

Next, a girl called Margy did it, then one called Babe. Then Babe's sister Rhoda. She was only nine – and small for her age. She dithered on the ledge for a minute, but then the branch swayed back from Babe's jump and she was almost able to grab it without diving. Her trouble was, she wasn't heavy enough for her feet to trail on the ground so she was left dangling. Willie and Babe reached up and caught her.

Rhoda had done it. Little Rhoda! How could I chicken out? I stepped on to the ledge. Willie let the branch swing back towards me. It was only as high as my waist and looked miles away.

"Go, Lindy! Now!"

I shut my eyes. Truly, I did. I didn't dare not do it and I didn't dare do it so I shut my eyes and threw my hands out, hoping like an idiot that the branch would magically come into them when I jumped. Of course I missed the branch, but I'd leant out far enough to lose my balance so I half fell, half jumped off the ledge, feet first.

Luckily, I landed on the pile of sand. The others all laughed and ran to help me up. All except Willie.

"Do it again. You didn't do it," she said. She sounded just like a sergeant in an army film we'd seen the week before at the Daylight.

I would really much rather have died than do it again.

"I can't," I said. "I'm too scared."

The others stopped laughing and looked at Willie.

"Then you can't be in the club," she said furiously.

Was that so? I forgot my fear. "The club was my idea. It isn't about daring people to do silly things." Then I had my brainwave. "It's about doing things for the war."

Willie's mouth fell open. "What, for the war?" she said.

"We should earn money for war bonds," I said. "There's some *point* in that."

This time it was Willie who left. She scrambled up the bank and stormed off. The rest of us trailed back up to the road, all talking about what we could do to earn some money.

"We could sell candy and lemonade."

I remembered a sale we'd had at the convent. I said, "We could all *give* things – clothes, books. Stuff our mothers would give us."

"We'll talk about it at the next meeting," said Margy.

I was worried Willie wouldn't come back. But she did, of course, the next day – riding into the little park on a very old bicycle with a loud bell, and her little brother Alfred on the back. She'd had the best idea of all.

"There's a drive on to collect scrap metal. For melting down and turning into war stuff. We could do that. We'll use Alfie's go-cart, to put it in. Only we'll have to let him join."

Our scrap-metal drive really started something. We even got our pictures in the paper: 'Crescent Club Does Its Bit' read one headline. But that was later.

Other kids, especially boys, noticed us trundling our cart through the back alleys and over the rough ground near the railway, collecting all kinds of scrap, and asked what we were doing. When we told them, they went haring off to get carts of their own and before long every kid in the neighbourhood seemed to be collecting scrap.

Soon there wasn't even any silver cigarette paper left lying about, let alone any screws or nails. As for tin cans, nobody would be throwing any at the trains for a while.

Margy's father said we should be proud of our war effort. He took the scrap in the boot of his car down to some central collecting place and came to the next club meeting to tell us the man there said we'd probably collected enough to build a couple of tanks.

"Slight exaggeration," said Cameron when I told him. But then he said, "Well done, though. Wonder if the ginks across the river have thought of it?"

The 'ginks across the river' were regarded as aliens, ruffians, gangsters – but Cameron didn't care. He caught the streetcar over Broadway Bridge, accosted the first boy he saw in the street and suggested they do a scrap-metal drive too. When he told his pals on our side what he'd done, they gaped at him. None of them would have dreamt of going into west-bank territory.

He admitted to me he'd tried to take Spajer with him, as a guard dog, but Spajer wouldn't get on the streetcar. When Spaje came home alone, Luti was upset with Cameron for the first time and he was quite crushed for once. We were fond of Luti. She was sweet to us. She loved cooking things that we'd never had before, and got pink with excitement whenever we liked them. She didn't take us around and show us off like Gordon did; she just made a home for us. I think she minded a lot, not having kids of her own. Maybe all this 'Poppa' and 'Momma' stuff Gordon played at just reminded her.

Chapter Eight

Fall (OK, Cameron – Autumn)

In October, the leaves on the maple trees turned to beautiful paint-box reds and oranges and yellows. Mummy just couldn't get over it. That was when she changed her mind about the riverbank. She took us down there herself, to get closer to the magic, and for the pleasure of sitting on the beach and looking across the river to the trees in the Bessborough Hotel's park. She said each tree was like the Burning Bush in the Bible, blazing but never getting burnt up. Dear old Spajer used to lie across her feet on the sand, panting gently while she played with his ears.

But Spaje *was* old now. One morning, we came down to breakfast to find Luti crying into the scrambled eggs.

"My poor old darling's gone," she sobbed.

We looked at each other in horror. I think we all thought, just for a second, that she meant Gordon.

When Luti showed us Spajer dead in his basket, we all put our arms around her. Well, Mummy and I did. Cameron walked out of the room on stiff legs and later I found him out in the garden helping Gordon to dig a grave.

Men don't cry, I thought, except that both of them were. You never saw Cameron cry. I thought it wasn't very manly of him, to cry for a dog when he didn't cry for other things.

I told Mummy about it.

"He's so horribly homesick," she said. "It must've been like burying Bubbles."

I felt a shock of shame. Why hadn't I realised that? I was very, very careful not to use any Canadian slang for a long time after that, not to annoy him.

There were only two times a week, apart from meals and outings, when Cameron and I got together: funnies-time on Fridays and letters-time on Sundays.

We both fell in love with the funnies. At home we'd had Pip, Squeak and Wilfred in the *Daily Mirror*, which we missed, but here there were tons of different ones. We read the daily strips in the local paper, the *Star Phoenix* – Li'l Abner, Blondie, Bringing Up Father. But our favourite – our passion – was 'The Spirit' in Friday's edition of the *Montreal Standard*.

Of course all of us kids – even Cameron, though he pretended not to – followed the adventures of Superman and the Masked Marvel and Wonder Woman, but the Spirit was a crime-fighter with a difference. He didn't have any superpowers and he didn't wear a costume, just a mask. He was so funny and believable that even Cameron wasn't ashamed to love him, and we had tugs-of-war every Friday when the paper came – who would get first go at the comic section? Gordon used to hold it above our heads to tease us.

The Spirit's artist used to make things fly from one square frame to another, sometimes breaking all the frames when there was an explosion or a fire or something crazy. There was one story about a sad jazz musician who played his saxophone in New York.

> "The shadows loom
> within my room…
> And canons boom
> their dirge of doom…
>
> WIDDIYA
>
> WODDIYA…"

(That was the saxophone playing.)

The words and notes spilt down the page, breaking the frames.

Quotes from The Spirit became Cameron's and my secret language. When Gordon was in a mood, and Mummy kept shushing us, we'd whisper, "The shadows loom!" Or, if he raised his voice to Luti, "The canons boom." Sometimes, when the whole house seemed to be crackling with tension, we just muttered, "Widdiya woddiya" and kept to our rooms. But at mealtimes we had to come to the dining table and if Gordon was still in a mood, 'Widdiya woddiya' could go on till bedtime.

The worst times were when Mummy was with me in our room after supper, and Gordon would call up the stairs, "Where's my kids? C'mon down, Poppa wants his family!"

Mummy would call back, "They're in bed, Gordon."

But Gordon would insist. "Then you come down, Alex, why don't ya! Poppa don't like to drink by himself! He wants a li'l company!"

Mummy used to go down, but I could tell she didn't want to. Luti would apologise at breakfast the next day and say that Gordon worked so hard he needed a little drink to unwind.

Gordon was nice at other times. And Mummy kept reminding us that he was keeping us. That we had to be grateful.

On Sundays we'd sit down after breakfast to write our weekly letters home – me to Daddy (and sometimes, at first, to my old best friend, Sue) and Cameron to his parents. Mummy of course wrote to Daddy and Grampy and her sisters all the time. Letters took weeks to get to England, if they got there at all – Mummy said the ships were full of stuff for the war, including food parcels, because food in England was getting really short. I used to have dreams about my family looking like skeletons.

What she didn't mention was how much shipping was being sunk, but Cameron soon found this out and told me about it.

"Rotten German U-boats! They're sea-devils, creeping up on our ships. You can't see them, you can't stop them – hateful, lousy, *bastard* things!"

Mummy usually stopped us swearing, but this time she let him. "He needs to," she said later when I asked her why. "That's what swearing's for. He's finding it hard to accept that we can't go back till the war's over. But it doesn't stop him wanting to."

The best letters we got – and how precious they were! – weren't from Daddy; they were from the aunts. Auntie Millie in particular. She told us everything that was happening, always trying to make even air raids and rationing sound like lots of fun. She sometimes put in Bubbles' latest car-crimes. He was a car-chaser – if the front gate was left open he would tear into the road and chase after cars, barking madly up their exhaust pipes. Letters with Bubbles in them were Cameron's favourites. He used to take them to his room to read over and over.

Occasionally there were photographs. One lot showed the two aunts standing by the Galloping Maggot, our old Austin Seven car that Mummy had left with Auntie Millie. They wore long raincoats and army helmets and were surrounded by buckets and hosepipes, ready in case there were incendiary bombs, the kind that burst into flames when they land. They were all smiling as if the war was a game. And there was one with Auntie Bee and Uncle Will in his naval uniform, with our little cousin Ray in his siren-suit.

My uncle Jack, Cameron's father, wasn't in any of them. I wondered why. He never wrote to Cameron, who got all his news from Auntie Millie.

Grampy, however, did write. He wrote in the most beautiful writing and put in lots of detail. Mummy was wrong about Redcliffe Square not being bombed. His big house had had all the front windows broken by a bomb. *But don't worry! The government will pay to have them all put back*, he reassured us.

He told us his housekeeper, Gene, was working in an aircraft factory, that Daddy was working 'all the hours God sends' and that he, Grampy, was an air-raid warden, going out at night on his bicycle to make sure people didn't show lights in their windows to guide the German bombers. *My dear old faithful Shott runs alongside my bike and keeps me company in the dark hours.*

Cameron and I sent him a postcard with all the autumn tree colours. We never heard that he got it. Maybe it ended up in the Atlantic Ocean.

At the end of October we had our first Hallowe'en. I'd never heard of Hallowe'en. Mummy said that as far as she knew, it was something to do with souls of the dead, from pagan times, or maybe witches. When all the other kids started getting really excited and told me that I'd have to dress up to go trick-or-treating, I was completely bewildered.

We asked Luti about it, but it was Gordon who answered.

"Oh, gee whiz, you folks don't have Hallowe'en? It's pretty near as big as Christmas, here! The kids'll have a ball. We must go downtown to the costume shop and buy you something to wear! What do you fancy, Cameron? Would you like to be a ghost, or a vampire, or maybe a skeleton?"

I thought Cameron wouldn't want to have anything to do with it, but when Mummy said he'd have to go trick-or-treating with me or I wouldn't be allowed, he said, "I'd like to dress up as The Spirit."

"Well, all you'd need for that is a suit and a hat and a mask," he said.

"That's fine. That's all I want."

Gordon turned to me. "What about you, Lindy? You'd like something a bit fancier, I bet!"

I said I'd like to be the ghost that walked the Bloody Tower with my head tucked underneath my arm.

Luti jumped. "Lindy! How awful! Whose ghost was it?"

"Anne Boleyn," I said. "Mummy'll sing the song for you, if you like."

"Perhaps some other time," Luti said.

But Gordon loved Mummy doing party-pieces and made her sing the whole song, which she did with a Yorkshire accent. He clapped like mad at the end.

"How would you do the head?" he asked.

"Maybe a football?"

He thought that was a wonderful idea. "So, we get you an Anne Boleyn costume, if they've got one, and paint a football to look like a head! That'd knock 'em cold – they'll never've seen anything like that!"

"But what about your real head?" said Cameron.

That stumped me, but only for a minute. "I could have a very long costume that came right up over my head and put a coat hanger in for the shoulders."

"How would you see out?"

"I could make little tiny holes in the top."

"And where would your arms go? More holes, not so tiny?"

"Be a shame to spoil the dress…" said Luti. "If you've had to buy it…" Suddenly she stood up. "I'll make it for you!" she exclaimed.

And she did. She got out her sewing machine and a long evening dress she'd worn when she was young. It was made from a beautiful blue silky fabric with a pretty pattern on it. She unpicked the seams, found some paper patterns and managed to make a new dress out of it that looked almost like a real Tudor one. But the clever part was the sleeves; I was able to put my arms through some holes in the sides and into the sleeves that hung down from the coat hanger that had been sewn in to look like shoulders. It had to rest on my head, so Luti used a padded hanger with the hook cut off.

Gordon bought a football specially, stuck some false hair on it and painted a face. At Cameron's suggestion, he even painted some red for where it had been cut off by the executioner.

When I tried on the costume for the first time and came downstairs, holding on to the bannister because I could only see a bit through the eye-holes, Mummy gave a little scream.

"That is the most *horribly* realistic thing I've ever

seen!" she said. "You're really going round the houses at night, knocking on doors? You'll frighten the wits out of people!"

"We should put some red paint round the neck of the dress too," Cameron said, getting carried away.

But Luti said no, that was going too far.

On the night of Hallowe'en, the Crescent Club came to collect me, including Willie's little brother Alfie, dressed, for some reason, as a gnome. They all thought my costume was 'fantabulous' — even Willie, who was dressed as a witch with a pointed hat and a false nose with a big black wart on it, said it was the best. They all wanted to look at the head, which really was horrible. Gordon had gone to town, making the eyes and tongue pop out and using lots of red paint for the blood around the neck.

Cameron wore a boy's blue two-piece suit that Gordon had borrowed from somewhere, and Gordon's fedora hat pulled down over his mask. Of course he wasn't too pleased about having to go trick-or-treating with a bunch of girls, instead of with his own gang, but Mummy was firm; she wasn't keen on the whole business, but Gordon told her that nothing could happen to us if we stayed in "our nice neighbourhood" around the crescent.

But, of course, Willie had other ideas. She wanted to go to the neighbourhood across the tracks where she lived with the Warrens. Most of the club lived there too, so Cameron, Patricia and I were out-voted.

We tramped through the lamp-lit streets, passing groups of kids, all in weird costumes and scary masks. We saw them on doorsteps, ringing bells, and shouting "Trick or treat!"

Cameron said, "Let's do a few on the way," so we did, and were given handfuls of sweets to put in our collecting bags – orange and black lollies, white ghost-chews and chocolate skeletons. Everyone who opened the door got a satisfying fright when they saw me. One man wanted us to come inside so he could photograph me, but Cameron said we weren't allowed.

We were already feeling like candy millionaires by the time we crossed the railway and arrived on Willie's home turf.

It really was a lot darker and drearier around there than in our area. But Willie and the others were quite at home, and Willie said there was an old man living next door to her house who was 'real mean' – he'd complained about Alfie making a noise.

"Yeah. I *hate* him!" said Alfie. "He won't give us any treats. Let's fix him!"

Willie and Alfie had it all worked out, what the trick would be.

"We'll twist toilet paper in his hedge," she said. She had a roll ready under her witch's robe.

Cameron and I exchanged uneasy looks. But Margy, Babe and Rhoda (who was a ghost) said he deserved it.

We left him till last, in case we had to run.

There didn't seem to be anything mean about the people around there, who gave us just as many candies as we'd got at the richer people's houses. Nobody didn't give, so there were no tricks, and Willie was just warming up to go to the old man's house when we heard a hoot from across the street, and there was Patricia's brother Bob and Cameron's gang from Nutana. Some of them lived in this district too. They came running over.

They looked very big to me, being proper teenagers. In their zombie and vampire and monster costumes they were really scary. We girls all backed away, leaving Cameron in front.

"Hey, Cam, whatcha doing with a bunch of girls? C'mon with us! We're getting plenty, and we've done some great tricks too!"

Cameron hesitated. "I'm on duty here, looking after my cousin," he said.

I'd never heard his English accent sound so out of place.

The boys all laughed. "'On duty!' You gotta love him. Heck, she'll be OK – she's got Willie the Witch to mind her! You'll take care of her, won't you, Willie?"

"Sure," said Willie.

"C'mon, Cam, 'old boy' – we'll use you as our front man! The smaller you are, the more they give ya!"

And before he could protest, Cameron was almost carried away. The last I saw of him was the Spirit's fedora hat surrounded by teenage giants, rushing through the lamplight and off into darkness, whooping and hollering and making ghost noises.

There was a moment's silence, and then Willie said, "Good, we don't need him. Let's go do it." And she led the way up a path to a little house made of wooden boards, like most of them.

We climbed the steps to the porch and Willie boldly banged on the screen door. Then she kind of pushed me to the front.

"He'll just die when he sees you!" she whispered gleefully. "Hold the head in front of you!"

By this time the coat hanger that was across the top of my head had slipped a bit and in reaching up to try to straighten it, I dropped the head. It fell right on the doorstep, and when the porch light came on and the door opened, it sort of rolled forwards and landed at the feet of the person in the doorway.

It wasn't an old man. It was an old lady.

She stared at headless me, and then looked down and saw the football head, in all its gory glory, staring up at her with its popping eyes. She gave a scream and the next minute she'd folded up and was lying on the porch.

What happened next was a kind of blur. We backed down the steps — Alfie actually fell down them. The old man came rushing out when he heard the thump of her falling. As he did, he accidentally kicked the head, which rolled down the steps. He didn't even notice it. He went down on his knees beside her and started crying, "Mae! Mae! Oh God, make her open her eyes!"

We all stood there, frozen. Little Alfie was the first to come to his senses. He picked himself up, then the head — and ran away with it, off into the darkness.

Then Willie came to life. She raced across to the house she lived in, next door, and in a minute or two her mother and Mrs Warren came running out and bent over the old lady. All the grown-ups had their backs to us. I could barely see what was going on, through the little eye-holes Luti had cut in the front of my dress. Or maybe I just had my eyes shut, so I couldn't see what I'd done.

What if I'd killed that old lady?

Suddenly we heard a police siren blaring, and turned our heads like startled deer.

Willie hadn't come back, but Margy and Babe suddenly grabbed me and started pulling at my dress. Margy ripped open the snap fasteners at the front and Babe tore the hanger out and then just pulled the material down to my real shoulders. The dress trailed on the ground. Babe stuck the hanger into her collecting bag. I took a deep, shaky breath, and realised I hadn't breathed properly for the past hour because my face was covered with cloth.

The police car drew up and two policemen jumped out, pushed past us, and went up the steps. By this time the porch was empty. The old lady had been carried into the house. A third policeman stood near us to stop us leaving. After a few minutes the others came out again and started asking us questions and looking at our costumes.

"Is she all right?" I managed to ask.

"She's had a bad shock. Maybe when she saw the ghost—" looking at little Rhoda standing there in her sheet, as un-scary as a tiny tent with two holes in the top. I wanted to say, *It was me, it was me!* I'd never felt so frightened and guilty in my life.

Word travelled fast. Before long other cars were drawing up and out of one of them leapt Gordon. He had a word with the policemen, and shepherded me and Patricia into the Hillman. On the way back to the crescent, he said, "I got a phone call. What've you kids been up to? I *told* you not to leave the crescent!"

Gordon dropped Patricia off and drove home. Mummy was waiting on the doorstep. Willie's mum had phoned her to tell her what had happened.

She thanked Gordon and rushed me up to our room. I kept tripping over the dress, now at least a foot too long.

"Where's Cameron?" was the first thing she asked.

"I don't know."

"He was supposed to stay with you!"

My first snitch bumped against my teeth. But I bit it back.

"Well," she said. "The poor old girl you frightened the wits out of is all right, I gather. I shouldn't have let you go. Silly dangerous nonsense! Thank heaven we don't have Hallowe'en at home!"

She was peeling the dress over my head. It got stuck on the collecting bag, which I'd somehow kept hold of.

"What's all this? Holy smoke! Have you been robbing a sweetshop?" she said, peering in. She brought out a chocolate coffin, stared at it, and then bit it in half. "You could have done for the poor old thing. Apparently she's got a weak heart."

"Can I have a sweet?"

We sat there on the bed, silently munching. And crunching. The lollies were the best.

"I'll murder Cameron," she said.

"Oh, no, don't!"

"He shouldn't have left you! And I had to let Gordon go to fetch you in the car, even though—"

"I know, I could smell it," I said.

"Did the police see you headless?"

"No. Alfie ran away with the head."

"I must remember Alfie in my Will," she said.

Just then we heard the front doorbell ring, and Gordon talking to Cameron.

Mummy went to the top of the stairs.

"Cameron! Come up here!"

He came up and Mummy took him into his bedroom and shut the door.

I couldn't resist. After a few minutes I put my ear to the wall and listened.

"Who do you owe your loyalty to?" Mummy was saying angrily. She wasn't fooling – I knew that voice. "To Lindy or to a bunch of street urchins?"

I guessed he said me. I mean, muttered.

"I gave you a job to do. I don't ask much of you, Cameron. Something really bad nearly happened, and you could have prevented it."

"I'm sorry, Auntie."

"Go to bed."

A bit later I bumped into Cameron in the bathroom. We brushed our teeth, which needed it after stuffing our mouths with sweets till I, at least, was feeling sick. I whispered, "It's OK."

He didn't say anything. His face was still red. Mummy hardly ever told him off – not half as often as Auntie Millie did at home. But Auntie Millie, Cameron figured, had the right.

Chapter Nine

Snow

Autumn changed to winter early in the prairies that year. Cameron and I were probably the only ones who were pleased. The first snowfall came in mid-November.

We'd been dreaming of the snow Gordon had promised us, that was higher than a man's head. When we woke up one morning to find a white world, we were thrilled.

We put on our snowsuits – thick baggy woollen trousers and hooded jacket for me, something like plus-fours with thick socks and a leather fur-lined cap for Cameron – and rushed out into the garden. The cold was strange – very, but somehow not very. We could hardly draw it into our lungs, and yet we didn't feel shivery like in cold weather at home. Our breath made dense clouds and I could feel my eyebrows kind of pulling.

Our excitement turned to dismay when we realised the snow – fine white powdery stuff, not the big wet flakes we got at home – wasn't head-high or anything like it, and lay only about six inches deep. It fell and it fell, but, just like in one of our favourite spoof radio commercials: *Other cereals snap, crackle and pop. Our brand just kinda* lays *there.*

We rushed back in again and consulted Luti.

"Well, give it time," she said. "It'll snow for days now. It does mount up. But for really deep snow, there has to be wind, to pile it into drifts."

Ah, yes, I remembered. *Drifts.*

We rushed out again and tried to have a snowball fight, but to our amazement, this snow didn't make snowballs. Nor could you make a snowman with it, let alone a fort. This snow was so dry it wouldn't stick together. We'd never seen snow like it.

It was good for kicking through, though, rising up in slow clouds, and it didn't make you wet if you rolled about in it. Luti came out in her own snow-clothes and showed us how to make snow angels, by lying on our backs and making wing-patterns with our arms.

"My Spajer used to love playing in the snow," Luti said. Then, not to make us sad, she added, "It's good for sledding. There's a sled in the garden shed."

I rushed into the house while Cameron got it out. Mummy was in the living room listening to the news on the radio.

"Have you seen the *trees*?" I asked excitedly. "Every twig has a white coat! Can we go sledding on the riverbank?"

"Sure," she said. Even she was picking up Canadian by now. She jumped up, stubbing out her cigarette. "I'll come with you!"

We carried the sled through the little park towards the river. We saw that men were making a kind of wooden frame, all round the open part of the park, just about a foot high. Mummy asked them what it was for.

"It's for the skating rink," they told us. "We'll flood it tonight and by morning you'll be able to skate on it."

Cameron was keen. I wasn't so sure; Gordon had bought skates for us, and was 'rarin' to go', teaching us, but his joke was, "What's the hardest thing about learning to skate? The ice!"

We made our way to the top of the bank, beyond the road. There we stopped. There were dozens – maybe hundreds – of kids and a few grown-ups, all with sleds and flat wooden toboggans. They'd already made slopes through, and over, the undergrowth and there were screams and laughter and swishing sounds everywhere as they went bumping and whizzing down towards the snowy beach.

And beyond!

Mummy was staring over the trees at the river. "Look!" she said. "Can you believe it?"

Nobody had bothered to tell us about this. The great South Saskatchewan River was frozen! All that rushing water had been caught and tamed by the freezing cold and was still and white and solid. I don't suppose it was frozen right to the bottom, but certainly deep enough for people to walk and sled on it. If it had been smooth, I bet you could have driven a car across it.

But it wasn't flat. It was as if the cold had caught the river in all its waves and eddies – as if it had been frozen not little by little, the ice weighting it to flatness, but suddenly, all at once. There were humps and panes of ice sticking up and even driftwood logs jutting out of the mass.

We just stood and stared.

"The temperature must be much lower than it feels," said Mummy. Her winter coat was wide open, showing her jumper and trousers, and her scarf wasn't even wrapped round her neck properly. Right on cue as she said this, a strange man came up to us. To all our amazement he pulled the edges of Mummy's coat together.

"My dear lady," he said, "you mustn't expose yourself like that! You must be from the Old Country. You don't feel it because your blood's still thick, but this below-freezing cold is treacherous! Please fasten your coat and wrap something round your face!"

Mummy did as she was told. "How cold is it?" she asked.

"It's twenty degrees below zero," he said.

Mummy stared at him as if she couldn't believe she'd heard right.

"*Twenty below zero!* Why aren't we all frozen like the river?" she laughed.

"It's no joke. You can get frostbite. Don't let the kids take their gloves off." He turned to us. "Son, cover your ears. And whatever you do, kids, don't touch metal with your tongue or your bare fingers. They'll freeze to it." And he tipped his cap and walked away.

Cameron brought the ear flaps on his cap down and tied the tapes under his chin. "Ow," he said suddenly. "My ears are hurting! Auntie, do you think they've frozen already?"

She rubbed them briskly through his cap. "Go and sled," she said. "Go on. Get in the queue. And don't forget, I want a turn after you."

I wanted Cameron to go first, but at the same time I hated waiting. It was too cold to stand in a queue; however much you stamped your boots your feet got colder and colder. When Willie – who I hadn't seen since That Night, when I'd considered she'd deserted us – came up to me and offered me a go on her toboggan, I took her up on it. I generously decided to forgive her. I'd missed her, anyway.

I sat on the toboggan, which was flat with the front curled over and a bit of rope to hold on to, and Willie gave me an almighty push. Before I knew what was happening I was hurtling down the slope, bumping over snow-covered bushes and just missing a young tree halfway down. It was as exciting as my first proper bicycle ride, down the hill from my old school. Was that only five months ago? It felt like a lifetime.

I saw Cameron careering down the slope on the sled. Its metal runners took it much farther and faster than the toboggan, right out on to the river! It was crazy. It was wonderful. I dragged the toboggan back up the hill.

"Can I have another go?" I asked, panting.

"After me," Willie said.

Then she did an amazing thing. She *stood up* on the toboggan, holding the rope, and went down like that, her pigtails flying under her woolly cap. This time she didn't make a Tarzan cry, but shouted, "Hi-ho Silver! Away!" like the Lone Ranger.

Even the boys gave a cheer.

I thought, *If she can do it, so can I.*

Meanwhile Cameron had handed our sled over to Mummy. She sat on it, pushed off with her heels and went shooting down the slope, which was now icy and very slick. She kept her heels off the ground and didn't try to brake and in a few seconds she was out on the river.

"Your mum's a good sport, isn't she?" said Willie admiringly.

Well, I could be a good sport too.

I took the rope and stood on the toboggan. Its nose pitched down and it began to fly, with me standing on it. But not for long; halfway down the slope I lost my balance and sat down. Hard.

I felt my tailbone crack against the wood, and a sharp pain shot up my back. I let out a howl. The toboggan was still going. At the bottom I fell off and lay on my side in the snow. I was in agony.

Willie and Cameron came galumphing down, kicking snow all over me. "Are you okay? Did you hurt your bum?" Willie shouted as she reached me.

Yes, I'd hurt my bum. I thought I'd broken my tailbone.

Cameron hiked me to my feet. "Can you walk?"

I found I could. But oh boy. Did it ever hurt!

Mummy hadn't seen what happened. She was back at the top, talking to Willie's mother, who had come to fetch Willie home for tea. When the others hauled me back up the slope, crying with pain, Mummy turned a face to me that told me something had happened already to shock her. Of course, she was shocked more when she saw my tears. She and Cameron practically had to carry me back to the crescent, where I was put to bed with a hot water bottle on my tail and two 'pinkies' – tablets Mummy had brought from England, Daddy's magic pills that were supposed to cure everything, and often did.

Later, when she came to bed, I sensed she was worried about something that wasn't me.

"Poor Irene," she said. Irene was Willie's mum. "She's in a terrible state. Mr Warren has lost his job. She says it's simply impossible for them to keep her and the children any longer. She'll have to get a job, and she's like me – no qualifications! She married straight from school. What on earth will she do? Oh, God, I do wish our government would change its mind and let our husbands send us some money!"

"Can't O'F help us?"

"He already does as much as he possibly can. I don't like asking Gordon for money either."

"At least Gordon has a good job."

"Yes." After a bit she said, "Lindy, what would you think if... if we left here and got a place of our own?"

"That'd be perfect! Then we wouldn't have to keep quiet when Gordon's in a mood."

"You do know that that's a euphemism, don't you?"

Euphemism was one of Cameron's words. It meant saying something nice to cover up something worse.

"Well..." I said. "Is it whiskey?"

"He's fine when he's sober. But he goes on benders. He drinks too much and then he..."

"What?"

Mummy lay still in the darkness.

"He gets... difficult. Luti has to tiptoe about, not to upset him, and I do too. He – he wants me to drink with him. He insists. He pours me a very large drink and puts ice in it and then he gives it to me. I don't want it so I sit there with the glass and I try to hold it steady, but... I can't. I'm so tense, my hand shakes. And he watches. He watches the glass. And the ice... tinkles... and I'm *ordering* my hand to keep still... and then suddenly he starts to roar."

I'd heard this. At night. It had woken me once or twice, Gordon's roar. But I could never hear the words. Now she told me.

"'Look at you! You're shaking! You're scared of me! I scare my women! What kind of swine am I? What kind of beast?' And then he starts to cry. Once he threw his own glass on the floor. And Luti rushes to comfort him as if he were her little boy."

I forgot my sore tail and moved over to cuddle her. "Can't we leave?"

"If only I could work to keep us! But I've never had a job, except acting, and I can't act here. How can we live if we have no money?"

This problem should have occupied my mind all the time, but it didn't. The weather was too exciting.

Whatever his faults, nobody could say Gordon was a tightwad. Our winter clothes that we'd brought with us simply weren't warm enough – he had to buy proper Canadian stuff for all of us. Not to mention three pairs of skates.

Everyone went to school dressed for the cold in snowsuits over their ordinary clothes – skirts for the girls – with fur-lined boots. When we got there we had to strip all this off in the cloakroom. The school was heated, like the houses, by a furnace in the basement. Gordon taught Cameron how to 'feed' ours with coke – "I guess you didn't do that kinda work at home, but here, that's a man's job." Shovelling the endless snow was another!

Luckily for Luti, Mummy and me, women weren't expected to do men's work.

The little park turned into a skating rink, sure enough, and was alive with skaters most of the day and into the evening, when there were special floodlights. The 'wall' round the rink wasn't high enough to hold on to so Gordon had to be our support. Cameron, of *course*, wouldn't stoop to hanging on to anyone, though. When he was determined, he didn't waste time, and was soon sailing round on the ice with his hands behind his back, as if he'd done it all his life. I clutched Gordon and didn't so much sail as stagger.

Mummy learnt to skate too. Gordon far preferred giving her his arm and helping her round the rink than me, so I didn't get as much practice as Mummy did. Still, the little park gang was nice and would get each side of me and kind of pull me along until I got the idea. My ankles burnt like fire at first, but after a while they stopped and I could slither around the rink on my own.

I did go sledding again when my tail-bruise healed, but didn't do any more stand-up stunts. I'd gone off Willie, a bit. She was too reckless for me. I missed her in a way, but as we didn't go to the same school, and as she lived across the tracks, I didn't see her unless one of us made an effort.

And one terrible night, that's what she did.

★

Gordon loved board games like ludo and chequers and snakes and ladders, and card games like gin rummy, at which he always beat me. I didn't like this and sometimes sulked. I might have been a better sport, if he hadn't *crowed* when he won.

One night we were all around the dining table playing snap when the doorbell rang. Luti went to answer it.

I heard a shrill voice at the door. A voice I knew! I jumped up and ran through the living room. There on the porch in the lamplight was Willie.

She had Alfie with her. They had no proper snow clothes on – they had snow on their bare heads and on their shoulders. When redheads cry their faces go a kind of red that clashes with their hair. This makes them look extra desperate. But Willie and Alfie couldn't have looked much worse – sobbing and shivering, like orphans out in the snow.

Luti called, "Gordon! Alex! Please come!" She looked, and sounded, frightened. "Something's happened to Mrs Lord!"

Gordon took charge. He brought the kids in, wrapped a rug around Alfie, and sent Luti to the kitchen to get them something hot to drink. He asked Willie a couple of questions, which she was crying too much to answer. He practically ripped Cameron's sweater off him and put it round her. Then he muffled himself up, and drove off in the car. Mummy carried Alfie, all bundled up and shivering, into the kitchen, while I took Willie into the dining room and shut the door.

"What's happened to your mum?" I asked.

"I don't know. I think she's dead," Willie sobbed.

The word 'dead', connected with a mother, hit me like an electric shock.

"*Dead?* She can't be! What do you mean?"

"She's lying on the floor. Nobody's there. I couldn't go next door. I didn't know what to do."

Willie put her head down among the cards on the table and sobbed out loud. I pulled my chair closer and put my arm around her. I could feel her shaking. I tried *not* to imagine Mummy lying on the floor in an empty house, maybe dead. *The worst. The worst.*

Cameron came in. "Luti says, come into the kitchen," he said. He looked at Willie's bent shoulders for a minute. Then he said, "Willie, Alfie wants you."

Willie stood up. She wiped her dripping face on the sleeve of Cameron's sweater. Then she stumbled into the kitchen, Cameron and I following. Alfie was there with Mummy and Luti. He threw himself at Willie, nearly knocking her over.

"I want Mum! I want Mum!" he kept shouting.

Willie held him tight. She looked at me over his head.

I knew I could never forget the sight of her red face and wild green eyes.

Luti was hovering helplessly near the stove. Mummy said firmly, "Sit down, children. Gordon will be back soon and I'm sure he'll bring good news."

They sat down close together. At first they didn't drink the hot cocoa Luti put in front of them, but Mummy wrapped their cold hands around the cups and after a while they carried them to their mouths. Mummy made a few hopeful remarks, but nobody else spoke. We just had to wait till Gordon came back. It seemed to take for ever. Cameron couldn't stand the tension and went upstairs.

When we heard the car, we all rushed to the front door. Gordon came in with a policewoman.

When I saw her, I thought, *She* is *dead!*

The policewoman asked Luti if she could be alone with Willie and Alfie, then she went into the dining room with them and shut the door.

Gordon poured himself a stiff whiskey.

"She's alive," he said. "She took too many sleeping pills. By accident, let's hope. The doctor said when they do it on purpose they always do it in bed."

"Where are the Warrens?" Mummy asked.

"I don't know. They weren't there. I just don't know."

"The poor little things! Poor little things!" Luti kept saying, wringing her hands.

At last the policewoman came out.

"I'll take them to the hospital to see their mom," she said. "Can we borrow some warm top-clothes till I can sort something out?"

I rushed to give Willie, who was now grey in the face instead of red, my snowsuit and warm boots. I hugged her as I gave them to her, and helped her put them on. Alfie just had to make do with being wrapped in a blanket. Gordon carried him to the police car.

"It's a wonder they didn't freeze," he muttered when he came in and shut the door on the winter night. "It must be thirty below out there. Indoor shoes and nothing on their heads or hands... They must've run all the way..." He swallowed his whiskey in one gulp. "Gahd. This is awful! I never thought those Warrens were suitable folk to have war guests, but I didn't think of anything like this!"

"That poor woman must have been desperate!" said Luti. "What do you think, Alex?"

I hadn't looked at Mummy properly since it started because I'd been looking at Willie. Now I looked, and got another shock. She was white as paper.

"I think I need a whiskey," she said.

Chapter Ten

Changes

Mrs Lord got better, but a lot of things changed after that night. Mainly slowly, but they did change.

Willie told me that the Warrens had gone to live with relatives in Alberta. Before they left they'd told Willie's mum that she could go on living in their house for the moment, and that that was all they could do. But how was she to pay for things?

Well, that got sorted thanks to Luti and her bridge club. She persuaded some of her friends to get their husbands to make Mrs Lord an allowance to help her and the children to live. Willie said she had to take the money but that it had made her different.

I don't want to sound like Pollyanna, but there was a good side to the awful business.

We never knew if Mrs Lord took too many sleeping pills on purpose, but word reached her family in England, and they made a big fuss. Willie's dad was an officer in the army and when he came back from France (what a relief *that* was!) and heard, he was furious. There was stuff in the papers at home, about what a scandal it was for the government to send people overseas without any money. This made our families, Cameron's and mine, panic – specially the aunts. They, along with Grampy, complained to their members of parliament. And there were others. It seems Mrs Lord wasn't the only evacuee English woman who was finding it all too much.

"We're just not built for being dependent," Mummy said. "It's bad enough being far away from home. Living in a strange country, among strangers, having to ask for every cent you need... No wonder."

"You'd never take sleeping pills, would you?" I dared to ask.

"No," she said. "But I might take to drink."

She was joking. She could joke because news came that our government was going to let men send money to wives who'd taken their children abroad to be safe.

In the meantime, I was finding that coping with Gordon's 'moods' was getting harder. For Luti too. You could see. Cameron swore that her going-white hair was going whiter.

I was friends with Willie again. I started to visit her house, taking the puddle-jumper out to where she lived, because it was so hard to walk on the icy sidewalks. I used to look out through the showers of sparks sent up by the wheels – it was to do with the frost – and think of her and Alfie, running through the cold that night, believing their mum was dead.

Willie had calmed down since what happened. She told me she used to rush home from school every day with her heart thumping, afraid of what she might find, though her mum had promised and sworn she'd never take even one sleeping pill again in her life. She liked me to visit, telling me once, "Willie needs friends."

Willie had never been short of friends before, but word had got round that there was something 'weird' about her family.

Cameron thought it was funny, 'Lords' living in a little, poor house. It was a bungalow with three bedrooms, a small back yard and an open porch. Everything in it was shabby and half worn-out but somehow I liked it – it was homely and friendly. Willie said that they were much happier there without the Warrens, even though they'd been very kind to them.

"It's just lovely to be on our own," she kept saying.
I thought, *Yes, I bet.*

O'F began to come round more often. He couldn't ride
streetcars because he had arthritis, so when he did visit,
he had to take taxis, and this was a luxury for him.

"He gives me bits of money," Mummy told us. "He
can't really afford it. I know he's feeling the pinch because
he doesn't smoke his pipe any more."

"Couldn't you stop your Black Cats and let him smoke
his pipe instead?" I asked.

She gave a huge sigh. "Don't give me more guilt,"
she said. "If I couldn't smoke, I'd be a nervous wreck."

When we visited him in his little flat he always
apologised because it was so small, but he made us
welcome and had cookies and milk for us and lots of
good strong tea for Mummy. He made it properly too.
(Luti never could.) He'd sit with us and talk to us about
England (which he'd left forty years before) and the
'situation', meaning the war. Sometimes we listened with
him to his favourite radio programme, *Fibber McGee and
Molly*, which made us all laugh. Or if it was lunchtime
on a Saturday, he'd take us out for a meal at a café called
the Elite. My favourite lunch was a chicken sandwich
with hot gravy poured over it, and French fries, followed
by a marshmallow sundae.

We obviously much preferred this to the rather stiff visits to us, when the Laines would always be on their best behaviour; Gordon didn't boss Luti about and there was no whiskey because O'F was teetotal, which meant he didn't drink alcohol at all.

We asked why he was coming over more often now, and when Mummy told us he was 'feeling guilty', we couldn't see why.

"Well, of course he couldn't have known. He thought Gordon and Luti were the right people for us."

"He was right about Luti!" said Cameron staunchly.

"Yes," said Mummy. "Anyway, I've been unloading a bit to O'F. He's the only family I've got to unload on—"

"Except us," I said, rather hurt.

"Darling, when I do unload on to you, it's me who feels guilty. Of course, O'F had no idea about Gordon's... problem."

"You mean the benders," said Cameron.

"Mm."

The way she said 'Mm' made me wonder if there was some other problem she hadn't unloaded on to me but had on to O'F.

Christmas really brought out Gordon's best side. He played Poppa and was extra nice and generous to us.

He brought home a tree, which we helped decorate,

and not only invited O'F to Christmas lunch, but went and collected him by car from the other side of town. It was quite a party because Luti insisted on inviting the Lords, and there were presents for them under the tree.

Cameron and I got stockings, which we thought were our presents. But after lunch we were sent outside, and on the porch were two nearly new bicycles, all wrapped up. Even Cameron gave 'Poppa' a hug for that! We couldn't ride them yet because the roads were sheets of ice – all the cars had chains round their tyres to keep from skidding. But we really were very excited and grateful.

Mummy got a bottle of perfume. Her favourite, *Je Reviens.* She seemed completely overwhelmed, as if she just didn't know how to react, but when Gordon caught her under the mistletoe she couldn't very well not kiss him, and everybody laughed and clapped. Well, Luti didn't, but she was busy clearing away the turkey bones.

Gordon only drank a small glass of wine over Christmas. On New Year's Eve there was a grown-up party and judging by the noise there was quite a lot of drinking then, but for several weeks there were no benders and things were nice at home. Mummy was calmer, and smoked less, and in January she let Luti take her to the bridge-club, though she didn't play. But she met a woman there called Stella who loved acting.

"But there are no theatres," I said when she told me about her.

"Well, not professional ones. But there is a little theatre and there's an amateur dramatic society. Stella asked me if I'd go and give them a talk. They're getting ready to do a new play and —" She wiggled her eyebrows at me — "they're looking for a director."

Mummy had been a leading actress in London before she was married. I wouldn't have thought she'd be interested in a lot of amateurs, but as Grampy used to say, "Any port in a storm." She went downtown one evening and when she came back she was all sort of glowing.

"They're a nice lot," she said. "Very keen. Of course I don't know if they're talented… They've given me the play to read. Look." She showed me a little paperback called *Penny Wise*. "It's an American comedy. I read the beginning on the streetcar. I kept laughing out loud."

"Would you like to direct it?"

"I don't know. I've never directed. But they loved the talk. I need something of my own to get my teeth into."

One way and another, as we began to look forward to the end of winter, I forgot about our plan for moving. Mummy agreed to direct *Penny Wise*. This took her out of the house and into town twice a week for rehearsals. She was loving it. She said the amateurs were "remarkably good" and "as keen as mustard", and that she felt useful again, even though she didn't get paid.

And then the money came through from England.

This was something to celebrate! It was as if Daddy (and Uncle Jack) were reaching out with love across the world and putting money in our hands. I didn't know how much it was, only that it came to the bank every month. For the first time, Cameron and I got pocket money! Mummy didn't have to get hand-outs from Gordon for 'bits and bobs' she needed to buy. She even offered him money for our keep. Big mistake. He got insulted and sulked for two days. But then Luti persuaded him that Mummy hadn't meant to hurt him, and things got easier again.

Or would have, if he hadn't started buying her presents.

This made her nervous, and even I could see Luti didn't like it, because they were things like a new handbag and silk stockings and a scarf-and-glove set. Mummy had to use them because if she didn't, Gordon would hint and make remarks until she did. Then he was very smiley and kept saying flattering things to her. Two or three times he asked her to take her turban off so he could see her 'lovely hair'.

★

Still I didn't have a single idea what was coming. I must've been stupid.

It happened after a party.

· We were shunted off to bed soon after supper. The Swedish daily lady had come in for the evening to serve. She and Luti got the living room ready, with little tables and coasters for the glasses, so they wouldn't leave rings on the polished wood, the floor rugs all straightened out, the cushions plumped, and everything dusted and shiny. Gordon put the radio on to some dance music. All the downstairs lights were blazing (Luti often went around switching them off to save electricity) and the radiators were on at full blast.

From my room I could hear people arriving. Mummy, of course, was the guest of honour. She'd put on a dress that she liked – blue-green, her favourite colour – but then, after a few minutes, she came back upstairs and changed.

She glanced at me, watching her. "Gordon said I should wear my yellow dress," she said shortly.

I noticed she didn't put on any eye-stuff, but she touched up her nails. She always wore bright red nail varnish. She put on different earrings to match the dress.

"Aren't you going to put on your Christmas perfume?" I asked.

"No," she said, kissed me goodnight, and told me not to read too late.

There was plenty of noise coming up the stairs. Cameron came in after he'd cleaned his teeth.

"What a racket," he said. "Why do they have to shout so much?" Then, "What're you reading?"

"*Anne of Green Gables.* It's a lovely Canadian story."

"I've got to read *Prester John* for school," he said. "It's quite good..." He sat down on the bed. This was very unusual. "Lind, do you think we'll be staying on here, with the Laines?"

"Why not?" I said carelessly. "Things are OK now, aren't they?"

"Well, I mean, haven't you noticed that Gordon's got a pash for Auntie Alex?"

I stared at him. A pash? I couldn't think of anything to say. Surely such a thing couldn't be. He was married. Mummy was always talking about Daddy.

"Did you know the Lords are leaving?" Cameron asked next.

The change of subject threw me. "How do you know?"

"A boy in my class's mother knows Mrs Lord. They're moving to New York, to some other relatives."

Willie hadn't said a word about this to me. Maybe she didn't know. But I was still thinking about the pash.

"But – so what?"

"Well. Auntie said if we did move, it would have to be somewhere not as posh as here. I was thinking, maybe we could go to live in the Warrens' house. Rent it I mean."

My book had fallen off the bed. Cameron bent, picked it up, looked at it rather scornfully, and gave it back to me. There was a loud gale of laughter from downstairs.

"Maybe I'll suggest it," he said, standing up. "'Night. Not that we'll get much sleep."

Despite the racket, I had almost dropped off to sleep, very late, when I heard footsteps clacking up the parquet stairs. Then someone in high heels ran past my door, and Luti and Gordon's bedroom door along the corridor slammed.

I lay still, frowning. It must have been Luti. Though she never slammed doors. I noticed that the voices downstairs had gone quiet, then some odd, nervous laughter. Then talking started again, but not so loud. After a few minutes, I heard more footsteps on the stairs – a man's this time. It could only be Gordon. He went to the bedroom. I heard Luti's voice raised, but I couldn't hear the words. You never heard Luti shouting, but now she did, and right away the door opened again and I heard Gordon walking quickly along the passage and back down the stairs.

I was sitting up by now. But when nothing else happened, I lay down again, and after a bit I dropped off to sleep.

When I woke up next, it was still night, but the little light on the dressing table was on, with a headscarf over it to shade it. Mummy was there. The wardrobe was open and so were the drawers. There were suitcases lying open on the floor and she was throwing things into them.

"Mummy! What are you doing?"

"Lindy, please go to sleep. It's half-past one in the morning."

"I want to know why you're packing! Are we leaving?"

"Yes. As soon as it's light. Now go to sleep, *please*."

"But what's happened?"

"I can't tell you now. Please do as you're told."

I lay silent, my heart thumping, watching her. I suppose I must have dropped off because the next thing I knew was her gently shaking me awake. There was light coming through the thickly frosted window.

"Get up and get dressed," she whispered. "Snowsuit too, and your boots. I've put your things out for you. Cameron's nearly ready."

The room was cleared, except for my clothes. No, not quite. All the presents Gordon had given her – the bag, the stockings, everything – were piled on the dressing table. I noticed the bottle of *Je Reviens* in the middle, reflected in the mirror.

Mummy said, "Go to the toot downstairs. I don't want the flush to wake them up."

But she must have forgotten to tell Cameron that, because I heard the flush in the bathroom between our bedroom and the Laines'. And just as we were creeping out on to the landing with our suitcases, Gordon, in his pyjamas and with his dark hair on end, burst out.

"Where are you going?"

"We're leaving, Gordon."

"No you're not! By Gahd, you're not! I won't let you!"

"There's no way on earth you can stop me."

She gave Cameron one of our suitcases and me another, and between us we staggered down the stairs. Gordon was behind us. He was shouting, and actually grabbing Mummy's arm. She shook him off. At that moment, the doorbell rang.

"Who's that!" shouted Gordon.

"My taxi, I imagine," said Mummy.

Gordon stopped cold. "Alex," he said in a strangled voice. "Don't do this. I beg you. Where are you going? You've nowhere to go."

"Don't worry about that. We're not your business any more," Mummy said.

Just then Luti appeared at the top of the stairs in her nightie, pulling on a dressing gown. "Gordon! Leave her alone!" she cried.

He ignored her.

We were down in the living room by now and Mummy pushed Cameron ahead to open the front door.

"Give the driver the suitcases," she said. "Tell him to load up as quickly as possible."

Suddenly Gordon left us and dashed up the stairs again, shoving Luti aside, and ran into our room. A moment later he reappeared. He was holding the handbag he'd given her. He almost fell down the stairs.

"You left my presents! Couldn't you have spared me that? Did you have to insult me? Don't you realise I was drunk? I'm sorry, I'm sorry! Oh my Gahd, what'll I tell people? Don't go, please don't go!" He was crying.

Luti stood on the stairs, just staring down.

At least I should say goodbye to her, I thought, but Mummy was herding us out into the cold morning and I couldn't turn back.

The air outside was almost as white as the snow with early-morning mist. Our breath came out even whiter as Mummy urged us towards the taxi that was waiting at the kerb. I nearly slipped on the icy path as I half ran down towards it, following Cameron. I could hear a commotion behind me, but I didn't look back until I was sitting in the taxi. Then I looked out through the open door.

Gordon was struggling with Mummy. He was trying to hold her and Luti was trying to stop him. He was begging, pleading, shouting. He wouldn't let go. Suddenly, Mummy snatched the handbag from him and slapped him across the face with it.

There was a terrible moment — frozen, like the air — then he let her go. The bag fell on to the front step. Mummy, in her snow boots but with her coat still open, ran down the path, jumped into the taxi, slammed the door, and said, like in a movie, "Drive! Anywhere! Drive!"

Chapter Eleven

Across the Tracks

So what had happened?

We didn't find out right away. We sat in silence as the taxi took the scenic route around Saskatoon on the empty early-Sunday-morning roads for twenty expensive minutes, while Mummy had a good cry and a good rave: "Stupid, wretched man, how dared he! How dared he!" And then a frantic think.

"I suppose we'll have to go to a hotel," she said, after blowing her nose for the third time.

"Why not to O'F's?" I asked.

"Oh don't be silly, Lindy! He hasn't got room for us, and it'll only make him feel terrible that we've had to run away!"

And then Cameron piped up with his idea.

"Why don't we go to the Lords'?"

"The Lords? You mean, the Warrens?"

"They've gone, and the Lords are going. They've got three bedrooms, haven't they, Lind? Maybe they could share, just for a few days till we think of something, and maybe we could stay on there when they leave?"

Mummy stared at him, thinking.

"Well…" she said at last. "Any port in a storm… What's their address, Lindy?"

"Thirty-eight Taylor Street."

Mummy repeated that to the taxi-driver. He turned the taxi around on its crunchy, chain-covered wheels, and drove towards the Exhibition Grounds. Across the tracks.

By the time we reached the little clapboard house on Taylor Street, Mummy had smoked half a Black Cat, calmed down, and put on some make-up. Cameron and I were breathing normally again and I, at least, was beginning to enjoy a feeling of relief. I felt as if some heaviness I hadn't known I was carrying had been lifted away.

Willie came to the door. She was still in her pyjamas. (Imagine! Answering the door on a Sunday morning in your pyjamas! Luti would have had a fit.)

She gaped at us, and then behind us to the taxi, still standing there.

"Hi! What gives? What are you guys doing here?" she said, looking pleased.

"Can we see your mum?" asked Mummy.

But Mrs Lord was already coming down the passage from the kitchen. She was still in her dressing gown. "Alex! Lindy... What...?"

"We've run away from the Laines'," Mummy said.

Her jaw dropped. But then she said: "Good for you! Come in! Come in!"

"We've got all our luggage—"

"Bring it in. Pay off the taxi – good heavens, get rid of him before he beggars you! Alfie! Come and help!"

Between us we carried all our stuff on to the open porch and piled it amid the snowdrifts, before going into the little house, which was warm and welcoming. There was a good smell of coffee and toast and bacon.

"Willie, make more breakfast. Sit down – Alfie, bring the other chairs in from the sitting room."

Soon the six of us were gathered around the wooden table, which was covered with scratched oilcloth. Mrs Lord poured coffee for us, while Willie stood by the old-fashioned gas stove throwing eggs and bacon into two frying pans.

"So, tell me at once – I can't wait to hear! What happened?"

Mummy didn't speak for a minute. Cameron and I waited breathlessly.

"He made a pass at me," she said.

Nobody spoke, but I heard my breath come noisily into my throat.

"You mustn't tell anyone. It would ruin him, and I don't want that. He's been very good to us on the whole."

"I won't tell a soul, though I'd like to know how you're going to explain it! The whole town'll be talking! Go on, what happened exactly?" She seemed to snuggle down in her chair, resting her chin on her hand.

"There was a party. Gordon drank too much. Much too much. He was sort of – showing me off, as usual, and – flirting with me. You know, making silly remarks, about me being 'Poppa's best girl' – dreadfully embarrassing, and Luti suddenly lost her temper and ran upstairs and didn't come back, even when Gordon went after her. Then they all went back to drinking and there was some dancing and Gordon wanted to dance with me but I wouldn't. I wanted to go up to Luti, but he wouldn't let me. He literally stood over me and wouldn't let me.

"At last all the guests left. I was just dying to get away but Gordon asked me to help to clear up, because the maid had left hours before, and I couldn't not do that. So I was in the dining room with a tray, piling dishes, when he came tiptoeing up behind me and – suddenly he put his arms around me and tried to kiss me.

"I dropped a plate and pushed him away. And then – oh, Irene! It was so absurd! He started chasing me round the dining-room table."

Cameron snorted. I dared not look at him. I was so shocked, and yet it was funny. I could just picture Mummy running round the table with Gordon after her.

"Go on, go on!" said Mrs Lord.

"Do you know what he said? And this was what did it, for me. He said, 'You oughta be grateful to Poppa for saving you from the bombs!'"

"Oh, no. Not that!"

"That and more. 'If Ice-water Alex would only join him in a li'l snifter she'd soon give him a li'l kiss.' Really, it was too much, Irene! I couldn't stand it. With Luti upstairs, probably crying her eyes out! Impossible. I couldn't stay under his roof after that."

"Of course you couldn't. Ask me, he deserves to be ruined!" She leant back in her chair. "I think I'll send the story to the *Star Phoenix* to put on their front page!" She made headlines with her hands. "'Dawn Escape of English Fugitive! War guest Flees Crescent Lothario!'"

We all burst out laughing, even Alfie, who was listening with all his ears. Willie said, "What's a Lothario?"

"A lover-boy," said her mother.

Willie giggled and dished out the eggs and bacon. We fairly wolfed them down. There's nothing like escaping at dawn for giving you an appetite.

We had a wonderful first day with them – Runaway Sunday. There were no shops open so Mrs Lord – Irene, as I was told to call her – cleared out the cupboards of tins and packets and we made a crazy mixed-up main meal, like the first supper in *The Railway Children*. I remember pancakes from a packet, made by Willie and me (I really admired Willie for being able to cook – I'd never cooked in my life before), and tinned peas and some popcorn that we popped and poured maple syrup over, and plenty of saltine crackers and butter. Alfie found some old dog biscuits at the back of a cupboard, ripped open the box and chewed on them as if he were starving. We laughed *so much*, like people let out of—

No. I knew I shouldn't think that. I did have good memories of our time at the Laines', and sadness about Luti. *What must she be feeling? What will she say to Gordon?* I wondered. *Will she miss us?* Well, I knew she would. She loved us. And we'd loved her, in a way. But that didn't make me sorry we'd left.

Cameron had something else on his mind.

"I suppose we can't go back for the bikes," he said.

"I'm afraid not," said Mummy. "We can't go back at

all. Which is tiresome, because I couldn't bring everything. There's another suitcase, down in the basement, with our summer clothes in it."

"You should ask Mr Laine to send it on," said Irene.

Mummy shuddered. "I couldn't."

But she didn't have to.

It took Gordon about forty-eight hours to find out where we'd gone. Then, on the Tuesday afternoon when we were at school, he came knocking on the door.

He'd brought our summer suitcase – *and* the bikes *and* the skates *and* the sled. He stood on the porch, where he'd unloaded all this from the Hillman before he knocked, so Mummy would see how reasonable he was being. He was totally sober, totally calm. He didn't beg or plead or make any fuss at all. He just stood there in his heavy overcoat, and said, "Alex, I've brought your things. May I have two words with you – that's all I ask."

"Of course," said Mummy, and stood aside.

Irene hovered in the background, but she had the tact to leave them alone in the little sitting room. Gordon didn't take off his outdoor things except his cap. They sat down and Gordon put his hands on his knees, the way he did when he had something important to say.

"I won't trouble you with apologies. You must know how ashamed I am about what happened. Not just on

Saturday, but other times. I'd just like to say that your leaving my house is just about the most shaming thing that's ever happened to me. No, don't say anything. I understand you had to leave. But I have some standing in this town, and if people find out that you left because of anything I did, my name will be mud, and I will probably lose my legal practice. So for old time's sake – and there have been some good times, you can't deny that – I ask that we cook up some story between us to explain why you're not living with us any more."

Mummy nodded. "I wasn't going to spread stories, Gordon. You've been very kind and generous to us and I won't forget that. The last thing I want is to harm you. Let's just say that since our money came through from England we all agreed it would be better if the children and I had our own household. If you like, you can say that either you or Luti haven't been well, and that I didn't want to burden you with having kids in the house. Everyone will just think you've done very well to keep us for six months. And so you have."

Gordon stared at her for a long time. She was shocked to see tears behind his glasses.

"You are so kind, and so pure, and so much, *much* too good for me," he said. "The kids were no trouble. Luti is heartbroken. And I did this. With my damned stupid drinking. I'm a changed man, Alex. I swear it. You've changed me. No, I'm not asking you to come back. I don't deserve it."

And with that, he got up, shook hands with her, and led the way to the front door. He asked if he could help bring the things in, but Mummy, who was overwhelmed by the scene, and only wanted him to go, said no. He walked down the path to the car and drove away without looking back.

We never saw him again. Even in a small town, it's possible to avoid someone you don't want to bump into.

Chapter Twelve

Our New Life

'Bunking-in', as Cameron called it, with the Lords was great fun. At least, I thought so, and so did Willie. The Lords were really welcoming and absolutely fantabulous about it, treating our stay as a sort of game.

The 'three bedrooms' were actually two and a half. The two both had twin beds in them, and had been occupied by the Warrens, and Mrs Lord and Willie, with Alfie having the little bedroom, which wasn't much bigger than a large cupboard.

What happened now was that Alfie moved out of his little room and handed it over to Cameron, while the two mothers slept in one of the twin rooms and Willie and I in the other. Alfie slept on the floor in the mothers' room, on a blow-up mattress between the two beds; the mothers just had to get in and out of their beds from the bottom, or risk treading on him.

Every now and then, Mummy told me, she would go and peep into Cameron's tiny room at the back of the house and remember the cabin on the ship that she'd refused to sleep in, and be grateful for a double room, even though it was so small the beds were pushed against the walls. I knew it must feel pretty claustrophobic for Mummy, but Mrs Lord gave her the bed next to the window, so it wasn't too bad.

Sharing was great for Willie and me, because we could talk at night before we fell asleep. We giggled and gossiped, talked about our schools and sang to each other.

> "I got tears in my ears
> From lying on my back
> In my bed while I cry over you-oo!
> And those tears in my ears
> Are off the beaten track
> Since you said, it's goodbye,
> We are through!"

We talked about our fathers too. I didn't talk about Daddy much to Mummy because it made her sad, but to Willie I could tell all the nice things I remembered about him.

I told how his patients loved him, how one of them once told me over the phone, "Dr Hanks only has to come into the room and you feel better." How he had to get up in the middle of the night when someone rang up. How he delivered babies, and how he taught me to dance.

And she told me about her dad, who she was very proud of for fighting the 'filthystinkingGermans'. She never said 'Germans' without the other two words, as if they were one.

I felt sorry for Cameron, with no one to talk to in the night, and once when I went to the toot and saw the light under his door, I fetched Willie and we crept into the little room and sat on his bed to keep him company. But you could see he wanted us to push off so he could read *Prester John*. Cameron was a loner, and that's all there was to it.

It was a good time, staying with the Lords. We loved being just English people and not having to be on best behaviour. It was our house, small and shabby as it was, and we felt free in it to do what we liked and be ourselves. Nobody ever said "Shhhh!" As for "Widdiya woddiya", that was forgotten. There were no more fights over The Spirit because we decided buying the *Montreal Standard* was a luxury we couldn't afford.

★

One good thing the little house made me do.

The old man Willie had wanted to scare at Hallowe'en still lived next door to us. The first day I saw him coming out on to his front path to shovel snow, the memory of what happened that night hit me afresh and I felt my heart start thumping with guilt at the old lady falling down in a faint. I hadn't seen anything of her since we'd moved in. I took my conscience to Mummy as I always did.

"Yes, and? What do you want me to say?" she asked.

"What can I do?"

"Oh, come on, Lindy. You don't need me to tell you that."

It took me a week to get up courage – a week when I was going to school every day on the streetcar, answering questions from the little park gang about why I wasn't showing up for skating. About *that* Mummy had given me very strict instructions what to say.

"We moved to Taylor Street. We decided it would be good to try living on our own. Not to be a burden."

No doubt primed by their curious parents, one or two of the kids asked, "Did the Laines agree you should leave?"

"Well, in the end," I said. "They didn't want us to, but Mum thought we should try to be independent."

It was Patricia who pressed me more. "Was there a row?"

I remembered the scene on the doorstep, with Gordon shouting and clinging. I remembered the noise the handbag made on his face. But the houses in the crescent weren't that close together, it was misty, and very early, so I said firmly, "A row? Of course not. They gave a party to say goodbye to Mum, and the next morning we left."

(Willie had advised me to start calling Mummy 'Mom' but I couldn't. Mum was the best I could do.)

The principal had to know my new address. Mummy sent her a note. She called me in.

"So you've moved to Taylor Street, Lindy," she said. "That's really out of our catchment area. Are you planning to change schools?"

"Do I have to?"

"Well… you're settled here… we wouldn't like to lose you. We could probably make an exception… But it's rather far for you to come."

"I don't mind. The streetcar nearly passes our door."

The truth was, although I'd have liked to go to school with Willie, I didn't want the hassle of getting used to a new school. I loved Miss Bubniuk (I had a bit of a crush on her, as a matter of fact, she was so beautiful and so much fun) and there was going to be a play at the end of the school year that I had a good part in.

So I stuck. The goings-on at school gave Willie and me something more to talk about after 'lights out'. Her school was a bit rougher than mine, and once she came home with a black eye. She said some fat boy called Cecil, who kept jeering at her and calling her Scarlett O'Hara because of her red hair, went too far, so she socked him, and he socked her right back.

If any boy had socked a girl at Buena Vista he'd have been expelled, but nothing happened to Cecil, who kept right on, only now he called Willie Joe Louis, after the famous world heavyweight championship boxer. He kept dancing about in front of her shouting "Put 'em up! Scared to sock me again? You better be!"

But she didn't care. She just said, "I am Joe Louis and I only pick on people my size. You're too feak and weeble." She'd got that from me, of course. Cecil didn't know what it meant and it drove him crazy.

One night in bed I talked to Willie about my guilt about the old couple next door. She was quiet for a bit, and then she said, "Do you think I haven't been feeling bad about it too? That night, when I didn't come back, I was sitting in the kitchen in my witch costume crying because I thought we'd killed her. I just couldn't face going out there again." After a few moments, lying there in the dark, she added, "I guess you all thought I'd run out on you. Huh?"

"Well...."

"What shall we do?"

"Say sorry, I guess."

"Yeah. You did the scaring, but I did the planning. We should both do it."

We made up our minds to do it the next day before school. We got up early. There had been quite a heavy fall of snow in the night, and the paths and pavements were a good five inches thick with it. Again. This job seemed to be endless... Now that the only 'men' about the place were Cameron and Alfie, they couldn't do all the furnace-feeding and snow-sweeping, so we all took turns at it, letting Cameron off most of it because he had so much homework.

That morning, as we were getting ready to go to say sorry to the old couple, Willie said, "Tell you what – let's sweep their path as well as ours. Let's do that first."

So we did. But while we were doing it, the door flew open and the old man came fuming and panting down the steps.

"What the Sam Hill do you girls think you're doing on my property?"

"We're sweeping your snow for you, Mr Hembrow," said Willie.

"And why the devil should you do that? Do you think I'm too ancient and helpless to sweep my own snow?"

"No. We thought we'd do it to show how sorry we are."

He jerked his head back and stared at us with his mouth open. He was a tall, rangy man, with hard lines on his face, and a mop of white curly hair. He must have been handsome once. But now he was about eighty years old. Maybe more.

"Sorry? For what?" he barked.

Willie put down the yard broom she was holding and went up to him. I followed, clutching the shovel.

"Mr Hembrow, it was us – on Hallowe'en. We were the ones who scared your wife. We didn't mean to. We're very sorry."

He went on staring at us for a long time. Finally he said, "Then you can finish the work. Do the sidewalk too. I don't want to see one scrap of snow on either of 'em when I look out again." And he turned on his heel and marched up the steps and slammed the door.

We both heaved deep sighs. "Well. That wasn't very nice," I said.

"No. But still, we'd better do it."

We were doing the last bit, pushing the snow from the pavement into the gutter, when he came bursting out again.

"Hallowe'en was *three goldarned months ago!*" he yelled. "If you're so all-fired sorry, where've you been for three months?"

There was no answer to this. I hadn't said anything so far, and I knew I needed to.

I said, "How's your wife now, Mr – Henbow?"

"She's sick," he said, and went in again.

I'd overheard Mummy ring O'F to let him know about what happened with Gordon, to explain why we'd moved. I could tell she was trying not to make him feel any worse about it than he was bound to, for putting us with the Laines in the first place. I heard her swear him to secrecy, and then tell him we were coming over to see him at the weekend. But he insisted on coming to us.

"He says he wants to see the house," said Mummy. She gave me a look. "We must make him understand how happy we are here, because when he sees it, he may think we've moved into the sticks, and that it's his fault."

So the house wouldn't look too crowded, Irene took Willie and Alfie out skating to the big rink downtown; she really was a very tactful person. We made a special tea for O'F and laid it nicely on the kitchen table, which was where we all ate as there wasn't a separate dining room. Mummy used some of her lovely scarves, in rainbow colours, that she'd had since she was a famous actress, and draped them around the living room to make it look a bit exotic and not shabby.

O'F arrived by taxi, as always. He'd had even further

to come than before and Mummy rushed out to try to pay the driver but O'F shook his head.

"Call it a 'taxi' on my stupidity," he said.

He hugged Mummy, and then me, and shook hands with Cameron, who he knew by now was not the huggy type.

We had tea. O'F was quieter than usual. Normally he'd tell us a joke – he loved jokes, especially Irish ones. But today he didn't tell us any jokes and seemed very down.

"Darling," said Mummy at last. "You must not blame yourself. How could you know?"

"I should have. I should have made enquiries. I'm sure everyone who knows him, knows about his drink problem. I just never thought they'd volunteer to have war guests when… I'm really afraid he only did it to impress all his cronies."

"Well, even if he did, he was a good host. He did everything he could for us. We must have cost him a lot of money. If it hadn't been for that one thing—"

"That one *vital* thing," said O'F. "That one *terrible* thing. The thing that made me give up alcohol altogether. The thing that cost me my job and my marriage…"

"O'F! Darling O'F – you didn't tell us!"

"No, of course not. And I won't. It's all ancient history.

Having you here, my dear ones… It's made such a difference to my old age. Like a blessing. And in return I land you in a situation like that!" He shook his head. "What a fool. What a prize idiot." He sighed. "Oh well. No good crying over spilt milk, eh? Tell me some gossip. Have you got some nice neighbours here?"

I hung my head.

"Go on, Lindy," Mummy said. "Tell him."

So I did. He sat there, sucking on an empty pipe, drinking his tea. When I finished my sorry tale, he said, "What did you say their name is?"

"Henbow or something," I said.

"Are you sure it's not Hembrow?" he said, sitting up.

"Yes! That's it."

"Good lord. I wonder…" He stood up, and moved to the kitchen window. "Could it be? Is his first name Bernard?"

"I don't know…"

"Bernard Hembrow! Do you know who he is?"

We shook our heads.

"Bernard Hembrow was one of the pioneers of the town. A true old-timer."

"What?" Mummy said. "But I thought it began back in the eighteen hundreds!"

"Well? Bernard Hembrow is eighty if he's a day. That

takes him well back to when this place was little more than bare prairie."

"And his wife?"

"A Metis."

"A what?"

"The Metis are people of mixed race. I believe Mae Hembrow was originally Ojibwe."

We looked blank.

"It's one of the tribes who used to live around here."

"You mean – she's – Red Indian?" I cried, forgetting Hank's advice.

"If that's what you want to call them. They don't like it, being called Indians. I call them First People, or Native Canadians."

I nearly died on the spot. I'd frightened a – what had he said? A First Person? Whenever I saw a western movie, I was always on the Indians' side, even against Errol Flynn. And that woman who fainted when she saw me headless – she was a real, live one! The first and only one I'd seen since we got here, which is to say – ever. Outside of the movies. It was as if I'd frightened some god-like being from legend.

"You know, Lindy," O'F went on, taking my hand in his papery one, "it wasn't your fault, at all, what happened. But it was a very sweet thing, to try to apologise. I'm sure Bernard Hembrow appreciated it, really."

"I don't think so. It just made him mad at us."

"You have to make allowances for old people." He smiled suddenly around his cold pipe. "Like you have to for me, and my foolishness. If I say I'm sorry, now, for my mistake, please don't yell at me and make me shovel the snow!"

Chapter Thirteen

The End of Winter

I think our mothers seriously considered our all going on living together. When the two lots of money from England were put together, we felt almost well-off! But really, I knew the little house on Taylor Street *was* too crowded with six of us, and poor Alfie finally settled it by going on strike, saying he couldn't sleep on the floor any more and racing Cameron every night for the bed in the cupboard-bedroom. Since Alfie went to bed hours before Cameron, he always won, and Cameron had to sleep on the blow-up mattress in the sitting room. He was OK with that because at least the sitting room had a desk in it, but it meant the mothers had to spend the evenings in the kitchen. The radio was a huge old thing that couldn't be moved, so that meant they had to miss all their favourite programmes. Irene said very seriously that living without Jack Benny (her favourite comedian) was a deprivation too far.

"I have to laugh once a week for my health," she said.

So in mid-February the Lords left for New Jersey. Captain Lord, from England, had found another relative for them to live with. A richer one, they hoped, or at least one who wouldn't have to 'beggar themselves', keeping them. Cameron looked at the map and saw New Jersey was near New York.

"I'd like to see New York," he said. Then he said, "Is Willie going to write to you?"

"I hope so," I said. "She said she would."

"Can you ask her to describe New York? Then you can read me the letters," he said.

Ha! Little did we dream!

We remained happy in Taylor Street – maybe even more after the Lords left, though Willie and I cried buckets when we said goodbye, promising to write 'every day'. But I knew from Sue, my best friend from my old school, that we wouldn't. I only ever had one letter from Sue and I only wrote to her twice.

And Willie didn't write for a while. I guess they were too busy getting settled.

"America isn't Canada," O'F said. "And New Jersey sure isn't Saskatchewan. They'll have a lot of getting used to to do."

I missed Willie a lot at first. Whenever I had a problem, I asked myself, *What would Willie do?*

Well. The problem of next door was easy to answer, so I bought a box of Laura Secord candies – the best candies in the world, all kinds, like a patchwork quilt of different-coloured sweets and chocolates – with my pocket money and marched up the scuffed wooden steps and knocked on the screen door. After a while, he came – Mr Hembrow.

"Well?" he barked.

"Mr Hembrow, will you please give these candies to Mrs Hembrow? And here's a card I made. It's to say sorry. I really am," I said.

He worked his tongue around his teeth for a bit, glaring down at me. "You've got a nerve, I'll say that for you. Coming back here after the way I acted." He reached out slowly and took the box and the card. "You folks living next door now? What happened to the others?"

"They've moved to America," I said.

"Yeah? Well, Little Noisy Mouth will like that. They don't mind noise, down there – make so much of it themselves they won't notice."

I guessed Little Noisy Mouth must be Alfie. Then,

just as I was turning to leave, Mr Hembrow said, "You want to come in? Mae'll want to see you."

I'd secretly hoped for this. I'd asked Miss Bubniuk about the Ojibwes. They were one of the fiercest tribes around, she told me, for hundreds of years before the white men came.

I followed Mr Hembrow into the house with a thumping heart. It was cold and cluttered, as if no one had cleaned or tidied up for a while. The furniture was even older than ours, and all higgledy-piggledy, and the place was sort of dark, because of the thick frost on the inside of the windows. I knew that only happened if there were no storm windows – a second window that nearly everyone put up when winter came. It was a heavy job, though – maybe Mr Hembrow couldn't manage it.

There were interesting things there too. A big, framed, brown photo in the tiny hall caught my eye. It was of an Indian – I mean a First People – chief. On the floor in the sitting room was a rug made of some kind of fur that must have come from some really big animal. Could it be a buffalo? There was a stuffed moose-head on one wall. It had glass eyes and looked real. It was quite low down, so it seemed as if the whole moose was pushing through from outside and would soon be standing in the sitting room.

Mr Hembrow led the way through to a bedroom at

the back. The house wasn't like ours. It seemed to have only one bedroom, but it was a good big one. It looked out over a snow-covered yard at the back with quite tall trees, which ours didn't have. At least it was warm in here. The frost on the inside of the window was half melted, the meltwater trickling down the wall into a mass of old towels.

Mrs Hembrow was lying on the bed, not in it. She was dressed in a long warm skirt and a heavy blouse with a bright orange shawl wrapped round her shoulders.

I could see at once that she was a First Person. She had dark skin and eyes and although her hair was grey, I could see it wasn't a white person's hair – it was too heavy and straight. And long. It was in a long plait, hanging down over her shoulder, tied with a ribbon. She was leaning against a pile of pillows and had another fur rug over her feet. Next to her bed was a little table with a lamp and a lot of bottles and boxes of medicine. She was listening to the radio and making something that looked like a basket.

She looked up as we came in.

What would Willie do? I went right up to her. "Mrs Hembrow, I'm Lindy Hanks from England. It was me who scared you that time when you fainted at Hallowe'en. I'm sorry. I didn't mean to."

She didn't look surprised or angry – or anything. She

didn't have an expression. Her face was just smooth and blank. Her eyes looked like black holes.

"How did you do it?" she asked.

Mr Hembrow coughed. "My wife always says she saw a woman without a head. I don't guess she really did. It was the witch, wasn't it, Mae? Sorry, honey, I mean the bad woman."

She didn't say anything. She just kept her eyes fixed on me. And I suddenly realised no one had believed that she'd seen what she said she'd seen. That must have been awful, if they kept telling her she'd imagined it. So I told them the whole story.

"Prove it to him," she said at the end.

"How? How can I? I haven't got the dress any more."

"The head. There was a head cut off – I saw it on the ground. Show him the head."

Well, there was a thing. The head! I hadn't thought about it since that night.

"Alfie – er – Little Noisy Mouth – ran off with it. I never asked him what he did with it – I never wanted to see it again. And now he's gone to America and I can't ask him."

Mr Hembrow thrust the box of Laura Secord into my hands. He nudged me. "Give her the candies."

So I did. She opened the box and looked at the yummy pattern of fondants and nougat and chocolates with violets and rose petals made of sugar on the tops. She didn't say thank you. She took one of them out, bit into it, looked to see what was inside, and then popped it in her mouth and ate it slowly. She looked up at me with those blank eyes.

"Prove it to him. Find the head."

"I'll try," I said helplessly.

When he was showing me out, Mr Hembrow said, "Mae's people don't thank you. Saying thank you is kinda rude, like saying you didn't expect someone to do a nice thing. But she was pleased. We don't buy that kind much."

I knew what that meant. That small box had cost nearly three weeks' pocket money.

"You believe her now, don't you?"

"Sure I do. It just sounded kinda crazy. Mae's folks, you know, they're mortal scared of ghosts and witches and such. They don't even like to hear 'em named. I shouldn't have let her go to the door that night but I had my rheumatics real bad."

Just as I was going down the steps, he added, "You girls did a real nice job that time. I'm sorry I was such a sore-head."

"That's OK, Mr Hembrow. I wish I could do it every time."

He looked at the sky. There was some blue showing.

"Be break-up soon," he said. "Another month or so.

Winters sure go on a piece, hereabouts. Winters go on so long in England?"

"No. What's break-up?"

"The river. You'll see. Best sight in the world, when the river breaks up."

I went home, and I looked for the head.

I searched the whole house – every cupboard, under the beds, down in the basement where the furnace lived. I wondered if maybe Alfie had put the head in there and burnt it up; that's what I'd have done. But if that was where it ended up, that was the end of the story. I didn't think it really mattered. Mr Hembrow believed his wife now.

But every time I visited, she looked at me out of those strange holes of eyes and I knew she wanted to see that head again, to look at what had frightened her half to death. She needed to. And I couldn't help her.

Cameron came home from Nutana telling us all the boys, and some girls, in his class were betting real money on the exact date and time the river would break up. It seemed the ice didn't just melt slowly. It broke up all at once. I thought this must be something to see, and I asked Mr Hembrow if he knew when it would happen, or if maybe his wife did. I thought First People might have an instinct for something like that.

But he just said, "Wait and see. And when you hear it's happened, get down there. Stand on the bridge and watch it come."

One Saturday morning in late March, I heard the phone ring early. Cameron came into our room looking quite excited.

"The river broke up in the night!" he said. "I guessed midnight last night! I bet a quarter on it. If nobody in our class came closer, I've won. Twenty-five cents by nineteen — that's four seventy-five. I can put that down on *Jane's Fighting Ships* at Broadway Bookstore."

I leapt out of bed and threw on my clothes. Taylor Street was further than the crescent from the river. We had to take two streetcars. Everyone on board was talking about break-up. When we reached our end of Broadway Bridge we got off. We could already see what was happening: the river was one heaving, crashing mass of enormous blocks of ice. It was the most fantastic sight! We joined a crowd trooping to the middle of the bridge, and found a place against the parapet.

"It's like being on an ice-breaking ship in the Arctic!" Cameron shouted above the noise.

As far upriver as we could see, the tumbling, heaving blocks came rushing towards us, some as big as cars. They hit the pointed piers of the bridge, rose up against them with the force of the current, smashing and falling back, one after the other in an endless tumult. It felt as if we were moving – it really did seem as if we were on a ship that was ploughing through the ice, helping to break it up as we went.

"Oh boy," breathed Cameron. "Oh boy, oh boy, oh boy. This is really something you can't see at home!"

We stood there until we were half frozen from the cold wind blowing in our faces. We didn't want to leave. But at last, we had to. We walked back as far as Five Corners and went into Pinder's Drug Store, where we pooled our pocket money for hot chocolates and waffles with maple syrup. A very rare treat, but we were too excited to just go home.

"Are you really going to buy *Jane's Fighting Ships*?" I asked.

He'd been talking about wanting it for ages. It gave details and pictures and diagrams of all the battleships in the world. It was terribly expensive. Four seventy-five wouldn't be nearly enough.

"Yes, of course," he said. "I'm going to do a paper round for the rest of the money. But they'll let me have it for a five-dollar deposit."

I didn't say anything. I thought he should give the money to Mummy. I remembered he'd bought her sweets with the thirty cents he got from the gopher tails. But this was real money. Then I thought of O'F's empty pipe and suddenly wished we hadn't bought the breakfast.

What would Willie do? Get a job. Obviously. At twelve you could. At ten you probably couldn't. But I decided to try. As soon as the Easter holiday came, I'd try.

My friendship with the Hembrows impressed O'F. First because he thought helping to found a whole town was a big deal, and so he admired Mr Hembrow a lot; second, because he said very few people nowadays got to know any of the First People. Most of them were on reservations, way out of town.

Someone else was impressed. Miss Bubniuk.

We were given homework for history about finding out the history of the town. Of course I went straight next door with a notebook and pumped Mr Hembrow for details about what it was like to come west when he was a trapper, back in the 1880s. I wanted to know more about the wars of the Metis with the settlers who were moving north and west to take over more land for farming and hunting.

He told me how he decided to side with the Metis after he met Mae – who had a different name then that meant 'Leaves Tears Behind' – and married her. And how he fought against the Mounties in the North-West

Rebellion, and about two Indian chiefs called Poundmaker and Big Bear.

Then he told me about the early days of Saskatoon, and a wonderful story about how, after the town started to really be a town, and even to 'boom', he was out walking during break-up when the lumps of ice that were bashing against the new railway bridge made it collapse and fall into the river. He actually saw it happen.

I wrote all this up in my terrible writing (I was trying to learn Canadian cursive) – pages and pages. When Miss Bubniuk gave me it back, at the bottom, where I'd been sure there would be an A, was an F, and the words: *Have a care for your poor teacher. I can't see the content for the bad writing.*

I burst into tears in front of the whole class and threw my exercise book into the wastepaper basket.

Miss Bubniuk said, "Oh, Lindy, stop – turn off the waterworks!" which made the class laugh, and then she rescued my book and said, "All right. I can't read your scrawl but you can, so read it to us."

So I had to go up to the front of the class and read aloud my long, long account, which used up nearly the whole lesson, and at the end I got clapped and Miss Bubniuk took my notebook, scratched out the F and gave me an A plus, telling me to go home and copy it all out again, "In writing worthy of what you've written." (I didn't. I couldn't.)

That night I visited next door and read it again to the Hembrows. I expected another round of applause, but Mr Hembrow looked uncomfortable, and Mrs Hembrow hid her face because she was trying not to laugh. I'd never seen her laugh before.

"What's wrong?" I asked, ready to be very hurt if they criticised it.

But Mrs Hembrow said, "Bernie, tell the truth."

And Mr Hembrow said, "I didn't know you was going to write it all down like that and tell people. I never fought the Mounties, not actually *fought* 'em. But I did see the railway bridge go down, that I did do, and the rest is the God's truth. All the history part is right, because what I didn't live through, which was most of it, I read up on."

I didn't tell anyone this at school. But Miss Bubniuk was so excited that she and the principal arranged to send a car for Mr Hembrow to come to school and give a talk to all the grades four and higher, in the big hall. And he talked beautifully, not only about the early days of Saskatoon but about how bad it had been for the First Nations.

"We should never forget what we done to them poor people, and how our country was built on others' displacement and hardship and losing their whole way of life that'd lasted for thousands of years," he said.

Then he told Mae's story, which was so sad – till she met him and he married her – that a lot of the girls were crying. Me too, because I hadn't known till then that all her family was killed, and that that was why she was called Leaves Tears Behind.

Chapter Fourteen

Penny Wise *and Other Dramas*

Mummy suddenly became very busy; directing *Penny Wise,* which was coming along marvellously apparently, was hard work and she had to leave us two evenings a week to go to the rehearsals. Having the Hembrows next door, and with Cameron now being twelve, she thought that was safe. A lot of kids of Cameron's age babysat for money. She found this weird, but as she said, "Kids seem to grow up quicker in Canada." And Cameron, of course, was very grown-up for his age.

I didn't think it was very grown-up of him to put every cent he earned towards his silly old book of battleships, though he did buy O'F some pipe tobacco for his birthday, after I told him he should. I bought O'F

178

pipe cleaners and made him a card with a poem I'd written in it.

> Dearest O'F, best of friends
> Best of uncles till life ends
> On this very special day
> May contentment come your way
> And fragrant pipe-smoke wreath your head
> Promising happiness ahead.

I *really* liked 'wreath your head'. Even Cameron said that was good. We gave him a tea party with a cake and candles and Mummy gave him a book as well – Ernest Hemingway's *For Whom the Bell Tolls*. Cameron read it first and said that, second to *England, Their England*, it was the best book he'd ever read, except the love stuff. Before I could get hold of it to see what the love stuff was, it was too late.

Cameron could do his paperboy job during school time, because it happened early in the morning, before it was even light until spring came. He borrowed Mummy's alarm clock and got up so early he was never around for breakfast except on Sundays.

What job could I do? I kept thinking. I asked around, and then Marylou, my desk partner, suggested the stables.

I liked horses, and I knew how to ride, and Cameron had already heard about a riding school out by the Exhibition Grounds that he said he might ride at when he'd finished paying for *Jane's Fighting Ships*. (I really thought Jane must be a funny sort of woman, to write a huge book about battleships.) So, when the streets started getting clearer of ice and snow, I rode my bike out there and asked for a job.

I'd already tried getting easier jobs — like in Pinder's serving ice cream and in a shoe shop — but they just said I was too young. Letty, the woman at the stables, didn't say that. She asked if I'd had any experience, and I told her that once, at my convent, I'd had to muck out a stable as punishment for playing a joke on one of the nuns. She asked what the joke was, and when I told her, she laughed and said, "Well, you look like a good strong girl — I'll give you a trial. Saturday mornings, nine till one. A dollar an hour. And in school breaks I can use you more."

I said, "And can I ride?"

"If you pay."

"No, I mean, a little ride, without paying."

She looked at me with a grin on her face. "You strike a hard bargain. OK. Twenty minutes round the riding school. You can ride Bonny. She's just had a foal, and she needs exercising."

She showed me a Shetland pony with a tiny foal, no

bigger than a large dog. He was so, so sweet. I petted Bonny and she let me pat her little one, whose name was Piper. I rubbed the baby's-hand-shaped white star on his forehead and he pushed against me.

This is going to be OK, I thought. *I can do this. This is definitely what Willie would do, and it'll give me lots to write to her about.*

In my first letter to Willie, I'd asked her to ask Alfie what he'd done with the Hallowe'en head. But when her first letter arrived, she didn't mention it. She wrote lots about her new American school, which she said was the noisiest place she'd ever been in and that she wasn't going to learn a thing. But she sounded – well, excited. About everything. She said their new family were "not just richer than the Warrens, they're rolling!" and had taken them to visit Manhattan. She couldn't believe the buildings.

Under the ground, you could understand it. But not up in the air like that. Why don't they topple over? We went up in a lift to the top of the Empire State Building. I left my tummy behind it went so fast, and when we looked down, I got dizzy. It's super-duper-fantabulous. I wish you were here. There's loads of room, they've got five bedrooms and FOUR BATHROOMS. No more queuing up to pee! I'm going to ask them to invite you!

"I hope she won't!" said Mummy, when I told her.

But knowing Willie, I thought she might.

★

It still bothered me a lot that Daddy hardly ever seemed to write. I'd had only one letter from him the whole time we'd been in Canada, and Mummy the same, I knew – they came together in one envelope with a tuppenny stamp on it, as if it was being posted to somewhere in England. I thought that was funny, that tuppence brought an envelope thousands of miles.

I asked Mummy if the letters were being sunk. She said "Possibly", but it was something she obviously didn't want to talk about.

Then one day I came home from school at lunchtime because I'd left my sandwiches on the streetcar. I thought it'd be fun to have lunch at home and maybe listen to some of the soap operas Mummy and Irene used to talk about. But Mummy wasn't listening to the radio. She was in our bedroom, sitting on the bed. She was bent over something clutched in both hands. She was sobbing.

I rushed to her. "Mummy! What's the matter?"

She straightened up.

"Wait a minute," she said.

She went out of the room and I heard her in the bathroom running the tap. Washing her face, I supposed. She'd left what she'd been clutching, crumpled up on the bed. It was letters from England – two of them. One I saw was from Grampy. The other was from Daddy. I noticed that Daddy's was the crumpled-up one. Grampy's was just lying there beside its envelope.

When Mummy came back, she said, "Bring the letters and come into the kitchen. I need a cup of tea."

I sat at the table. Mummy didn't ask me why I was home at lunchtime. She just gave me a couple of cookies and a glass of milk, and made herself a pot of tea. She was smoking furiously while she did it.

"What's happened?" I asked.

"Nothing. No bad news. No news at all, really."

"So why were you crying?"

She took the letter and smoothed out the creases.

"I've waited weeks and weeks for this," she said. "And when it comes – what is it?" She crumpled it up again and her face was all screwed up like the letter. "I *know* he's run off his feet. He's doing double shifts at the hospital – your Grampy says so. On top of his usual surgeries and visits. He's not living at home, by the way. He's living with his awful vinegary old Scottish auntie. She's supposed to be housekeeping for him, but I bet she eats half his rations or feeds them to her rotten mangy old cat... She always hated me. Never wanted Daddy to marry an actress... Ooh, I could tell you a thing or two about that woman! That's why I hardly ever saw her, and why you didn't. Oh, never mind all that!"

She took a big gulp of tea and a drag on her cigarette. "But look! Lindy, it's not fair! I wait and wait, and write and write, and when *at last* I get a letter, what is it? It's nothing but two long, boring *golf stories*! And one of them's *very rude*!"

I was stunned. "No news? Nothing – loving?"

"Oh – yes – I suppose so." She smoothed the letter out again slowly. "He says he loves us and misses us. He says the bombing's been 'a bit of a nightmare'."

"If he's not at home, how can he go into our Anderson shelter?" I'd helped to dig that, in our garden, when the war started. When we left, I thought it would keep Daddy safe.

"His aunt has one. Ours…"

"What?"

"Well, it's been flooded. A landmine landed in the reservoir behind our house."

Through dry lips, I dared to ask: "Is our house still there?"

"Oh, yes. All the back windows gone, but they'll be repaired."

"But – then – Mummy – isn't it good Daddy was with his auntie?"

"Yes. But please don't ask me to love her because I can't."

"But you – you do love Daddy?"

"Love him!" she shouted suddenly, so that I jumped and spilt the remains of my milk. "I adore him! He's my darling, and the best doctor in West London – all his patients say so! I've heard him called a *saint*! I just wish he was a bit less saintly and a bit better at writing *letters*, that's all!"

So I didn't get to hear any of those soap operas, after all. But Mummy said that evening, when she'd calmed down, that talking to me had helped, and that I'd come at the right moment.

"He can't help it," she said. "He's not good at expressing his feelings."

"Like Cameron?"

"A bit. Funny – he's more like Cameron than Uncle Jack is. Uncle Jack is *very* good at expressing *his* feelings."

I didn't even try to guess what she meant by that.

At school it was 'aggie season'.

As the thick, packed, dirty snow slowly melted and ran away in streams, it left parts of the playground bare. As soon as there was a patch of dirt where the mud had dried, out came the aggies. They were marbles, all sorts – big ones the size of gob-stoppers, little peewees, and everything in between. In all colours and with all kinds of squiggles and swirls inside them. The object was to win them from each other.

A small aggie-sized hole was dug in the dirt, and you had to try to knock aggies in with your crooked finger. There was a skill to it and a hundred rules that kept changing. I was hopeless at the game. But I became addicted to it. All my pocket money went on little net bags of aggies. I neglected my homework, I neglected everything. If I won some aggies, I felt like a millionaire, and if I lost, which I usually did, I was plunged into despair. Oh, I understand gamblers! I played all recess, and after school I was late home. When I started creeping out of bed half an hour early so as to get to school in time for a couple of games before lessons, Mummy got seriously worried.

"This is ridiculous," she said. "Stop it! You'll start playing on Saturdays next!"

No I wouldn't. Saturdays were sacred to the stables.

I did my work, and my arm muscles got strong and hard, lifting the forkfuls of bedding and bales of hay. I groomed all the ponies and got to know them. Of course Bonny was my favourite, right? Wrong. Bonny was one big pain, and nearly made me quit my job. She was a terrible ride, because she was a wonderful mother.

Piper wasn't allowed to run alongside us when I rode Bonny around the 'school', which was a kind of oval ring with a low barrier around it, because Letty wanted

Bonny to get ready for a gymkhana, where having her foal with her wouldn't be allowed. So I'd mount up and ride away from the stall where Bonny had left Piper, but she wouldn't go — not a step — unless I whacked her with a crop. I hated doing it but Letty said I must make her obey. So it was *Whack, whack, whack!* and *Kick, kick, kick!* all the way up one side of the ring. Then, as we turned at the top, heading towards home and Piper, she'd take off, and gallop pell-mell down to the far end, where she'd stop dead with her nose pointing to her stall, until I'd drag her round and start whacking her again.

Letty just stood there roaring at me. "Why is she galloping? Pull her up, can't you? Make her walk! You're the boss, not her!"

Like fun I was the boss! Bonny was the boss, and in the end I told Letty I'd do without my ride if I couldn't ride a pony who didn't have a foal in the stable.

Letty said, "All right. You can ride Dolly."

Dolly was a nice, well-mannered little pinto.

"But — only if you agree to ride Bonny in the first pony show in two weeks. I have to show her because she's my only Shetland, and there's a Shetland class."

"I can't! I won't show her well. She does what she likes with me. If she races for the stables I won't be able to hold her."

"OK. No ridey Bonny, no ridey Dolly."

Then I thought of something.

"My cousin's a better rider, and he's stronger. He might be able to make Bonny behave."

"Right. If you can get your cousin to ride Bonny, I'll let you have a go on Dolly. You can ride her in the show too. You're not a bad little rider," she admitted.

"I'm just too feak and weeble," I said, and she laughed.

I earned my four dollars a week and gave half to Mummy. I felt very virtuous compared to Cameron. I thought he was selfish – he spent hours poring over his battleships. But after a while, when he'd seen them all, he tried to take the book back to the bookstore. They wouldn't take it and told him he still owed them money.

"How much?" I asked.

"A lot," he said glumly. "I'm doomed. I didn't work it out properly. At this rate I'll be doing my paper round for the rest of my life before I've paid it off."

This was the first time I'd ever heard Cameron admit he'd made a mistake. I remembered I loved him and said, "I've got some saved. I'll lend it to you. You can give it me back a bit at a time."

He looked at me. "Thanks," he said. "But that's what I'm doing now. I think I'd rather owe the bookstore. If I owe you, I might feel, subconsciously, that I don't really have to pay you back."

"Maybe you could go out and catch some more gophers," I suggested.

"At ten cents a tail? *Two* lifetimes. There must be better ways."

He never found one, and in the end Mummy had to cough up the rest of what he owed. But meanwhile he was very cheered by the idea of riding in the gymkhana.

"I'd like to win a few Canadian rosettes to take home," he said. "I wonder if Mum's kept my old ones."

I kept trying to tell him about Bonny, how hard it was to make her go properly because of the foal, but he wasn't listening.

"A Shetland? Come on! I've ridden fifteen-hand hunters."

I shut up. Fifteen hands? That wasn't even a pony, it was a horse.

On the day of the show, we cycled up to the stables. The roads were pretty clear now, though there was still snow in the shadow of trees, and the gutters were roaring with meltwater. There was no real sign of spring – no bulbs coming up, or buds on the trees. And it was still pretty cold.

I remembered our garden at home. It would be all golden-white with daffodils and narcissus by now – unless the flood from the reservoir had killed everything. But surely no flood could have stopped our pear trees from blossoming. Suddenly, tears that weren't wind-tears came to my eyes.

I miss it, I realised. *If Daddy isn't living there, if our house is empty, who will take care of the garden? Who will put bread out for the birds? Perhaps the noise of bombs has scared them all away. London without birds!*

Letty was waiting at the stables. She lent Cameron a pair of boots, some string gloves and a crop.

"Don't be afraid to give her a smack if she needs it," she said. "As for when she wants to run, I'm putting a curb bit on her, instead of her snaffle. So don't pull too hard, she's not used to it."

There were lots of ponies and kids milling around the ring. It was quite a big event, I saw, with judges and an announcer with a loudspeaker. I felt a bit nervous, but I'd ridden Dolly a few times and she was an angel compared to Bonny. When it was my class ('Ponies fourteen hands and under, riders under twelve years') I led Dolly out. She still had her winter coat but I'd given her a good brush and plaited her mane and put oil on her hooves so she looked really smart. I'd even given her white bits a wash. I gave her a handful of oats to make her love me, and mounted up.

I remembered Auntie Millie's advice: "Head up, heart up, hands down, heels down – and don't poke your chin!"

I guided Dolly into the ring and followed at the proper distance behind a chestnut pony, watching its rump between Dolly's ears, which were pricked forward eagerly. I followed the orders on the loudspeaker – trot, collected canter, walk, straight into a canter again, stop, line up for the judges. And suddenly I had a blue rosette pinned to my bridle for second prize!

I felt a blaze of triumph. When we got out of the ring I almost fell off in my eagerness to hug Dolly and give her more oats, but Letty stopped me.

"Enough oats! You'll bloat her, and she's got jumping next. Well done. Now let's see how Big Cuzz duzz!"

The Shetlands walked out into the ring in a line. Bonny was last because, kick her as hard as he could, Cameron couldn't make her move till he used the crop. Then she kind of crawled along – if a pony can crawl – behind the last of the others, scarcely putting one foot in front of the other. Cameron was whacking her as hard as he could, while the people standing around started to laugh… The others got the order to trot, went round and overtook her from behind. It was like the tortoise and a bunch of hares. I could see Cameron, red in the face, whacking furiously. I waited till the turn at the top… And *wheeee!*, she was off.

And so was Cameron – because he pulled too hard on the bit, Bonny stopped dead with her head down, and over he went, bum over tip. I gasped, and so did the crowd. As soon as her mouth was free, Bonny raced past all the other ponies. The entrance was closed, but when she reached the barrier, which was quite low, she took it in one leap, switched her tail, and was gone. Back to Piper.

What a mother!

The announcer, when he could be heard over the laughter, said, "These ponies are for hire to teach children to ride!"

Meanwhile I'd scrambled over the barrier and run to see if Cameron was all right. He was already on his feet.

"Get away, I'm fine," he hissed at me. "You might have warned me that *thing* has the hide of a hippo and the mouth of a – a –" But he couldn't think what, so he just cursed under his breath.

There came a day when I left the house to go to school half an hour early – and there was no snow left in the back yard. It was all gone, leaving brown grass and lots of mud. And a football.

The head!

I stopped dead when I saw it, lying under a bush. Then I rushed to pick it up. Yes, it was the head, all right! I could see traces of the painted face, but most of it had been scraped off by the snow and there wasn't enough left for it to be really horrible.

Will it be enough to satisfy Mrs Hembrow? I wondered.

I knew Mummy would still be in bed. ("Like all actors I'm not a morning person.") For once I forgot about playing aggies and ran back into the house and woke her up.

She focused blearily on the washed-out-looking head.

"Mrs Hembrow needs it to be more frightening than that," I said.

Mummy got out of bed. "Have we got any paints? No, of course not… Well… Can I use your stable money to buy some today? And tonight we'll paint Anne Boleyn with her tongue sticking out and the blood round her poor neck."

But I had a better idea.

After school I collected the paints Mummy had bought, wrapped the head up in the *Star Phoenix* sports section, and knocked on the Hembrows' screen door. Mrs Hembrow came to open it; she had been getting better with the weather. She was very tall when she was on her feet and she looked like a princess with her long plait over her shoulder and her necklace. Both silver.

"Hallo, Lindy," she said.

"Mrs Hembrow, I found it! I've brought it."

She didn't ask me what – her eyes had already gone to the round shape wrapped in the *Star Phoenix*.

"Come in."

We went into their sitting room. The moose's nose stuck out so much I had to go around it. I put the head down on the table, with the paints beside it.

"Why did you bring paints?"

"Because we need to paint the face back on. I mean, I'll do it if you like. But I thought you'd like to do it. From what you remember."

She stared at me, and then reached out and took the newspaper off. She turned the ball over slowly until the washed-out face showed. You could still see the bulging eyes, a bit, and a faint red where the tongue had been.

"Yes," she said. "Leave it here. I'll do it. I'll do what I remember. Then I'll put it in the furnace. Then it goes away."

Suddenly she turned and kissed me.

Just as she did it, Mr Hembrow came in from the kitchen. He came up to the table and looked at the head. There was a long, solemn moment as we all stood there. I felt something important was happening, but I wasn't sure what.

Then Mr Hembrow silently took me by the elbow and walked me to the front door. He came out on to the porch with me.

"She kissed you," he said. "Mae don't never kiss strangers. When she did that, she took you into her nation." He smiled all over his face. "You're honorary Ojibwe now."

Chapter Fifteen

New York, New York!

Willie went and did it. She asked their new hosts, the Blundells, if they could invite us. And they did.

They not only invited us for Easter – or what would be left of our two-week school holiday, take away six days for the journeys – but offered to pay our rail fares. This gave Mummy a dilemma – the play was due to be put on for its three performances just after Easter, so she couldn't possibly go. For a whole day, Cameron and I went about with long faces, thinking we wouldn't see New York. I'd actually written to Willie to say so, but luckily I hadn't posted the letter.

Despite going to a convent school I'd never really got

into religion, and I didn't believe regular praying could get you anywhere, but I had this sort of superstition. It was about St Barnabas. I'd always liked him at the convent. He wasn't a patron saint of anything, but I knew St Jude was the patron saint of lost causes. And this was one. So I said a kind of prayer to St Barnabas, asking him to ask St Jude to get us to New York. I did it as a poem because that made it harder ·and I thought I needed to earn it.

"Oh St Barnabas, come to my help,
Cos I can't do this by myself.
Ask St Jude who's everyone's friend
To our lost cause his help to lend!
Way down south we long to go
To see New York which is a wonderful show.
We haven't much hope, but miracles can happen
So please make one to get us to Manhattan."

Of course I didn't tell this to Cameron. He'd have had something to say about a couple of the rhymes. Not to mention probably thinking my whole idea was silly. But on the third morning after the invitation came, Mummy called us both into the kitchen and announced that we could go without her. She'd found someone to accompany us – the sister of one of her actors was going to New York for Easter. This lady had been coming to rehearsals so Mummy knew her quite well. Her name was Geraldine.

This was so nearly a miracle, I felt quite sorry that I hadn't told anyone about St Barnabas. Cameron couldn't have laughed about it now!

We were simply *beside ourselves* with excitement. I hadn't seen Cameron so excited since the day he was in at the kill at a fox hunt when he was nine, and got the fox's brush. That time he jumped up and down in a circle holding his bottom. This time he just gave Mummy a big hug, which was equally unusual.

"It's three days on the train. Geraldine can't have her eye on you every minute. I trust you to behave yourselves and not do anything silly."

"Better drowned than duffers!" we both chanted. "If not duffers—"

"All right, all right. They're mailing the tickets," she said. She looked at us and then hugged us both. "Aren't we lucky – I mean, in a way? Canadians are so incredibly kind."

It turned out Americans were too. At least the Blundells certainly were.

They were also rich.

We were met at the railway station at Trenton by a chauffeur called Joe, in a huge car. It was something called a Cadillac, just about twice as long as a Hillman. Willie and Alfie had come to meet us. Willie looked like a teenager, in a beautiful blue sweater, sloppy-joe length, with pedal-pushers, bobby socks and saddle shoes. Saddle shoes! How I longed for a pair of those two-tone leather shoes. Even Alfie was clean and tidy and wearing new clothes, bought by their new hosts.

Willie was so excited she could hardly speak properly. And Alfie was so excited he couldn't speak at all.

"It's so great! You can't imagine! It's just so exciting – I have my own huge room, with wardrobes all across one wall! The bathroom's just for me! They are so rich and so nice – we're going to New York tomorrow – wait till you see it – it's the best place *ever* – Mum says the air makes her feel *intoxiated* all the time—"

We drove through some beautiful country. The spring was showing much more here than in Saskatoon – the trees were bursting into their different-green leaves, where ours were still bare. As we climbed out of the car, we could see that the house – *mansion* – was beside a lake. The water was perfectly still and the reflection was perfect – like a second house and woods, upside down. Apart from birds, skimming overhead, nothing moved. It was like a painting. I wished Mummy could see it.

Irene greeted us with hugs and introduced us to our hosts. Mr and Mrs Blundell were quite old, about fifty.

Mrs Blundell kissed us and Mr Blundell said he hoped we'd had a good journey. We proudly told them we'd done the last part, from New York, by ourselves — we had been very undufferish because we were scared not to be, so we had just sat there, primly. But it was only for half an hour. The main part, Saskatoon to New York, was so long we'd got bored. And been duffers. But we didn't tell the grown-ups that.

Only later, when I was alone with Willie, did I tell how we'd got off the train at a whistle-stop and the train started without us, and we had run alongside the track in a total panic, screaming and waving our arms until the engine-driver pulled up to let us back on again. Geraldine — who was really nice, she didn't deserve us — had almost pulled the communication cord when she thought she'd lost us.

I didn't tell even Willie what she said to us about getting off the train — how she wouldn't accompany us back to Saskatoon because we'd nearly given her heart failure. She said we could travel by ourselves and if we got lost she hoped we'd stay lost. Did she mean it? We couldn't know until it was time to travel back.

Mrs Blundell led us to our rooms. Cameron was to share with Alfie and me with Willie, but the rooms were so huge we each had a double bed. The bathroom was

absolutely amazing. It didn't even have a plug in the bath
– you had to pull a lever to let the water out. And there
was a separate little glass room near the bath, which was
a shower.

I'd never had a shower before. Willie said they were
fantabulous and made you much cleaner than a bath so
I had one straight away to try it out, and to get clean
after the train. If my first Canadian bath had been
wonderful, my first American shower was even more so.
The water nearly knocked me flat – it was like being
under a hot Niagara Falls.

Then we had our first American meal.

Almost every time we'd sat down to a big meal at
the Laines', Gordon would say one of two things: "You're
a good provider, Momma!" or, "Them's powerful vittles,
Mrs Laine!" (He'd always called food 'vittles'. I think he
was pretending to be a cowboy.)

Mr Blundell didn't say anything funny. He just said
grace, then beamed round at us and said, "Please make
pigs of yourselves now, kids."

Afterwards Willie took us off to look all over the
house. It was big, grand, modern. It even had a sort of
grown-up playroom, with a billiard table and one for
ping-pong. I liked the kitchen best. It had so many
gadgets! Willie told me what some of them did, but she
said, "I'm saving the best till last!"

Her best was in the living room. It was a piece of shiny wooden furniture with a small glass window-like panel in the top part.

"What is it?" I asked.

"It's called television," she said. "Mr Blundell's got one of the first ones in the whole United States. He's in the business! He says one day soon you'll be able to watch movies on it, at home."

"So you'll have Errol Flynn in your living room," I teased. Willie had a mad crush on Errol Flynn, after seeing him as Robin Hood.

Cameron said, "Can I see it working?"

"I daren't touch it! You can only see the news on it so far, twice a day. And last week we watched a baseball game. The pictures are a bit scratchy, but it's like magic to see a newsreel at home – don't you think?"

Cameron went to find Mr Blundell, to ask if we could watch the next news show on his television, so we could see what was going on at home.

They came back into the living room together.

"Are you worried about the war, Cameron?" Mr Blundell asked.

"Of course, sir," said Cameron, being extra polite. "Aren't you?"

Mr Blundell didn't answer. He put his hand on Cameron's shoulder. "Are your people at home safe so far?"

"Yes," said Cameron. "My parents live in Cheltenham. That's safer than the big cities."

"Write regularly, do they, with family news?"

"My mother does. My father's too busy."

"Look, Cameron. This is how to switch the set on. I'll tell you when you can. It's time for the news in a few minutes. Shall we all watch it together?"

Everyone in the house gathered to watch, including various people who at home would have been called servants, but Mrs Blundell introduced us to them as if they were family.

"This is Max, who helps me with the hard housework. Mary – she's a wonderful cook. Where's Joseph? Oh, there you are, Joe. Joe never misses the news. But you've met already. Joe drives the car and does the gardening for us."

Then we all settled down. I felt something extraordinary was about to happen. Mr Blundell nodded to Cameron to turn a knob, and, amazingly, the little glass window sprang to life! There was a rather wobbly picture of a man reading the news and some film of something that was going on in New York or Hollywood – I wasn't sure where, I just sat there, awestruck, my mouth open as I watched this little window as if I was watching the world through it.

But Cameron wasn't completely carried away.

"Isn't there any news from Europe?" he asked when it was over.

"I'm afraid there's not a lot of interest here about the war," Mr Blundell said. "President Roosevelt would like America to get into it but there are too many of us Americans who think it's nothing to do with them."

I hadn't known about this. In Canada, there was always a war-bonds drive going on and all the newsreels and papers were full of the war. And of course you saw lots of men in uniform. I told the Blundells about the Crescent Club and our scrap-metal drive. Cameron looked embarrassed, but Mr Blundell said, "Well done. Anything that helps beat those swine."

I didn't like listening to the news on the radio. Or watching the newsreels in the movies. I certainly never read the *Star Phoenix*, except the funnies. Seeing Mummy and Cameron glued to the radio at news time, I felt guilty, and when I eventually confessed to Mummy, she didn't make me feel any better.

"It's bad not to want to know what's going on in the world," she said. "You should try to keep up. It's the only way we have of sharing it."

At bedtime that first night, I knocked on Cameron's door. Alfie was already asleep.

"Mr Blundell seems to care about the war. Why do you think the Americans don't want to join in?"

"They're too comfortable. Why should they bother? The Nazis can't very well come over here."

"But isn't it a bit awful of them to let England be bombed and all the other beastly stuff, and not come to help?"

"Of course it's awful. But look at us. We're over here. Safe, and even…"

"Even what?"

"I was going to say happy. But I'm not."

"You're not?"

"Are *you*? *Really?*"

I didn't answer. He made me feel there was something wrong with being happy.

"When you think what's going on at home…" he said.

"But aren't you enjoying yourself here? I mean… it's fun, isn't it? And we're going to see New York, and…"

"Oh yes. It's fun. Fun's all right − being happy's something different."

Chapter Sixteen

Fairyland

The day after we arrived, Mr Blundell told us he had taken a whole day off work. He squeezed us all in the car and drove us into New York.

That first visit was so special. As we drove across the Hudson River I looked ahead and saw, for the first time, skyscrapers – dozens of them, like a forest of metal fingers pointing upward. They glistened and gleamed. I couldn't believe they were real buildings, with people inside them. Seen from far off, the whole of Manhattan was like a brilliant statue created by a single sculptor, who wanted to show that we could reach the sky if we stretched hard enough.

Cameron stared and stared as we drove across the bridge.

"If the *Luftwaffe* dropped bombs on this," he said, "it wouldn't take many. It looks so fragile. Not solid like London."

"They can't reach us," said Mrs Blundell. "Thank God."

We drove slowly down Fifth Avenue. On every side were wonders: shops full of glorious clothes; lit-up signs everywhere; huge crowds of people on the wide pavements, flowing like human rivers across the road at the crossings; and these huge buildings like topless walls that made the street dark enough to need lights in all the windows, though it was only lunchtime.

We had lunch in a restaurant called the Carnegie Deli. Mr Blundell said there were grander places but that this was more fun. The waiter was really rude! I ordered corned-beef hash, which was my favourite food that I hadn't had since we left England. When it came it was the biggest plateful I'd ever seen, enough for all of us! As the waiter plonked it down in front of me, he shouted, quite fiercely, "NO SHARIN'!"

I said, "Why not?"

"Because, ya dumb kid, if ya share, then nobody else'll order no food. Ya want I should lose my job already?"

I was shocked; we all were – Irene looked horrified. But the Blundells burst out laughing.

Mr Blundell said, "Benny, go easy on them, this is

their first time in New York. Teach them how to 'talk Brooklyn'."

The waiter stood up straight and cleared his throat loudly. All the people at the nearby tables stopped talking to watch.

He said, very fast: "Toity poiple boids sittin' on a coib eatin' woims and choipin', when along came Goitie Moiphy and her boyfriend Hoiman, who woiks in a shoit-factory in Joisy. When dey saw de toity poiple boids sittin' on a coib eatin' woims and choipin' –" He looked round at us all and shook his head sadly – "Wuz dey pertoibed!"

Everyone around us clapped! It sounded like a foreign language, but so funny I got the giggles. Alfie fell off his chair and had to be hoicked up again. (Or do I mean herked?)

I hadn't understood more than the odd word (woid), but I asked, "What's 'pertoibed'?"

"Perturbed, of course," said Cameron, who hadn't laughed. "It means disturbed."

"Distoibed!" the waiter corrected him loudly. "You ain't got it yet, kid. Eat your pastrami and wise up." And he left us.

While Mr Blundell 'translated' for us about the thirty purple birds, and Gertie and Herman, we tucked into our enormous portions. Eating corned-beef hash again reminded me of coming home from boarding school and Mummy cooking my favourite dish, after saving up her rations to get the corned beef.

I told about that, and how she'd got some whale-meat off the ration and tried to hide the fishy taste with lots of curry-powder, but how Daddy said, "If this is beef, it must come off a cow who's been eating fish and chips!" This made everyone laugh some more.

But there was something sort of nervous about the way the Blundells laughed. Later when I remembered that lovely meal, I thought it was strange, sitting there in that bright, noisy restaurant full of happy people stuffing themselves and having fun, while talking about London in wartime. For once I was glad Mummy wasn't with us; it reminded me of that restaurant in Montreal, when everyone sang 'There'll Always Be an England', and she had cried.

I couldn't get halfway through my mountain of corned-beef hash before I was full. Well, not too full for a sundae, but afterwards I dropped off to sleep in the car. Willie shook me awake.

"Are we going up the Empire State Building?" I asked as we climbed out.

"Next time. First we'll shop for a nice dress for you," said Mr Blundell.

A dress? For me?

We went into the most beautiful shop I'd ever seen. It was huge, full of light and colour and lovely clothes on dummies. As we walked through it, I felt as though it must be a dream.

Mr Blundell took Cameron off to buy him a sweater, and Irene went off to the kids' department with Alfie, leaving Mrs Blundell with Willie and me in the teenage department.

"Brian wants you to have a formal, Lindy," she said.

A formal! I didn't even know that meant a long evening dress. Did girls of my age wear such things in America? They certainly didn't in Saskatoon! I just gaped at her. I should have said something – like that I'd rather have had a pair of saddle shoes and a sloppy-joe sweater. But I felt helpless. If Mr Blundell wanted to buy me a long dress, well, it was all part of being in this fairy-tale place. Here in New York, it didn't seem impossible that I might be invited to a ball!

I tried on three beautiful long dresses. They were all too big for me, but Mrs Blundell said, "In a year or two you'll need a long dress to go to school proms. Take it and put it away." So I chose a white one, with a full skirt made of layers of netting. I looked at myself in the long glass. Mrs Blundell took my hair, which I still wore in a thick brown plait, and held it in a kind of hairy flower on top of my head. It was like a trailer of me as I'd be when I was grown-up. The saddle shoes and sloppy joe floated away (for the moment). Who wanted to look like a teenager when you could look like a woman?

In the six days we were in New York, the Blundells looked after us and spoilt us.

We were taken to see the sights – the Empire State Building, of course, and downtown, by subway, to see the Statue of Liberty. And Broadway to see all the lit-up signs. In Central Park, we made a gangster movie with Mr Blundell's home-movie camera. Cameron stopped holding back, for once, and really entered into it. He didn't do The Spirit, he did Al Capone. He jumped out from behind a tree, shouting, "Take that, ya rat!" and shot Willie, who did a great heart-clutch and fall, only as she landed she kicked her legs in the air, and when Mr Blundell showed the movie on our last night, she was so embarrassed at her knickers showing, she ran out of the room.

I think my favourite of the things we did, was seeing a play called *Life with Father*, which was so funny we simply sat there screaming with laughter for two hours. Even Cameron couldn't resist it, and laughed every time the father shouted, "OH, GAHD!" which he did every time anything went wrong. We had stopped saying "Widdiya woddiya" since we'd left the Laines', but from

now on "OH, GAHD!" would be our secret code word.
Sometimes we just rolled our eyes and mouthed it.

Another night Mr Blundell took us to Carnegie Hall
for a classical concert. I'd never seen a full orchestra
before and I was too busy watching it to listen much,
but the music absolutely *sent* Cameron. He came out
with red eyes and didn't talk the whole way home. He
thanked Mr Blundell as if he'd given him his whole
house, practically.

On the Friday night, which was Good Friday, we had
a special dinner. We were asked to dress nicely for it and I
wore my new formal, with a sash round the waist and the
skirt tucked up so it didn't trail along the floor. Willie had
one too – a tartan taffeta one. We both put our hair up –
Mrs Blundell lent us pins and helped us.

"We must dress up for Easter," she said.

The table in the dining room was laid with a beautiful
white cloth with embroidery on it, and we had nice
linen napkins and fancy plates, knives and forks, and there
were tall silver candlesticks with red candles in the middle.

"Why red?" I asked.

Mrs Blundell whispered, "For the blood of Our Lord."

The meal, prepared by Mary, was specially delicious
– roast chicken, with a fancy, creamy dessert. After we'd
eaten, Mr Blundell asked if we'd like to read the story
of Easter in the Bible, round the table. Of course I knew

it from the convent. We read it in the proper Bible – the King James version, Mr Blundell called it. The language was strange and hard, but of course Cameron read it beautifully and the Blundells complimented him. I fluffed mine a bit – the Crucifixion always gave me the utter creeps – and Willie asked to be excused; she said she wouldn't read it well enough. At the end, after he had said a special prayer for people in Europe who were suffering, Mr Blundell added, "May we be forgiven for not being there."

Cameron looked at him and then at me. Pursing his lips, he suddenly bowed his head and said, "Amen."

Chapter Seventeen

Back to the Real World

Mr Blundell drove us to New York to catch the train back to Saskatoon. We were scared stiff that Geraldine wouldn't turn up to escort us, after what had happened on the way there, but when we got to our platform, there she was.

Phew.

She didn't meet our eyes, but chatted away to Mr Blundell, while I looked around the enormous station and nervously hummed 'The Chattanooga Choo Choo'.

Cameron muttered, "Shut up, Lind. We have to think. Shall we say anything?"

"Yes. When we're on the train we have to say again that we're sorry."

So we did, the first minute we were alone with her. It turned out she was still mad at us, after all.

She said, "You stupid thoughtless kids scared the life out of me. I couldn't let you travel back alone, but I am not speaking to you."

Well, although I felt guilty, in a way it was good. Because on that long train ride back to Saskatoon, Cameron and I ended up having to talk to each other.

There was a lot to talk about. Cameron had gone mad about music while we were in New York. He said he was going to go back to his paper round and use the money – and more; his dad's money – for piano lessons.

"Is this just because of the concert at Carnegie Hall?" I asked.

"No, of course not. I was in the music club at school. I'm going to start one in Saskatoon."

"What'll you call it?"

"I'm going to call it the Classics-lovers Club. To be a member, you have to be able to sit through an entire Beethoven symphony without fidgeting. Or a concerto."

I wished I'd listened more to the music at Carnegie Hall, instead of watching the musicians and the instruments. But I loved show tunes and Frank Sinatra and Bing Crosby so much I doubted if I'd ever qualify for the Classics-lovers Club.

★

The long, long journey left me a lot of thinking time. As we were chugging through the pinelands of Ontario, I said to Geraldine, "Are whoever you stayed with in New York very rich?"

"No," she said.

'Yes' and 'no' was all we could get out of her.

That night as Cameron and I were getting ready for bed – I mean berth – I said, "It'll be as big a change going back to Taylor Street after the Blundells' as it was when we got there from the Laines'."

"Yes, it will. We'll feel like Bubbles in a tiny kennel."

"I wasn't thinking of space, so much. It's everything. It's like another world." I buttoned my pyjamas. There was something tickling my memory. "Don't you think they were maybe a bit *too* rich?"

"How d'you mean?"

"Well… I mean, it's not really fair, is it? Them so rich and us…"

"Are you jealous?"

"Dunno. I just don't think it's fair."

"Dad always says life isn't fair and you shouldn't expect it to be."

Lying in my swaying berth, looking out at the dark landscape and being suddenly reminded of Uncle Jack, I faced up to what I'd been remembering: Cameron's home in England compared to mine. Both our fathers were doctors, but his was a surgeon, doing operations on rich people, while mine was a GP in a poor district of London. I loved our house, but compared to theirs it was small. We weren't poor, but they were rich, almost (but not quite) like the Blundells. Big rooms, a vast garden, servants, two enormous cars, Auntie Millie's full-length fur coat – lots of lovely things. Luxury. *Glamour.* I'd never made a comparison before. But when I thought of Taylor Street, and Mummy struggling, and England fighting and America staying out of it while the Blundells got really, *really* rich, well… it didn't make me jealous, exactly. But grown-ups were always telling us kids to play fair. And this just wasn't.

Later, chugging along through watery Manitoba, Cameron suddenly said, "Did you talk to Joe at all?"

"Who's Joe?"

"The Blundells' chauffeur. Obviously you didn't, but I did. He's German."

"What, 'filthystinking'?"

"No. They're not all filthystinking. Some of them are against Hitler. Joe's family is. That's why he's in America. But they stayed."

He stared out of the window for long minutes, watching the lakes go by.

Then he said, "Just imagine if when we thought about

our families we had to think about them in Germany. Or Poland. Or anywhere where those rotten Nazis are. Instead of in England, where at least it's just rationing and bombs. Joe is *always* thinking about his family in Germany. They're probably in a concentration camp by now."

That was the first time I'd ever heard those words. I was ashamed to ask, but he must have sensed my puzzlement and told me anyway.

"They round them up and take them to these camps. Joe says they're awful places. The Nazis pretend they're some kind of holiday camps but they're really prisons. They take everything away from them, they have to wear uniforms, they make them work, they don't give them enough to eat. Imagine if you had to think of Uncle Jamie in one." He turned and looked at me. "But you know what, Lind? Sometimes I'd rather be a resistance fighter in Germany than be here. At least then I wouldn't feel like a…"

"A what?"

"A *bloody deserter.*"

We were travelling first class, thanks to Mr Blundell. At meals in the dining car we kept trying to make conversation with Geraldine. We had a secret pact to try to make her say something besides yes and no. One lunchtime I asked her if she was interested in acting.

"Yes," she said. After a few more mouthfuls, she unbent

enough to say, "That's why I go to watch rehearsals of your mom's play. My sister says your mom is the most wonderful director. I wish I could be in one of her plays."

"She should let you, after this," I said.

And she nearly smiled.

The conversation reminded me that the play would be starting its three-day run the night after we got back; I'd had two postcards from Mummy, which had been all about it. As the train drew near to Saskatoon, I got the postcards out and read them again. There was a bit on the last one that I hadn't noticed before. It said, 'Surprise when you get back!'

Of course I thought it was a present.

Chapter Eighteen

All Change

Mummy met us at the station. Since we'd left England, I'd never seen her looking so happy and alive.

It must be the play, I thought.

She had a big bunch of flowers and a box of candies for Geraldine. She thanked her and we thanked her and we waited for her to snitch, but she didn't – she just sort of rolled her eyes at us behind Mummy's back as she hurried away. Luckily, Mummy hadn't thought to ask her how we'd behaved.

We went home on the streetcar, me chattering away about New York and my new dress and everything. But soon after we crossed the bridge, Mummy stood up and rang the bell, miles before the Taylor Street stop – at Eleventh Street.

"Aren't we going home?"

"Darlings, that's my big surprise! Taylor Street isn't home any more. The Warrens decided to sell it and we've had to leave. I've found a flat for us! It was all very sudden. I don't know how I'd have managed if it hadn't been for— Well, that's another surprise!"

Cameron and I exchanged bewildered looks, and Cameron said, "OH, GAHD!" like in *Life with Father*, only quietly, for me.

We humped our suitcases along Eleventh Street. We were back on the right side of the tracks. This was a pretty nice neighbourhood – but I didn't notice that yet; I was too *incredulous.*

Mummy was talking gaily but I wasn't listening.

No more Taylor Street. No more Hembrows. And Eleventh Street was miles from school.

Cameron suddenly pointed. "Look, there's Nutana, right at the end of this road! I can walk to school in five minutes!"

"And so can you, Lindy," Mum said. "You've left Buena Vista. You'll be going to Victoria next term. It's all arranged."

My world took another tilt. Had we been away for years, not days?

"But Miss Bubniuk – all my friends—"

"You'll make new ones," said Mummy cheerfully. "You couldn't possibly carry on going to Buena Vista – you're out of their district."

Before I had a chance to object, we arrived at a large house and Mummy continued her revelations. "This is it! We have the first floor. It's quite big enough. And, Cam, you won't have to do the furnace – that's our landlord's job now. You can take it easy."

We hadn't asked about the play, but as we went into the hall of our new house, Mummy was saying, "*Penny Wise* opens tomorrow night. You've got front-row seats!"

And then we saw him.

He was standing at the top of the stairs, grinning at us. He was wearing the uniform of a naval officer. I didn't know him for a minute, but then he said, "Hi, kids," and of course I remembered.

It was Hank, who'd bought us our train meals, and told us all those tall stories about gophers and hunting our breakfasts!

He came down to meet us. He kissed the top of my head and shook Cameron's hand. Then he picked up the suitcases – all three of them, the extra one Mrs Blundell had given us for our presents too – and carried them up the stairs.

We followed him, absolutely speechless with surprise.

At the top of the stairs was a 'front door' that opened into our new flat. It had a living room, a kitchen at the back with a balcony, and two bedrooms. And a bathroom, of course, which looked like a closet compared to the one we'd had in New Jersey. In fact the whole flat seemed small and cramped. There was nothing familiar in it except the photos we had of Daddy and Grampy and the aunts. Everything we'd got used to in Taylor Street had been left behind.

Mummy was bustling about showing us things, pointing out that the furniture wasn't as shabby as in Taylor Street, that we had a beautiful tree outside the front window, that the balcony was big enough to eat meals on, that the kitchen had a machine for washing clothes. Mummy was very excited about that.

"I hope you like it!" she said. "It'll be fun, not living out in the sticks any more!"

Meanwhile I kept glancing at Hank. Despite his grey hair, he looked very tall and handsome.

Cameron was the first to ask. "What are you doing here, Hank?"

"Your aunt got in touch. She asked me to come and help her to move."

Mummy had got in touch with him? He'd come all the way from Alberta to help her?

"Are you on leave?" Cameron asked. I could hear the

admiration in his voice. I knew, because of the battleship book, that joining the navy was Cameron's ultimate dream. "Are you a captain? Of a battleship? Which kind?"

"I'm not a captain, just a humble lieutenant. And I don't go to sea, I'm too old. I've got a desk job. Yes, I am on leave, but I have to go back soon. I'm posted to Regina, luckily."

Regina was the capital of our province, Saskatchewan. I wondered what was lucky about it, because Regina was called 'Hogtown' by people in Saskatoon. And it was certainly nowhere near the sea.

Mummy had prepared a cold supper for the three of us − not for her, because she had to go to the dress rehearsal.

I felt completely turned upside down. But Hank was very nice and friendly.

"Are you staying for the play?" I asked.

"Sure am. Wouldn't miss that!"

Before I went to bed in the new bedroom that night, I phoned Willie.

I knew I shouldn't because long-distance phone calls were so expensive, but I was missing her and I needed to talk to someone about what had happened.

She listened in silence and then said, "Never mind the new school and the move and all that − you'll get used to it. But you want to watch out for this Hank bloke."

"What do you mean?"

"Well – you say he's so handsome. I'm always watching out for handsome men hanging around Mum. If this Hank came running when she asked him, after all this time, he's probably buggy about her."

I was just about to say, *But he knows she's married!* when I remembered Gordon. A sudden cold flash of fear went through me. Mummy hadn't liked Gordon. But she did like Hank. She must have liked him, a lot, or she wouldn't have sent for him.

I was still awake when she came back from the dress rehearsal. I heard her arrive. Hank was sitting in the living room with the radio turned low, babysitting us. I heard them talking quietly, and then the front door closed again and after a few minutes Mummy came into our dark bedroom.

"Mummy?"

"Oh, hallo, poppet, are you still awake? It's awfully late."

"You can switch on the light."

She did. She didn't look a bit tired. She looked excited. She took off her coat and hung it up.

"How was the dress rehearsal?"

"Terrible! Unspeakable! Everything that could go wrong, went wrong!"

"So why are you looking so happy?"

She turned and stared at me.

"I do? I don't! I'm exhausted, and scared stiff! I can't imagine the play's actually going to happen before an audience tomorrow!"

"You're all lit up."

She came and sat on the bed.

"You funny little thing!" she said. "All lit up, am I? Well! I'm back in my world, the theatre world – at least on the edges. I love it. Even when I'm frustrated and despairing."

I clutched her hand. "Where's Hank gone?"

"Hank?" She stood up and started getting undressed. "He's got himself a room in a hotel downtown. I hope he hasn't missed the last streetcar… Really, he is a treasure. He's been such a help."

"It's weird. You sending for him."

"Oh, I know it was cheeky of me, Lindy, but I was desperate! Mr Warren suddenly rang up and told me he'd sold the place and that I had three weeks to get out. I started house-hunting the same day, and found this quite quickly, but there was so much to do! With rehearsals and everything, and having to pack up, and leave the house clean, and get settled in here before you got back – I felt overwhelmed! And I had to register you at your new school. I just didn't see how I could do it all on my own. I had no one to turn to!"

She was slathering her make-up off with cold cream.

"And then — it was like destiny! — Hank's card fell out of my handbag. I didn't stop to think about it, I just rang him. Someone gave me his number at the naval office in Regina, and the next day, he arrived. All got up in his uniform — I hardly knew him! Talk about the cavalry riding to my rescue! Dear, kind Hank! I just don't know how to thank him!"

I heard Willie in my head, saying, *I bet he could think of a way! Kissy-kissy!*

I said, "Why did he come?"

"Because he's Canadian and the kindest man on earth."

"Kinder than O'F? Kinder than *Daddy*?"

Mummy climbed into bed.

"No, but they weren't around. I needed a kind man who was around. Now go to sleep. You've got school tomorrow."

Chapter Nineteen

Worries

We went to the first night of *Penny Wise* with Hank. He took us in a taxi to the Regent, a real little theatre downtown. We sat in the front row, the three of us, with Hank in the middle, and the auditorium filled up with people and the play happened, and it was *brilliant*. I thought it was as good as *Life with Father*. Hank laughed in all the right places and clapped like mad and even cheered at the end. And through it all I was so unhappy I didn't laugh once. I just kept stealing glances at Hank, his eyes fixed on the stage, and thought, *Willie's right. He's buggy about her, you can see.*

After all the curtain calls, we waited for Mummy, who was glowing with triumph, and Hank took us all out to dinner at the Bessborough. He bought Mummy flowers from the flower stall in the foyer. He bought *champagne* to celebrate. (I had some. It went up my nose.) Then he took us home in another taxi and kissed Mummy goodbye. Only on the cheek, but they hugged each other, and he told her he'd come back if she needed him, "Even if I have to go AWOL."

AWOL (I asked Cameron) meant absent without leave. You could go to jail for it if you were in the army. Or the navy. He'd go to jail for her? Was he joking? I couldn't tell.

Willie was right. She was *so* right. I had to keep watch. Daddy couldn't help not being here, any more than Mummy could help it that she was. It was the war. But I wasn't going to let anything bad happen.

The next two months were probably the worst, for me, since we'd first come to Canada.

To be honest, I hadn't minded up to now, being away from home. I wasn't like Cameron. I didn't want to be in the middle of the war. The newsreels and the radio tried to bring it to me. I shut my eyes in the movies, and refused to listen at home. But it got into me somehow, making sure I didn't escape. Bombs and fire and smoke and darkness. Buildings crashing down. Big guns firing. Soldiers marching, people running, searchlights, planes in

the sky. Churchill's speech about fighting on the beaches…
I couldn't completely keep it out. And I couldn't help
being glad I was far away from it. I was on Mrs Blundell's
side. "They can't reach us. Thank God."

When I thought about how Cameron felt, I knew I
should feel like a deserter, too. But I couldn't. I wanted to
be happy. And I had been, pretty much, since we got here.

Mummy often said, "Our goal, and my war work, is
to see it through," which made me feel we were helping
the war by being brave.

But this sudden, violent change, when we moved away
from Taylor Street, made me feel seriously wobbly. If our
home could be sold from under us, forcing us to move,
if I had to go to a new school full of new kids who had
to get used to my English accent all over again, if I didn't
have Willie any more, or the Hembrows – I just felt I'd
been part of a complicated game where the grown-ups
made all the rules. I wasn't sure I wanted to play any more.

But there was something else, now. All that wasn't
so bad. Like Willie said, I got used to it. Victoria School
was near home. I made friends with a girl called Poppy.
Only a few kids teased me, saying my 'mom' coached
me after school to keep up my accent. I joined the
drama club. I got lousy marks in maths and good ones
in English. I was elected to the student council. What
can I say? It was school.

The bad thing was, I worried all the time about Hank.

He phoned Mummy. He phoned too often. I listened in to Mummy's end of the conversations. She laughed a lot.

I thought, *I should be glad he's cheering her up. I should be glad he's around if she needs him.* But I wasn't. I was frightened.

I kept thinking, *Why doesn't Daddy write oftener? Why does he waste his letters telling golf stories? Why isn't he more romantic?*

Didn't he know how *lonely* Mummy got, here on her own without him?

Suddenly a lot of little things I hadn't even realised I'd noticed, clicked into place in my head. Moods Mummy got into. Tears she tried to keep me from seeing. Getting cross sometimes over nothing. And now, from when we got off the train from New York, how she looked. *All lit up.* What if it wasn't the play that had lit her up, at all? What if it was Hank?

We went to the movies every Friday. One night at the Roxy, we saw a war movie. There was a British soldier in it who got a letter from his wife, telling him she loved someone else. It gave me nightmares.

In one of my secret phone calls to Willie, she said it's not safe for married people to be thousands of miles apart for months and months – and maybe, the way the war was going so badly, years. How could people wait that long for each other?

Cameron and I still wrote to our families every Sunday. Mummy never asked to see what I wrote to Daddy, although I usually read my letters to her because I was proud of them. But I stopped doing that when I began to write hints:

> *Darling Daddy-dinko,*
>
> *How are you? We're fine. Since the play, Mummy's been asked to do a special thing for a war-bond drive in June. It's about the Four Freedoms. That's something President Roosevelt said everyone in the world should have: Freedom of Speech, Freedom from Want, Freedom of Worship, Freedom from Fear. Mummy has to dream up four tablos in big box-things, like stages, that they'll build in City Park. Each tablo will illustrate one of the Four Freedoms. Nobody in the tablo will move. It'll be like a living picture. Mummy has to plan them all, and find the people and costumes. I'm going to be in one of them! I'll be a child in the Want one, looking hungry. Oh, and Mummy has to write a script and read it.*
>
> *Cameron's started taking piano lessons from a man called Mr Gustin. He can already play scales with two hands.*

O'F comes to see us more often in the new place because it's closer to his home and the taxi doesn't cost so much. So that's good. But I miss our neighbours from the old place, and our landlady here is a bit mean and bangs on our door early on rent day. It's too far to go to the stables, so I've got another job. I help out at the drugstore on Saturdays. I have to pretend I'm twelve. I don't serve at the counter, I just wash dishes in the kitchen. I can hear the juke-box. Lots of Bing Crosby and Tommy Dorsey. I love 'My Sister and I', which is about refugees. Is 'Deep Purple' still popular at home? And 'The Umbrella Man'?

Have you written to Mummy lately? I don't mind if you don't write to me, I can share Mummy's letters. Not if they're too private of course. I bet Mummy would like that kind of letter best.

I miss you. <u>Please write.</u>

Tons of love, and to Grampy and Auntie Millie and Auntie Bee. Lindy.

I didn't mention Hank. But I thought, *If Daddy doesn't write soon, I will mention him.* In a careful way. A warning way.

In June Mummy got very busy with the tableaux (I learnt how to spell it) for the war-bond drive and was out a lot. She had to write and practise the speech part of it, and have sessions with the people in the tableaux even though they didn't have to move or speak.

Cameron spent hours after school practising on the school piano. He'd gone completely daffy about his music. The Classics-lovers Club had three members and he spent time at his friend Aaron's house playing records on Aaron's record player, so I was on my own a lot.

Mummy had picked up on one Canadian custom. Nobody worried about leaving any kids older than about ten alone at home. And I was eleven by now. I was very free. I biked to Poppy's. She sure wasn't Willie, but she had a lovely house looking over the river on Saskatchewan Crescent. I thought rich parents like Poppy's would be strict, but they had busy social lives and we were left to do as we liked. We rode our bikes across the open front gardens, raided the fridge for picnics on the riverbank, and played Knock Down Ginger after dark – knocking on doors and running away, which I'm sure our parents would have had a fit about.

Alone in the house, we made trick phone calls. We'd ring any old number and pretend to be testing the telephone. We'd ask people to move around the room, whistling, and then we'd say, "Thank you, ma'am, we'll deliver the birdseed in the morning."

Or:

"Hallo? Are you the woman who washes?"

"No…"

"You dirty thing!" (Hang up.)

In between times, Mummy started worrying about the long summer holiday. We'd get the whole of July and August off. Any kind of going-away holiday was bound to be expensive and Mummy hated more and more to take money from O'F; he hadn't been well. She often took the streetcar across town to visit him, and sometimes I went too. They had friendly rows about him giving us money. She usually won, and didn't take any. So I knew a summer holiday for us was going to be a problem.

One day I heard her talking to Hank:

"These people in New York have offered to have us."

My heart leapt. But only for a second.

"But of course I can't accept…"

Of course, I thought.

"Well, they've done enough already, having the kids at Easter…

"Yes, I've heard it's terribly hot down there in summer. It's getting hot here too! Oh, how I miss the English seaside! Buckets and spades, rock pools, deckchairs on the beach, swimming in the sea… I never realised how lucky we were! Now my sisters say the beaches are all

covered with barbed wire and the sea's full of mines…
I'll have to think of something else… (Long pause.)

"Hank, I couldn't! It's too sweet of you, but no, really.
But thank you. You're an angel."

Mummy often talked 'actressy'. But I didn't like it
when she did it to Hank. Once I thought I heard her
call him 'darling'! I wondered what he'd offered. Money,
probably. I was so relieved she'd said no. I didn't want
her to owe him anything more. But I did want a summer
holiday!

I gave Mummy all my savings from jobs. It wasn't
much. I asked if there could be water in our holiday.
Her talking about the seaside made me long for it.

She said, "Wouldn't it be lovely… but there's no sea
for a thousand miles. It'd take a miracle!"

A miracle, eh?

I decided to see what St Barnabas could do. My new
class teacher, Mr Jansen, was keen on poetry, so I was
able to make my prayer-poem better.

> *Dear St Barnabas, be my speed,*
> *And come to me in my hour of need!*
> *To swim and fish is what we crave,*
> *But we haven't enough dollars saved.*
> *Please find us some water, salty or not,*
> *And I'll say you're a lovesome saint, God wot.*

> *As to the money I leave that to you,*
> *I'm sure you won't fail us cos you never* do."

I was so pleased with the first two lines, I put them in again at the end, to round it off.

This time I did read it to Cameron.

He said, "Why don't you pray to God?"

I remembered the 'Amen' and didn't like to admit I didn't believe in him. I said, "Because I didn't think it was important enough."

"Well, I did," he said, which surprised me a lot. "And my prayer was much more specific. It's interesting you asked for water. I want to go to Emma Lake."

I pricked up my ears. "Emma Lake? Where's that?"

"It's north of here. A huge lake in the woods. Mr Gustin has a cabin. He runs a summer school for young musicians. Maybe he'll ask me to go."

"All right for you then! What about us?"

"I'll pray again," he said, after a moment. I wondered if he'd forgotten all about us the first time.

"Do you really think God bothers about people's school holidays?"

"Of course, what a funny question."

But I didn't see how he could. With the war and everything, there must be millions of really important prayers being sent to him. And how could Cameron help

237

noticing that a lot of them weren't being answered, with so many people dying.

The War Bond Tableaux was another big triumph for Mummy. She read aloud what she'd written about the Four Freedoms. I'd heard it already when she'd been practising, but hearing it over the loudspeaker, in her English voice, it sounded beautiful. The people, sitting in rows of seats in the park by the river, listened very quietly. There was music, too… Beethoven!

I played my hungry-girl part. As I didn't look at all hungry, quite the opposite actually, I was partly hidden at the back of the tableau, which showed someone handing out loaves of bread to children with their hands stretched out.

The main thing was to keep absolutely still all the time Mummy was speaking. My nose itched horribly but I managed to will myself not to scratch it. One of the other hungry children got the giggles and I muttered furiously at her, afraid she'd spoil the tableau. Our arms were aching by the time the curtains dropped at the end, but our picture was in the *Star Phoenix* (though you couldn't see me). Mummy's name was printed. A lot of war bonds sold and Mummy became a bit famous.

People in other towns started asking if they could use

her script for their own war bonds pageants. There was talk of another play with the Regent Players, and maybe a Christmas show for what were called 'underprivileged children'. I was pleased because I liked feeling proud of her. And she had loads of friends now. She talked about 'my gang' – her group of actors, who used to come to the flat to drink tea and chat. If she did another play, they'd be coming over more, and maybe I'd get to hear their lines. But that wouldn't be till after the summer vacation.

What vacation?

At the end of the school year, Mr Gustin, Cameron's music teacher, gave a student concert.

Cameron had only been learning the piano since Easter, but he played easy pieces now, and Mr Gustin said he could perform at the beginning of the concert. It was held at his house on Tenth Street. All the family and friends of the students crammed into one end of the double living room on little gilt chairs. At the other end was a small grand piano.

Cameron didn't seem a bit nervous. He went up when Mr Gustin – a white-haired man with a sweet face – called his name and said, "First, my English pupil, who is making great progress. He will play 'About Lands and People' by Schubert."

He sat down on the piano stool and played something very pretty, without (as far as I could tell), a single mistake. Everyone clapped. He stood up and bowed.

I could see he was pretty pleased with himself. I knew it was wrong, but I felt a bit envious – I wanted the applause to be for me. Still. I was proud of him.

How come when Cameron makes up his mind, he can do anything he's decided to do? I wondered. I'd decided to be an actress when I grew up, but I wouldn't have betted on making it happen.

But what did happen was that St Barnabas, or God, or someone, came good.

Mr Gustin did invite Cameron to go to his summer school at Emma Lake, but only for a week. BUT! Mr Gustin also knew of another cabin, right next to his, that was for rent for the whole summer. Very cheap!

It wasn't cheap enough, but then Mummy was invited to do some talks on CFQC, the Saskatoon radio station, about her life as an actress, and about coming to Canada. Her talks were brilliant. In one of them she told about the conductor on the train who took her off for a cup of tea and comforted her. She didn't know his name but she said she hoped he'd hear the broadcast and know she was grateful.

She got paid for the talks and that's what helped us

to rent the cabin at Emma Lake, and gave us a summer none of us would ever forget. Our first full summer in Canada, and the last before what happened with Cameron.

Chapter Twenty

Emma Lake

T he day school ended, we spent the evening packing and the next day we set off by train for Prince Albert, a town nearly a hundred miles north.

We were very excited. At least, I was. Cameron had asked Mr Gustin what it would be like, but all he'd say was, "Well, for my money it's the most beautiful place on earth."

I couldn't believe it would be more beautiful than Felpham, the seaside town where we used to go for our summer holidays in England. Felpham was my standard for summer holidays.

I was soon to discover, though, that there was no comparison.

★

We left the prairies behind, and soon the train was chugging through forests. Not forests like in England with lots of different kinds of trees. Pine forests. Sitting out on the observation platform in the heat of midday you could smell the piny scent, overpowering everything. There was so much *space*.

Mummy spent a lot of time out there, smoking and writing.

"Are you writing to Daddy?"

"No. Auntie Millie. She's got troubles."

"The war, you mean?"

"Not only…"

She wouldn't say any more. And she didn't say that much in front of Cameron.

She'd had a letter from Daddy just before we left. I was so relieved when it came; I thought maybe there was a God after all. She read it and read it and then handed it to me. There was some news in it (our windows had been mended and the horrid aunt's cat had died, so at least it couldn't be eating Daddy's rations) and no golf stories, thank goodness, but there was nothing private. Just 'lots of love' and 'missing you a great deal' at the end.

When we arrived at Prince Albert, there was a man there to meet us. His name was Mr Kaldor. I think he was

Swedish. He had a truck with an open back. He piled our cases in and then helped Cameron and me up after them. There were some old tatty cushions to sit on, otherwise it was just bare boards. Mummy sat in front.

We drove through the town with the wind blowing pine-scent and wood smoke and horse-smell up our noses. Almost at once we were out in the country. Wild was the word! We drove for miles through the woods, not seeing any people, just the odd log cabin. The hard floor of the truck bounced under our bottoms. After a while it wasn't even a proper road, just a narrow, rutted track with the dark woods close on each side like walls.

"It's a bit like New York," said Cameron.

Like *New York*? But then I saw what he meant: the trees were a bit like tall buildings looming up with just a river of sky overhead.

Suddenly the truck jerked to a stop. Cameron stood up and peered over the top of the driver's cabin.

"Lind, come and look!" he hissed.

I got up beside him and saw a huge bull moose moseying across the road. It was the Hembrows' moose head come to life! The truck stood still till it had disappeared.

Exciting. But still, as we drove on I'd have been glad to see a few shops and lights and people! The word 'wilderness' kept coming into my mind. It made me shiver. It was about as unlike cosy Felpham with its beach balls and fishing nets and screaming kids and ice-cream sellers and donkey rides as you could imagine.

After about an hour, Mr Kaldor pulled up the truck with a squeal of old brakes. We craned over the sides. On mine, there was nothing but a solid wall of black forest. But Cameron, on the other side, said, "Look! There's the lake!"

And there it was, through the pine trees. A great spread like a huge silver tray, shining in the sun. And between us and it was our cabin. All built of pine logs with a roof of wooden tiles and a stone chimney.

Mr Kaldor had the key. He opened the creaky wooden door for us and helped us in with the cases. Right inside was a kitchen and beyond that, a big square living room with a stone fireplace, a big window you could see the lake through and a flight of backless wooden stairs leading up.

Cameron and I immediately raced each other up them to pick out our bedrooms. Upstairs there was no ceiling, just the sloping roof logs, and no windows, only skylights. Both rooms were the same size; one led off the other. There didn't seem to be a bathroom. We found it later in a separate shack outside, just a toot and a primitive shower.

Downstairs we could clearly hear Mr Kaldor's voice with a strong accent.

"I leave you a gud log-pile," he was saying. "I put some t'ings for you – bread, eggs, bacon, tea, coffee. Und milk. You need more supplies, you valk on down dat vay to my store. Yust about vun mile. You vant I light de fire for you?"

"If there are matches and some newspaper, I can manage," Mummy said.

"You don't leave open de doors, let in de mosquitoes. Dey get in anyvay… No electricity. You can manage de oil lamps? You keep cool de food in de safe in de ground outside. Keep closed or you get bears."

Cameron and I exchanged looks. Bears? *Bears?*

"You vant to go on de lake," Mr Kaldor went on, "der's a canoe by de jetty. Dat vun is yours, it go vit de cabin. De paddles is in de porch. You don't leave dem in the canoe or maybe somevun paddle avay it. For shvimming is best from de island. I go now or Missis be vorried vere am I."

"Thank you, Mr Kaldor. What do I owe you?" Mummy asked.

"Nothing yet. I put it on your slate at my store. You pay before you leave, ja?"

The truck went growling away, and we were on our own in our cabin by the lake. A lake with a canoe, and bears! We clattered down the stairs.

Mummy said, "Well! Here we are, children. I'm going

to get the stove going and make myself a cup of tea. Why don't you two go and do some exploring?"

I often felt freer in Canada than I'd ever felt in England. But the freedom to play Knock Down Ginger in Saskatoon was nothing compared to what we found here.

We were really in the wilderness. The forests this far north had hardly been explored or even trodden in, except by the First People and trappers. There were wild animals. And there was the lake. 'Better drowned than duffers' was absolutely true here! Duffers could drown easily.

We ran down to the shore, where there was a line of pine trees and then a short, sandy beach. The jetty, a narrow pathway of wooden slats on rickety posts, ran out into the water about fifteen feet. Alongside it, at the far end, was a beautiful red canoe with *Ondine* painted on the bow.

It was quite big and solid-looking. We stood on the jetty, staring at it. I looked out across the water to where a stand of tall trees seemed to be growing in the middle of the lake.

"That must be the island!" I said.

"He said the swimming was best from there," said Cameron.

We stood there for another few moments.

"Where did he say the paddles were?"

"In the porch."

We looked back towards the cabin. There was a wired-in porch facing the lake, at the back of the living room.

"I'll get them!" Cameron said. "And I'll dig out our bathing suits!"

"You'd better tell Mummy where we're going! And towels!" I yelled after him as he ran up the slope. He waved OK and was gone.

I took my socks and shoes off and sat down on the far end of the jetty. I dangled my feet in the water. It wasn't too cold at all. And clear as glass. As I looked down into it, dozens of little fish came to explore my toes. They nosed them and I could feel them gently nibbling, but it didn't hurt, only tickled. Then I stared across the lake. It was so calm, so peaceful – so beautiful. Mr Gustin was right.

After a timeless time – I mean, I forgot time and fell into a lake-dream – Cameron came panting back, already in his swimsuit, his arms full of towels and his hands full of paddles.

"Auntie says all right if we're careful. Go on, get in."

He threw my bathing things into the bottom of *Ondine*. I twisted my legs round till they were in the boat and, holding the sides, lowered myself in. She was lovely – wide and steady. Cameron was untying her. Then he stepped right into the water – it came up to his thighs – and pushed her further out, then sort of rolled in, rocking her madly. I clutched the sides and had a moment of panic.

"Here," he said in his calm way, handing me a paddle. "Do you know how to do this? OK, I'll show you – I did it when we went to Wales on a school trip. It's not like rowing. You face the way you're going." He sat at the back, on a kind of bench that stretched across, dipped the paddle in and pulled. The canoe surged forward, but at the same time, started turning.

"You have to paddle the other side," he said. "Go on, keep her straight."

We made a hash of it at first. Well, I did. At one point we were facing back the way we'd come because I wasn't paddling properly. I saw Mummy standing on the jetty, shading her eyes, her turban bright blue-green in the sun and her cigarette smoke rising straight in the still air.

I thought, *She's a brilliant swimmer. If we capsized she'd swim to the rescue!* which gave me confidence, and after that I pulled more strongly and was able to keep the canoe going straight. It was an amazing feeling.

We reached the island in about ten minutes. By the time we beached the canoe on a lovely sandy shore, I could paddle. I felt a wild, wonderful sense of adventure. *Swallows and Amazons* weren't in it!

I got into my swimsuit. By then, Cameron was just a bobbing head half a mile from shore.

"It's fantabulous!" he shouted.

He'd never used Willie's word before. I wished she were here! I wondered if she and Alfie swam in the lake at the Blundells'. No. I betted Irene didn't let them. I felt suddenly proud of Mummy because she did. She trusted us not to be duffers.

We swam and swam. It wasn't like the sea, it did nothing to hold you up, but it was much easier because there were no waves. And you could go far without getting out of your depth.

We came ashore, flushed with the grown-up-less-ness of it all.

"Are there fish, d'you think?" Cameron asked.

"Yes! Little ones at least, I've seen them."

"Let's go fishing tomorrow! We can make fires here and cook them! Isn't this incredible?" His wet face was all shining.

You know happiness when you see it, especially where it usually isn't.

There was no one else here. That was the biggest difference from Felpham with its crowds of holidaymakers, noise and colour. Here, the only colours under the sky were beige, dark green and silver... *Ondine*'s red was just a lovely alien splash. I wondered, lying in the sand after our swim, listening to the silence broken only by the voices of unknown birds, why I'd ever thought Felpham was the best place for a summer holiday.

That night we had supper by oil lamp in front of a log fire, blazing in the stone fireplace. Mummy had figured out the stove (which was wood-burning too) and managed to cook bacon and eggs and fried bread for us, which we ate on our knees. The night-sounds were strange – spooky. There was a bird that made the saddest, loneliest sound I'd ever heard, like a cry for help. We found out later it was a loon. And there was another like a creaky pump. That was a bittern.

Before bed, we went out on to the back porch. It had no glass, just fly-netting. There was a baby moon, reflected in the lake. And then we saw something amazing. Out in the line of pines between us and the lake we saw hundreds of tiny lights. We couldn't make out what they were – they looked like fairies flying in loops and festoons amid the tree branches.

"They must be fireflies!" Mummy whispered.

We sat there in the dark, not talking, just watching the fireflies play. It was magic.

In bed under the log roof, I heard another sound – a

faraway howling song. Was it a wolf? Another answered it. Wilderness! I wondered if I was scared, but I wasn't. I knew I was going to love this place.

I did love it. One of the things I loved best about it was that there was no phone, and so, no Hank. I stopped worrying about him. As to the war, it had never seemed so far away. We had no radio to bring it to us. It was as if there couldn't be a war, and this peace, in the same world.

The days all began the same in a way, and yet something different happened on each of them.

We got up early, when the sun came dazzling through our bedroom skylights, which had no covering to keep it out. We went out right after breakfast for a day on the lake, on the island. When we needed supplies we walked to the Kaldors' store along the dirt track through the forest, coming back loaded with groceries. We kept all the stuff that could go bad in a sort of metal box, like a huge Huntley & Palmers biscuit tin sunk in the sandy soil beside our log pile. The metal lid fitted tight, and a wooden one dropped down on top and fastened with a hook and eye, which we thought any reasonably clever bear could probably open, and we used to rush out every morning half hoping we'd been raided. But after a few days we decided that Mr Kaldor was kidding us. Like Hank about the gophers. Coyotes – not wolves, we learnt – yes, we could hear howling most nights. But bears? Surely not.

Most days we took *Ondine* on the lake. We paddled, we swam, sometimes just Cameron and me and sometimes all three of us. We found some fishing lines – not rods, just lines wound round pieces of wood, that you dropped over the side of the canoe, with little wire hooks in a packet. We threaded the hooks on, while Mummy attached small stones to the lines to take the hooks down into the water, and sticks for floats. For bait we caught crickets. We had to lie very still on the beach until we saw one settle, then pounce with an empty jar, then slide a plate underneath to trap the poor thing.

I couldn't do what had to be done next – even Cameron jibbed at it – but Mummy said, "Nonsense, we've got to catch some fish. What if we didn't have Mr Kaldor? We wouldn't just sit here and starve, would we?" And she did the deed, putting the squashed bodies in a box.

We paddled out to the deepest part, halfway between the shore and the island, and sat there in the quiet with our lines overboard, the floats sticking up… Clouds of insects buzzed and whined around us, but not mosquitoes – they'd been left behind onshore. In a few minutes, there was a plop, and Cameron's float disappeared. His line went taut. He reeled it in, hand over hand, and at the end was a grey fish about nine inches long.

"Right," said Mummy briskly. "Take the hook out of its mouth and bang it on the thwart to kill it."

Cameron held his fish in his hands. It was thrashing about. Suddenly he twisted the hook out of its mouth, and threw it back in the lake as if he couldn't bear to touch it.

"Oh, really, Cameron!" said Mummy. "Foxes and gophers, yes, fish – no! If you're prepared to eat things, you should be able to kill them!"

"I suppose so," said Cameron.

At that moment, Mummy's line went taut. She hauled her fish into the boat, took the hook out, and banged its head once on the edge of the canoe. It died. She threw it into the bottom and baited her hook again.

"Here, Cameron, hold this while I gut mine." She slit the fish's belly with a short kitchen knife she'd brought with her and shucked its innards into a bucket.

"How come you're so good at this, Auntie?" asked Cameron with a note of admiration in his voice.

"Dublin Bay," Mummy answered. "We used to take a rowboat out and fish for the family supper."

"Who? You, Mum and Auntie Bee?"

"Yes. When we were younger than you! Well, when Bea was."

No wonder she hadn't stopped us going out on a nice calm lake! Dublin Bay is on the sea.

"Why are you keeping the guts?"

"Throw some in and see what happens."

Gingerly I threw a bit of gut into the water, which seemed to boil as a mass of fish came to the surface to eat it.

"Little cannibals, aren't they? If we use the guts we don't need to kill any more crickets."

By the time we put in at the island, we had six fish. I hadn't killed any of them, even the two I caught. I liked catching them, but I didn't want to kill them.

"Almost anyone would kill a cow rather than not eat beef," Mummy remarked as she built the fire.

"*What?*" we both shouted.

"I'm quoting Samuel Johnson. Don't take me too literally. Crickets and fish are about my limit."

We wrapped our fish in wet brown paper, roasted them in the red embers, and ate them with our fingers. They tasted as delicious as only fish you've caught yourself can taste. After that we went fishing often, and before long Cameron and I could do it all by ourselves. What made me stop being so squeamish was what Mummy had said about not having a shop to go to. What if we really were all alone up here, with no luxuries, no conveniences – just ourselves and what the woods and the water could give us? Like the trappers and pioneers, like the First Nations, living free and *capable*, depending on our own life skills?

"I *think* I could kill a *chicken*, rather than not eat meat," said Cameron thoughtfully.

Chapter Twenty-one

Wooding

We began to measure well-being, security, even wealth, by the size of our log pile. With the big fireplace and the stove eating wood, it wasn't long before it started to run out. The chipmunks – adorable little things halfway between mice and squirrels – seemed to look at us reproachfully as the logs they loved to play in sank down near ground level.

"Time to go wooding," said Mummy. "Come on."

There was a toolshed with a saw horse, an axe and two saws in it, and a big canvas carrying bag for small branches. For the first time we set off not towards the lake or along the track to the Kaldors', but straight across the track and into the forest. The deep, dark forest, which stretched, so Mr Kaldor told us, on and on to the Arctic Circle.

We'd asked Mr Kaldor if it was safe, and he didn't say yes or no. He just kept up the bear joke. He said that if we saw a bear we should stand stock still, and if we saw a moose, we should run. "Don't run from de bear, she chase you if you run. If she chase you, you lie down, tell her you died. The moose don't chase you. If you go too near, it yust kill you."

We thought this was very funny.

"And mind out for de muskeg!" he called after us.

We were laughing too much to ask what kind of animal a muskeg was. We decided he was making it up. Who'd ever heard of a muskeg? We had some fun inventing a sort of mythical beast, a musk-ox with an egg-shaped head.

The trees grew so close together that no light came between the trunks, only from above, and not much of that. We found a faint track, but it didn't look as if people had made it.

"We need to mark our trail," Mummy said.

She made us collect pinecones in the canvas bag, and strew them along in our wake so we could find our way back. As the trees closed in behind us, we stopped talking. I remembered the iceberg, how everybody started whispering because it was so big and awesome. Our feet made no sound on the carpet of pine needles. All you could hear was the hungry whining of mosquitoes. (And the slaps as we tried to kill the ones that landed on us.)

"Better not get in too far," said Mummy. "Now start looking for dead trees."

We soon found one. Lots of the trees were dead — they just didn't get enough light.

"We're going to cut it down," said Mummy. "Cameron, do you know how to use an axe?"

"No."

"Watch. Because this is your job."

She pushed her shirtsleeves up and took hold of the axe by the long handle. She made us keep back, and then she swung it at the trunk of the tree. It landed with a deep *thunk*. She did this two or three times. A white diamond shape appeared in the brown trunk.

"See where I've cut a wedge? Now get hold of that saw, you two. One each end — that's right. Cameron — pull. Lindy — pull. Back and forth. That's it. Good, kids, you're doing fine."

It wasn't a very big tree, that first one. Before long we could hear it begin to crack. Mummy made us pull the saw out and stand back on the side of the wedge, and she went close and gave the tree a push. Slowly,

slowly, it swayed, cracked, and then came crashing down. Most of the way. But it got stuck in some other trees.

"Blast!" said Mummy. "Let's try another one."

The next tree we cut down fell properly to the ground with a satisfying crash.

"We ought to shout 'TIM-BER!' as it falls," Mummy said, "like real lumberjacks."

We sawed or chopped off all the dead branches we could reach and managed to drag or carry most of them back along our pine-cone trail. Then we put the long branches across the saw horse and Cameron and I took turns with the short saw to cut them into logs. This was very tricky at first, but we learnt. Mummy left us to stack them. We were just finishing, feeling very pleased with ourselves, and calling the chipmunks to come back, when we heard her from the front door.

"Come here!" she called, in a funny sort of voice.

When we got to her, she pointed. There alongside the cabin wall, near the door, was a dog.

It was a sort of collie, what you could see of it for dirt. It lay there, panting up at us. Under its long dusty coat it looked very thin, and its long tail was full of burrs.

"Look at it! What a picture of misery! Someone's abandoned it."

"Or maybe it ran away," said Cameron, bending to stroke it.

"Careful…"

But even if it'd been a snappish dog, it was too tired. It just lay there, as if it had dragged itself for miles and could hardly lift its poor head.

"Can we keep it?"

"Try getting rid of it! Lindy, go and get it a bowl of milk."

I ran to the safe and brought out a bottle of milk, and an egg. In the kitchen I beat the egg up in the milk. I knew that was good for invalids. I put the bowl down in front of the dog, which slowly stood up on shaking legs, put its nose down, and lapped up every drop.

"Probably covered with fleas… Oh well. Can't leave the poor brute out here…"

When we cleaned him up, we found he had a collie's mixed-colour coat, long muzzle, perky ears and long, sweeping tail. He looked a bit like *Lassie Come-Home*, which I was just reading, but he was a male dog, so we called him Laddie.

Next time we went 'into town' (as we called the Kaldors' tiny shack store) we asked if anyone had lost a dog, but they didn't know anything. There were other cabins spread out beside the lake, some let to visitors. Maybe one of them had lost him or left him behind.

Laddie was obviously young, and when he got over whatever he'd been through to get to us, he became very lively and loving. After two days of eating everything we offered him, and getting a lot of brushing and petting, he let us know he was our dog. But mainly Cameron's, like Spajer. If he had a choice who to walk with or sit with, he always chose Cameron.

When we took him out, he chased everything that moved. The chipmunks fled our woodpile and no bird dared land. We tried him in the canoe and he nearly capsized it when he saw a distant duck and leapt straight into the lake after it. We hauled him back, dripping wet and looking as if he'd like to say sorry. After that we left him barking on the shore, but we did take him wooding with us. Of course, having a dog made everything better, and if Cameron wasn't a little bit, I mean seriously, happy, well…. He was. That's all.

Mummy had settled down to do some writing in the mottled-red notebooks she'd brought with her, and let us go into the forest by ourselves, or rather, with Laddie, to fell trees and bring back wood. We didn't penetrate far into the dark woods – we still weren't quite sure about the bears – and when we'd got a dead tree on the point of falling, we'd yell "TIM–BER!" then listen to the crash as the tree fell. We'd keep perfectly quiet so Mummy would think we were squashed, till she'd come out and shout, "Are you all right?" (It never failed.)

"Of course!" we'd chorus innocently.

"Oh, you little villains, you scared me!" she'd grumble as she went back into the cabin.

I knew it was awful of us. How could we? But we did. And she never even punished us by forbidding us to cut down trees. I developed serious arm muscles, even more than from the stables, and I was proud of them. And proud of us – Cameron and me. It was another pioneering skill. I wondered what Sue, left behind at the convent, would think if she could see me now.

Chapter Twenty-two

Music Hath Charms (Even For Me)

After we'd been at the lake for two weeks, Mr Gustin arrived to open up the cabin next door and start his summer music school. And something new and exciting and life-changing happened to me.

Cameron was given a new teacher, because Mr Gustin was busy. His name was Leo and he was French Canadian. He was also tall and dark and if Willie had seen him she would have said "Hubba hubba!" and got a crush on him. *I* got a crush on him. But that wasn't what changed my life.

Music began to flow between the Gustin cabin and ours – only about ten yards away – all day and much of the night. It was all classical. Mummy adored this. I thought it was quite nice as a background.

Cameron was in heaven. That sort of music just sent him into raptures. He used to sit near the window facing the Gustin cabin reading, and when something he specially liked was being played, he'd stop reading and go into a dream. Once I dared to ask what he was thinking about.

"Depends," he said, and then clammed up again.

I wanted to know more. What was the big attraction? So when he went over next I crept through the trees and listened underneath the window of his lesson-room.

But it was Leo who started playing. I imagined beautiful dark Leo running his hands over the piano keys. And something happened. I just stood there while this skein of sound flowed out of the window and wrapped me up in its magic, lifting me off the ground and into a new world. When it ended I came back to earth with my ears still sparkling.

I shouted up at the window above my head: "What was it? What was it? It was so lovely!"

"*Berceuse*," Leo shouted back. "Chopin."

"Play more by him!" I shouted.

"Not now, we must have our lesson," Leo called back, and the next thing I heard was Cameron playing a chromatic scale.

That night, it rained. We hadn't had rain at all so far, but that night the clouds built up over the lake and the lamps had to be lit early. It was my job to clean the lamp chimneys with newspaper – oh, yes, we did have a newspaper, but only once a week and we read it a day late. I did read it now, some of it, so as not to feel stupid or be what Cameron called 'an escapist'. There wasn't much news about England. Most of it was about Germany invading Russia. Mummy said, "If it lasts till the winter, that'll teach them, like it taught Napoleon."

The rain started pouring down just before we went to bed. I was already *in* bed, when Mummy came up to kiss us goodnight and said that Cameron's teacher was at the door and wanted to see me.

I went downstairs in my dressing gown. Leo was there, the rain streaming down all around him from our little front-porch roof. Behind him the forest was just a black, solid wall.

"*Bon soir, mademoiselle* Lindy. You like Chopin? So open your side window and listen – I'm going to play something special for you."

He scurried off, his torchlight a thin white triangle streaked with rain. I went and opened the window in the living room that faced the Gustin cabin. Through the fly-netting I saw the window across the way light up with the cosy glow of an oil lamp, as Leo, a tall, ghostly figure, carried it in and put it on the piano. He sat down and began to play.

And suddenly, amid the raindrops that were pattering past my window, I heard musical raindrops.

I was enchanted. I stood, hardly moving or breathing, for the whole length of the piece, listening to how Chopin had turned the dripping rain into a beautiful musical poem. In the middle, the gentle dripping built up into a storm, just as our real storm broke overhead with crashing thunder and flashing lightning... I loved storms! The music underlined it, competed with it – and won! When the music ended, the real storm went grumbling off, as if it were annoyed at being beaten by the music, and I was so excited inside that I found I was crying.

When I turned round, Mummy and Cameron were behind me, silently sharing it with me. I put my arms around both of them. Cameron didn't hug me much. But that night, he did. For the first time, I felt, and shared with them, the absolute wonder of a piece of classical music. Maybe it wasn't a Beethoven symphony, but it was the beginning of a love that would last for ever.

Chapter Twenty-three

Laddie's Adventure

One morning, we found our ground safe had been broken into, or at least that something had tried to break into it, but hadn't got past tearing off the top cover. Mr Kaldor wasn't kidding, we realised then – there *were* bears in the forest. We found its tracks, big as side plates, and after that Mummy wasn't so happy about us going wooding without her, though she said having Laddie with us would probably make a bear think twice.

We never actually met a bear. We found something else, though. Or rather, Laddie found it.

We'd made a sort of path through the trees by now, to a bit of a clearing about a hundred yards in. We'd cut down two or three trees there and it was a bit more open to the sky. It was our special wooding place. One day while Mummy was busy writing, we crept off there with our tools, Laddie rushing ahead, his nose to the ground, hot on some scent. He went out of sight and we heard him suddenly start barking madly. I clutched Cameron's arm.

"Let's go back! Maybe it's a bear!"

But Cameron pushed on.

We came into the little clearing, and saw Laddie with his front paws against a big fir tree, his nose pointing up, barking his head off. We looked up into the lowest branches, and saw something huge and black and white, like a ball of spikes, clinging to the trunk about six feet above our heads.

At first glance I thought it was some kind of fungus or growth on the tree. But suddenly the spikes moved and spread, with a sinister rustling sound. The Thing let go of its hold on the trunk, and slid down to the ground, its four big paws rasping as they clawed at the bark. It lay at the bottom with all its spikes erect and its head drawn in, and its tail, also spiky, swinging towards Laddie. A big mound about two feet long, with a fan at its back end, a fan of quills as long as drinking straws.

"Blimey! A porcupine!" shouted Cameron. "Laddie! Leave! Leave!"

But Laddie didn't listen. He simply rushed at the porcupine. Its tail swung right in his face.

Our poor dog fell back with a sort of dog-shriek. He lay down, whining loudly, and began to rub his nose with both front paws. We could see the long tail-spikes bristling out of him. His face was like the porcupine's tail, a huge pincushion of quills.

"The beast! The beast! Look what it's done to him!" screamed Cameron. I'd never heard him scream like that. "Hold him, Lind! Don't let him go near it!"

And he dropped the tools and ran back along the path towards the cabin.

I crouched beside Laddie, who was writhing in pain and pawing his face frantically. I dared to try to pull one of the prickles out – but I couldn't. They were stuck in, and when I tried, Laddie yelped and half snapped at me. I just held him down on the ground in case he should try again to attack the porcupine, which was sitting at the foot of the tree as if it was waiting to stick more quills into him. Not trying to run away.

After what felt like an age, Cameron came back. I heard him coming by his panting breaths. He burst into the clearing.

He was carrying a *gun*.

It looked like a rifle. I couldn't believe it! Where could he have got it from? From where I crouched on the ground,

I watched helplessly as he walked quickly up to the porcupine, pointed the gun at its head, and fired.

The bang was a thunderclap, and it echoed back from the trees, smacking my ears. I jumped, and so did Laddie. He wriggled out from under my hands and ran into the woods yelping, his tail between his legs. I stood up. The porcupine's tail had dropped, its quills were sinking. Cameron put his foot under it and rolled it over. It was dead.

We both stood there in shock. I was staring at him as if I'd never seen him before.

"You didn't have to kill it," I whispered.

"Yes I did," he said. "Beastly, bloody thing. Let's go."

I saw he was shaking.

He stood there while I picked up the axe and the long saw. I put them into the canvas carry bag and lugged them back along our path. Cameron carried the gun.

Halfway back we met Mummy, running.

"I heard a shot!" she shouted as she saw us. "What happened? Where's Laddie?"

"Didn't you meet him?"

"No! Good God, Cam, what's that gun? What's going on?"

Cameron didn't answer. He just strode past Mummy. I dropped the bag, grabbed Mummy's hand, and led her back to the clearing. I showed her the dead porcupine and told her what had happened. She stood there staring at it for what seemed like minutes. Then she took a deep, deep breath.

"I will never understand that boy," she said. "He couldn't stun a fish. But he can shoot a porcupine."

"It hurt his dog," I said.

"Yes. And speaking of which – where is he? He'll be in a bad way. We'd better find him."

We searched the nearest part of the forest, calling and calling. Then we went back to the cabin. Cameron was next door. I knew his practising by now. He was playing scales. Furiously. The gun was nowhere to be seen.

Amazingly soon, we had a visit from a policeman. He said he was after illegal hunters, and had we heard a shot? Of course we told him everything.

"Ma'am... did you realise that killing a porcupine counts as illegal hunting?"

Mummy's mouth fell open. "You mean, we've committed a crime?"

"Porcupines can only be killed for food," said the policeman. "They're so easy to kill, and so good to eat, that you're only allowed to kill them if you're lost and hungry." But when he realised we were war guests, he just gave us a warning, and went into the forest to take the body away in case it attracted coyotes. He never thought to ask where the gun came from. Apparently lots of people up north had guns.

That night, I heard Mummy telling Cameron off after I'd gone to bed, because there was no door at the top of the stairs. It turned out the gun belonged to Mr Gustin. He kept it for students who wanted to shoot ducks, and Cameron had known about it; it seemed Mr Gustin was horrified, and angry, when he found out Cameron had borrowed it.

"Cameron, did you know the gun was loaded?"

"Yes."

"Did you know how dangerous it is to handle a loaded gun? Did nobody ever tell you that?"

"They told me you should never point a gun at anyone. And I didn't."

"Your mother begged me to take you to Canada for her. She trusted me to look after you. How would I explain to her that I let something happen to you?"

If there was one thing Cameron couldn't stand, it was being told off. And this was his second telling-off in one day. So he said something stupid to defend himself.

"Well, Auntie, you don't take very good care of me, do you?"

I sat up in bed with a jerk. Could he have said that?

There was a long silence. I knew Mummy must be terribly shocked.

"What do you mean?"

"You let us take all kinds of risks. You let us go canoeing by ourselves. You let us go into the woods, *by ourselves*. You leave us alone in the flat in Saskatoon. Mum would never do any of that."

The silence got so long and so *bad* I put my fingers in my ears to shut it out. But when I heard Mummy start talking again of course I took them out.

"Well, if it comes to that, your mother let you go fox-hunting when you were only nine. She sent you away to boarding school even earlier. I want you to learn independence and to have the freedom other kids in Canada have. But if you don't like it – if you think for *one moment* that I'm not taking proper care of you – I'm going to stop all that. From now on I'm not going to take my eyes off you."

"I didn't mean—" Cameron began, and I thought, *You prize chump, now you've done it!*

"I think you did," Mummy said. "Now go to bed. And don't you ever handle a gun again without proper supervision."

Cameron came up the wooden stairs and I saw his head and then the rest of him appearing through the opening cut in the floor of the bedroom.

"Come here!" I hissed furiously. "You fat-headed *fool!*"

But of course he didn't. He went into his own room and slammed the door.

Next morning there was an 'atmosphere'. I was so mad at Cameron I wasn't speaking to him at all. If he minded, or even noticed, he gave no sign. He went off to his piano lesson early. I half wanted to talk to Mummy, and tell her that she *did* look after us properly and that I was one hundred per cent on her side, but I didn't like to admit I'd listened – she hated that. So I went and sat on the jetty and read.

When Cameron came back he said, "Can we go wooding?" and Mummy (natch!) said, "No. Stay near the cabin where I can check up on you."

I thought, *That's it. The holiday's ruined*. But then Laddie saved us.

That night, after being missing for more than twenty-four hours, he came to the door and scratched to be let in.

Poor, poor Laddie. It was ghastly. The quills had worked their way into his nose, lips, cheeks. And we had to get them out. The policeman had told us we had to, or they'd get infected and our dog would die a horrible, painful death.

I found a pair of pliers. We took it in turns. Two of

us had to hold Laddie, who was a big strong dog, while the other one pulled out the quills. They had barbs on them – that's why I hadn't been able to pull them straight out before. The ones through his lips weren't so bad. We held his mouth open and drew each quill out the same direction it had gone in, so the barbs didn't catch. But the ones in his nose just had to be dragged out. It must have hurt terribly.

Every now and then he would pull himself free and crawl under the big dresser where we couldn't reach him, for a rest. But he always came out again, had a drink, and – I swear – as good as said, "Let's get it over." As if he knew it had to be done. And the thing was, he could have bitten us – we had to put our hands right into his mouth – but he never did. Not once.

He was such a good dog. And so brave.

Some of the quills had been broken off – these were the most difficult. It was hard to see them by lamplight, so Cameron sent me next door to borrow Mr Gustin's torch. Leo came to help us, but after about five minutes he said, "*Je suis désolé*, I can *not* bear this," and left again in tears. We were all crying by the end, even Cameron.

At last we got them all out. We bathed poor Laddie's nose with warm water with some disinfectant in it and fed him hamburger meat that was easy for him to chew.

The 'atmosphere' was over — it couldn't survive sharing something like that.

I swore to myself that night that I would never, never have a dog. Too much agony! But we went on being very glad we had this one. Laddie got better and was more our dog than before.

How can he forgive us for the pain we've caused him? I marvelled. But he did. He even learnt to ride the canoe to the island and go swimming with us.

And he was my best comfort after the fatal day we heard the growing roar of a motorcycle along the track. This was so unusual, we all ran out to watch it pass. But it didn't. It stopped. And who should be riding it but Hank.

Chapter Twenty-four

The Menace Returns

The first thing, the very first, that I did after I realised who it was, was to look at Mummy.

Would she light up at the sight of him?

Well, no. I wouldn't call it that. But her face didn't exactly fall, either.

"Hank! Dear Hank, what a nice surprise!"

I didn't like the 'dear', but at least it wasn't 'darling'. And 'nice' – Mummy always said nice was a feak and weeble word, when I used it in a school composition, or in a letter to Daddy. "Try 'wonderful', try 'marvellous', try 'fantastic'," she'd say. She didn't say any of those now.

Hank was getting off the bike. He kicked the stand

down, and lifted a rucksack and a bedroll off the back. He'd come to stay.

Of course he has! I thought. *You don't travel hundreds of miles from Regina to Emma Lake for a cup of tea.*

Then he hugged Mummy, and tried to hug me, but I sort of backed away – not to be rude, I just did it instinctively.

"How did you find us?"

"You told me Emma Lake. How I found you after that is the clever part!"

"Well, come on in."

Mummy led the way and Hank followed, grinning over his shoulder at us.

"Where's he going to sleep?" Cameron whispered to me.

"In the canoe," I whispered back sarcastically. "Or on the log pile."

As soon as Hank got into the cabin he took over all the 'manly' things. He made Mummy sit down, built the fire, trimmed the lamps (my job), got the stove going, put potatoes on to bake and started bashing the steaks he'd brought with him, while Laddie sat close to him, looking up at him hopefully. He also opened a bottle of red wine, and Cokes for us. I still hated Coke.

"You're going to have a rest," he said to Mummy. And after a bit: "What's that music?"

We explained.

Hank said, "Do we get anything from *Panama Hattie*? I love Ethel Merman, don't you?"

"No – it's all lovely classical," I said.

"Aw… well, each to his taste, I guess." He began to whistle 'Let's Be Buddies' very loudly, as if to drown out the music from next door.

I was *very* pleased about this as I thought it would put Mummy off him.

But it didn't seem to.

Mummy hardly ever drank, and after two glasses of Hank's wine she was tipsy, I could see. She actually got up, put her cigarette out, and began to dance to his whistling. *Of course* he came in from the kitchen, and next thing he was dancing with her. Laddie went under the dresser.

"What's your trouble, Cameron? Can't dance? Go on, man, ask your pretty cousin to dance with you!"

"No fear," said Cameron, and slouched off upstairs.

I'd rather Hank had offered me a ride on his motorbike, but still, I didn't mind having a dance. I wanted to learn to jitterbug – Willie had started to teach me. I just knew the basic step, so I started doing that.

Hank led Mummy politely to a chair, and said, "Look. More like this."

I couldn't resist. I let him show me how to jitterbug.

He even did the underarm thing so, thinking the next thing would be the bit where the man kind of slides the girl between his legs, I pretended to be tired, but that only made him go back to Mummy. Luckily, she'd sobered up by then and said it was time to lay the table. So Hank settled down by the fire and after a bit the lovely music from next door, and the wine, sent him off to sleep.

While we finished getting dinner, I said to Mummy, "He's nuts about you, did you know that?"

"Don't be silly," she said, which I expected.

"No it's not. Why do you think he came all this way to see you?"

"He's lonely."

"Isn't he married?"

"He's a widower. Anyway, he's far from home."

"Like you."

"Well, yes." She pulled the potatoes out of our wood oven, and then said, "You're not worried about it, are you? Even if he is a bit fond of me, I'm not fond of him, in that way, so you've nothing to worry about."

"Aren't you lonely?"

"Yes."

"Well then."

"I love Daddy," she said shortly. "Go and call Cameron." And she slapped the steaks on to the hot griddle.

★

Though Hank really did his best to fit in and be a manly helper, we had nothing but bad luck after he came – some of it *really* bad.

I do believe in luck. What else can you call it? So much that happens just happens – you can't stop it happening or make it happen.

We'd never had any trouble about swimming in the lake till he came. It was our happy watery heaven.

The day after Hank arrived (he slept on the floor in his bedroll in front of the fire) we went across to the island for a picnic. Laddie sat up in the bow of the canoe like a figurehead on an old ship. Hank insisted on sitting at the back, and he wouldn't let any of us paddle.

That was because he could feather. Feathering was a way of paddling that meant you didn't need two people to keep straight. He dipped his paddle in the water, pulled, and then kind of turned the paddle, so the nose of the canoe swung first one way and then back the other. Cameron was very impressed. I could see he was impressed with Hank altogether. Basically because he was in the navy.

When we reached the island Hank jumped out and pulled the canoe right up the beach. Then he helped Mummy out, and unloaded the picnic.

"First a swim, right, then lunch," he said, like an order. *Grrrrr!*

We took our top-clothes off – at the lake, all I wore were slacks rolled to below the knees, and a man's long plaid shirt – and ran straight into the lake at our favourite place, where the sandbar sloped gently into deep water.

Turning just before I went out of my depth, I saw Hank stripping off his clothes. He was what my Auntie Millie would have called 'a fine figure of a man', like Uncle Jack. Tall and muscly with a hairy chest... Mummy was sitting on the sand spreading out the picnic. Was she glancing at him? He did a few exercises (show-off!) and then raced into the water and flung himself face down and began to do a fast front crawl.

Cameron swam out after him, farther than he'd swum before. He was a good swimmer but they did seem to be trying to reach the far shore, which was miles away. I sat with Mummy, and watched them.

"Why's he taking Cameron so far?" I asked. "He shouldn't."

Then I stopped short because she might think I was really saying she wasn't taking care of him.

All she said was, "They're coming back now."

Sure enough, their heads began to look bigger, and after about five minutes they both rose up out of the water and waded towards us. That was when I saw them.

"What's that on Cameron's legs?" I said.

Mummy looked, and did a double take. She jumped

up and ran towards them. Just as she did, Hank noticed that he had the same thing – black lumps, like the Black Plague – among the hairs on his chest.

He let out a shout – a shout of fear. "Ugh! Hell's bells! Get them off me!"

"What are they?" Mummy asked, very calmly.

"Leeches! Vile brutes! Get them off'a me, get them off!" Hank was shouting.

He didn't try to get rid of them. He was flapping his hands like a girl.

But Mummy wasn't bothering about him. She was crouched in the sand looking at Cameron's legs. She tried to pull one of the black things off.

"Don't! You'll leave their heads in!" Hank almost screamed. "Use a cigarette! Burn 'em off!" He let out a stream of swearing.

Cameron meanwhile just stood there as if he was frozen.

Mummy stood up, took Cameron by the hand, and led him back to our things. She found her cigarettes and lit one. The match flame trembled.

"Hank. Come here and show me how," she said.

He ran up the beach, still flapping and swearing.

"Make the end glow! Just touch them! *Do mine first!* No, no, I didn't say that. Do Cameron's first. Be careful." He was making ugh-ugh groaning noises.

"Cameron. Stand still. Close your eyes."

Cameron was incredibly brave. He stood like a soldier, stiff, his fists clenched, his eyes shut. Mummy very delicately pressed the red glow to one of the black things. It shrank and dropped off into the sand.

"Did you feel anything?"

"No."

She did the next one, and the next, puffing in between to get a glow.

There were about six altogether – horrible black things, like long slugs. The thought of them, sticking their nasty little heads into Cameron's flesh and sucking his blood, made me feel sick.

When she'd finished with Cameron, she did the ones on Hank's chest. She singed some of the hairs, but she never burnt him. He stood there shivering like Laddie. When they'd all dropped off, he stamped them into the sand furiously.

"Of all the horrors in the world, I hate leeches most!" he said. Then he shook himself, looked at us as if he'd woken up, and suddenly said, "God, I'm sorry. They give me the creeps... You were so brave, Cameron, much more than me. Big brave sailor-man versus little English boy." He grabbed Cameron's wrist and held it up like a boxer. "The WINNER!" he shouted, and we all laughed.

"And you," he said, turning to Mummy. "You are a

heroine and a nurse and our saviour all in one. You're also beautiful."

And he put both arms round her and kissed her. A real kiss. Then, before even she could do anything, he snatched her Black Cat from her and had a good drag.

"Let's eat," he said.

I sometimes think I'm a bit of a witch. Not that I believe in witches. Still…

I have to be careful I don't wish harm on people. Even if I hate them. Because sometimes things happen to the people I hate. It started with Hank. After he kissed Mummy like a man kisses a woman, not like friends, I hated him.

I didn't wish he'd die. I just wished he'd go away. But if I *am* a bit of a witch, that was enough to make a very bad thing happen.

I didn't swim that day. Although Hank said the leeches probably didn't come close in to shore. He also told us that the best way to make them drop off was by shaking salt on them. We agreed to always take a bag of salt with us in future, as soon as we got over our fear. Hank said he'd never swim in a lake again.

That didn't save him, though.

Chapter Twenty-five

The Muskeg

Hank only had a short leave. He told us he could only stay with us for five days. On the last day he said he'd like to go for a walk in a part of the forest we hadn't been to, beyond the Kaldors' place.

"There's an artist called Ernst Lindner," Hank said. "He's got a cabin around here. I've seen his work in a gallery in Calgary. He paints old tree stumps and moss and fungus. I've never seen anything like that, in the pinewoods. There must be somewhere around his cabin where he finds these fabulous mosses."

We all walked to the Kaldors' store together. Laddie was bounding ahead. Cameron called him to heel every few minutes to stop him going into the forest. Mummy and Hank walked side by side. I was watching every minute to see if he touched her. Since the kiss, two days before, I was all screwed up inside. I hadn't slept properly. I lay awake, listening *through* the loons and the frogs to the grown-ups talking downstairs. I was listening for *silences*. I couldn't sleep till Mummy came to bed.

I was waiting for her to say again that I had nothing to worry about. She didn't say it. I thought that was because she knew, since the kiss, that I did.

I was mad at Cameron again, because he didn't have to worry about Hank and was free to like him. He was always sitting around with him, asking questions about the navy. The night before, he'd asked how old you had to be to join up. Hank had laughed and said, "Grow another few inches, and you'll pass for seventeen!"

Cameron was *twelve*. How dumb could you be, telling him that! He even joked that Cameron could already join the merchant navy as a cabin boy. I told Cameron afterwards that if he believed that, he'd fall for anything.

"Don't you remember how he pulled our legs about hunting our breakfasts, and catching gophers with condensed milk?"

"He wouldn't joke about the navy. Not in wartime. He loves the navy."

"You couldn't join the Canadian navy anyway!"

"You don't know anything about it, Lind, so be quiet."

"Quiet? Like you, you mean, telling Mummy she doesn't look after you, and spoiling any *chance* we have of doing stuff on our own!"

"You don't understand."

"What don't I understand? I understand you're stupid and ungrateful!"

"*I hate*—" he said violently, then stopped.

"What?"

"Every time anything bad happens I want to get away. I want to go home."

"Well, why don't you?" *Oh, why did I say that?*

For once I had the last word. He'd just walked away.

Now we were passing the store. Mr Kaldor was outside, watering his geranium pots. He'd heard all about the porcupine, of course. He said something to Cameron about being a big game hunter.

"Next time you shoot you a grizzly! Somet'ing to take home show your Papi!"

As we walked on past the store, he said again, "Look out for de muskeg, ja?"

I asked Hank, "What's a muskeg – are they dangerous?"

"Oh sure! They're bigger than grizzlies!" He did a looming monster.

"No, *really*."

"Truth to tell, I haven't an idea. Never heard the word. Maybe it's Cree for a beaver."

The track, after another half-mile or so, opened out into a strange, empty-looking place. The trees stopped, except for a few dead ones sticking up out of a bunch of grass and, yes, mosses.

And what mosses! I'd never seen anything like them. Big beautiful cushions of different kinds – pink, bluish, greens, browns. Some of the cushions had toadstools growing out of them, like the kind you see in fairy-tale pictures – red with white spots, pointed ones like elves' caps, white ones growing like tiny snow-covered Christmas trees out of the moss. I knelt down to look at them closer. They were beautiful. Mummy was kneeling beside me, letting out little gasps of pleasure.

"No wonder this Lindner man wants to paint them! They're amazing! Look at this one – have you ever seen anything so exquisite?"

Cameron and Hank hadn't stopped to look at the mosses. With Hank leading the way, they'd just gone striding ahead, jumping from one beautiful moss-cushion to the next, among the strange dead trees, laughing as they bounced. But suddenly the laughter stopped. Laddie started barking madly, the way he had at the porcupine.

Our heads had been bent low over the miracle mosses. We both straightened up at the same time. There was

Cameron, standing still about twenty yards ahead of us. Hank? Hank had become a dwarf. He was suddenly shorter than Cameron. Because he was sunk up to his hips in the moss-cushions.

Mummy and I jumped to our feet, but before we could move, Hank shouted at us: "No! Keep back! It's bog!"

"Cam, come back!" screamed Mummy.

He came running. But Laddie stayed where he was, close up to Hank, barking frantically.

"Laddie! Come! Heel!" yelled Cameron over his shoulder as he ran towards us. But Laddie didn't come.

As soon as he was within reach, Mummy grabbed him and clutched him to her in a frantic hug. Then she let him go.

"Run, Cam. Back to the Kaldors'. Tell him to bring a rope – and bring his truck! Run, don't stand there!"

Cameron took off. He got back on the track and disappeared round a bend. Mummy had hold of my wrist. We were both staring across the open ground at Hank. He was sunk up to his waist by now. He was heaving and struggling.

"Hank!" Mummy called. "Don't struggle. Help's on its way."

That was obviously more than she knew for sure. But she sounded calm and certain.

Hank was panting. His eyes were wild. "Spread your arms," Mummy called.

Suddenly I understood properly. *Spread your arms.* That meant he could sink in past his shoulders. He could sink in over his head. He could disappear.

"Mummy—"

"What?"

"We should help him! Cameron was standing right next to him, it mustn't be boggy there! Look – Laddie's standing next to him – he doesn't go in!"

"That's because they're lighter."

"I could go. I weigh less than Cameron. I could lie on the ground and hold Hank's hands." (Hadn't I wanted Hank to disappear? But not like this!)

"Don't you *move*."

She let go of my wrist. I panicked.

"Mummy! *You* can't go! You'll sink—"

"Stay here. Don't you *dare* move."

She walked carefully away from me towards him.

I followed at her heels. I could feel the moss-cushions giving under my feet. I realised this was the muskeg – moss growing on top of a deep mass of mud.

She turned on me. "Lindy. Go back. If you don't go back I can't go to help him. *Go back. Now.*"

When she spoke like that I had to obey her. I couldn't not. I started back. The ground felt *soft* – I sensed the bottomless bog under me. I'd never felt so afraid. I stopped dead. The moss-cushion rocked. I couldn't move. I couldn't turn to look at Mummy and Hank.

I stared at the track where Cameron had disappeared. I strained my ears. How far was it back to the Kaldors' store? How fast could Cameron run? How long would it take? I heard Laddie barking and barking behind me. Barking his danger signal. Its note seemed to go higher and higher.

I turned to look. Mummy had reached the place where Cameron had been standing on the moss. Hank had almost sunk to his armpits. His face was as grey as the dried grass. He had his arms stretched towards us. Could he sink all the way, with his arms stretched out like that?

Mummy lay down flat on the moss and reached out both hands. Hank gripped them with both his. Laddie stopped barking. He was running and jumping around the boggy hole. Every now and then he seemed to try to stretch his neck out to grab Hank. Once he reached too far and his front paws went into the mud, and he yelped and got himself back on dry ground.

Hank was still sinking. I've never seen such a look of terror on a man's face, even in the scariest movie. I was looking at someone I knew, who thought he was going to die.

What if he pulls Mummy in with him?

And then I heard it – the grumbling roar of Mr Kaldor's truck. Mummy looked over her shoulder. Hank's head came up. Laddie left the bog and raced over the mosses to meet the truck as it came round the bend. Cameron jumped out of the passenger seat. He was holding the end of a rope. He ran past me and seemed to bounce on the moss-mounds till he reached Hank. How lucky was it that Hank still had his hands free and could wrap the rope around himself under his arms and tie it!

Mummy crawled backwards. Mr Kaldor was frantically fastening the other end of the rope to the front bumper of the truck. He jumped back behind the wheel like a young man and I heard the gear lever grind. The truck moved slowly backwards. I watched the rope go taut with a sort of twang. And slowly, slowly, it began to pull Hank out.

The muskeg didn't want to let him go. It was like something hanging on to his body, gripping it, trying to suck it down. I couldn't look, I was so sure the rope would break! I did pray then.

"St Barnabas, I don't hate him, save him I pray, even if he kisses Mummy another day!" It was a desperate prayer, the best I could think of.

With a weird squelchy burping noise, the muskeg let

Hank go and he was dragged out on to solid ground. He lay there for a moment, his face in the moss. Then he slowly and shakily stood up. Below his chest he was a mud-man.

"Didn't I tell you look out for de muskeg?" Mr Kaldor scolded out of the truck window.

He gave us a lift home in the back of his truck. None of us spoke. Hank sat there with the mud drying on him and stared at Mummy without seeming to see her. I wanted to tell Cameron how wonderful I thought he was but I couldn't break the silence. It was too solemn. That was the closest I'd ever come to death. Even Laddie seemed subdued. He lay there with his nose across Hank's feet.

When we got back to our cabin Mummy said, "Hank, the best thing for you would be to go into the lake, and wash off the mud."

"Okay," he said. "Leeches can't seem so bad after what I've been through."

So he went for a swim in all his clothes. He stayed close to the jetty.

Mummy made supper and we ate it silently. Next door someone was playing something slow and sad... Hank said, "That's real pretty. Guess when you've nearly drowned in mud you can get a taste for the better stuff. Kinda brings you nearer to –" He pointed up towards heaven.

That was his last day. Next morning he packed up his stuff and kissed us all, even Cameron. The one he gave Mummy wasn't a kissy-kiss. But it was loving just the same. Then he rode away on his motorbike. I realised I'd never had a ride on it, and I'd wanted one. But I had a feeling of relief sharp as pain, that he'd gone.

Chapter Twenty-six

Bad News

When we got back to Saskatoon at the end of the summer, we found a pile of letters. Mrs Lynch, our landlady, hadn't bothered to send them on, so they'd just piled up. We often got them in batches like that, when a ship had come.

We couldn't open them at once – there was a fuss about Laddie to deal with first; Mrs Lynch objected to having a dog in the house.

We stood about in the downstairs hall with Laddie, who was panting with thirst, the letters clutched in Mummy's hand, while Mr Lynch argued with his wife. We'd hardly had anything to do with him till now, because he worked nights and slept all day. It took time, but eventually he won the row and Laddie was allowed inside. Then, finally, we went up to our flat, and, before unpacking or anything, we settled down at the kitchen table to read our mail from home.

I had a letter from Daddy! It was mostly about how he'd started 'going to the dogs'. This meant greyhound racing. He said he went with a bunch of men friends and that it was gambling. I didn't like the sound of that, but then he said, *Last night I won three-and-fourpence!* This silly amount was obviously to make me laugh, and it did.

He also told me our house was rented, and that the people had dug our lawn up to plant vegetables. *Dig for victory!* Daddy wrote. *Auntie won't dig up her prize hydrangeas but she scrounges stuff from my tenants. She cooks me a lot of vegetable stews. I wish you could still buy whale-meat off the ration; I wouldn't grumble now. I'm so sick of potatoes and carrots.* That was his only bit of a moan about the war.

Then he asked about school and how we'd spent the summer and sent love, and at the end, he wrote something odd.

Take good care of Cameron. He'll need lots of love just now.

Just as I read these words, Cameron, who was reading

a letter from Auntie Millie, suddenly jumped up from the table and ran out of the room. We heard his bedroom door slam. I stood up to go after him, but Mummy shook her head. She still sat there even after we could hear noises from beyond his door.

"He's crying! What's happened?"

Mummy was frowning and biting her lip. She reached for a cigarette. There was a long silence. Laddie went out and we heard him scratching at Cameron's door.

At last Mummy said, "Auntie Millie and Uncle Jack are getting divorced."

Divorced? Auntie Millie and Uncle Jack had been part of my life always.

"But *why?*"

"I can't tell you. It's private between them."

"But did they tell Cameron why?"

"I don't know," she said. "It's been coming a long time. I suppose Millie just—" She stopped.

"Just what?"

But she wouldn't say any more.

I could see that there was a letter from Grampy, a long letter. I wasn't shown it. When the days went by and Cameron stopped being Cameron and became a person shut behind a wall, not talking, not playing, not looking at anyone, hardly eating, I wanted so badly to read

Grampy's letter that I nearly stole it from Mummy's handbag where she kept it. But I didn't.

I asked Cameron. I wanted him to talk to me. I wanted to give him love and sympathy. But he wouldn't let me in. He told me to leave him alone. I could hear in his voice that any mention of his parents made him want to cry so I stopped. It was like living with a black cloud of unhappiness.

We were back at school. *My* life was normal. I was in Grade Eight now, at Victoria School. I served on the culture committee. I was in the drama club, doing a play called *Child Wonder*. (I was going to play the mother and was worrying how I could be made to look old enough.) I wriggled out of PE as often as I could.

Poppy and I were still friends and I had a bit of a new gang now. We had parties at her place. Before we came, her mother put polish on the parquet floors and then made us take off our shoes and shine it by dancing in our socks. We jitterbugged to records. I tried not to think of Hank teaching me. I tried not to think of Hank at all, and as he didn't phone any more that got easier.

"Why doesn't he phone?" I asked Mummy, and she just shrugged.

"They keep him busy, I guess," she said.

But I thought, maybe he'd realised he loved Mummy and it couldn't work except in some bad way.

I kept thinking of one of O'F's Irish jokes, about two IRA men who had orders to shoot someone from a rooftop. They waited there two days and nights and on the third day one of them said, "Sure and I hope nothin's happened to the poor fella!" I felt that about Hank. I had wanted him to disappear and he had, but now I wondered if anything had happened to him.

I went back to my Saturday job at Pinder's Drug Store and with the money I phoned Willie every few days, from a phone box so I could be private. I told her everything. She'd had a happy summer at a posh country club with the Blundells, but no adventures, and she was *agog* (our new favourite word) about ours. She said she'd give anything to have a dog like Laddie, but there was no chance in the Blundells' beautiful home.

Laddie was a special dog. He really was. He absolutely knew Cameron was miserable. He slept on his bed, and Mummy didn't say a thing, even though Mrs Lynch had said, "All right, then, but not on the beds!" Mummy just spread an old rug on top of the bedclothes and shook it out over the balcony every morning.

We went for walks on the riverbank. Cameron didn't

come, but he sometimes took Laddie for an extra walk by himself. One night, long after I'd gone to bed, I woke up to hear Cameron and Mummy talking. He must have got up and gone into the living room where she was writing.

"... Don't tell Lind," he was saying.

"I'm afraid I already have."

"But not why?"

"Of course not, Cam. I wouldn't."

"I don't want anyone to know."

"They won't know from me." Then she said, "Is the music helping at all?"

"A bit," he said.

Cameron, whatever else, never, ever missed his piano lesson. And when I asked him, he told me that the Classics-lovers Club had six members now. It seemed to be all that mattered to him. I asked if I could join, but he said, sorry, it was only for boys.

And then one awful day I came home late after a rehearsal of *Child Wonder* and met Mummy coming along Eleventh Street to meet me. She looked as if a giant leech had sucked all her blood.

"Cameron's run away," she said.

It felt as though my heart stopped. But not from surprise.

He'd left a note.

Dear Auntie Alex, I'm very sorry but I can't stand it. I have to try to get home. Please don't worry. I'll be fine. I'm sure I can get on a ship. I'm sorry I've been a trouble to you. Love Cameron. PS Did Mum tell you Bubbles is ill?

"Of course Bubbles would have been the last straw. Poor, poor Cameron! Oh, but he's crazy! He's so clever, he's so *clever*, and yet he thinks he can do a thing like this! Oh God, oh God, what am I going to tell Millie?"

I was so upset – and so furious with Cameron – I could hardly choke out words.

"Nothing," I said. "How can you? By the time you could write to her it'll all be over, he'll be back. Besides, it's *her fault*. How could she tell him about Bubbles *too*? And if she and Uncle Jack hadn't decided to get divorced he wouldn't have dreamt of doing this!"

"That's not true," Mummy said, puffing on her cigarette as if she was drowning and gasping for air. "He's never been happy here from the very beginning. He's *always* had it in his head to go back. I know he has. I just didn't think he'd be *stupid* enough not to realise he can't." And she burst into tears.

I put my arms around her. I didn't know what to say.

★

Mummy needed a grown-up to help her decide what to do, and I knew this had to be O'F.

I'd got a bit of a shock when we first went to visit him after the lake. He looked older somehow. And frailer. But he was still himself, kind and sweet as ever, sitting in his little flat puffing his pipe, petting Laddie, and telling us he'd missed us.

Now when Mummy and I rushed round to consult him he put the pipe down and roved about the sitting room.

"Where would he go?" he asked. "Where would Matt have gone? This is Matt all over again!"

"Who's Matt?" we asked.

"Matt was my baby brother. The youngest in our family — fifteen years younger than me. He ran away to sea when he was fifteen. Not the navy, the merchant navy. They take them very young. But not as young as Cameron! Oh, poor boy. He must have been desperate. His need to go home knocked all the sense right out of his head."

"What am I to do? We must find him!"

"Well. He can't get far without money. Has he any money?"

"No. He spends every penny he gets on his piano lessons."

"Then he'll have to hitchhike."

Mummy stared at him in horror.

"Now, Alex, my dear, don't get too upset. Everyone hitchhikes in Canada, and there's every hope that some sensible driver will find out what he's up to and will march him into the nearest police station. If you take my advice you'll stay close to the telephone."

I slept that night. But Mummy clearly didn't; next morning she looked a wreck. No make-up and she'd been smoking and pacing the floor all night.

"I thought he might just change his mind and come home sensibly, but he hasn't. I've got to report him missing."

After she rang the police and they came round and interviewed us, we just had to wait. And waiting was awful. Nothing that had happened to us so far since we arrived in Canada was as bad as this.

I couldn't even tell Willie. It seemed disloyal. So I didn't ring her. So then she rang me and I had to pretend nothing was wrong.

But she guessed.

"What's eating you? You sound funny," she said.

"Cameron's gone and it's my fault!" I burst out.

To Willie and Willie alone I poured out my guilt.

"I had this quarrel with him when we were at the lake! He said he wanted to go home and I said 'Go on then!' I was as good as egging him on to go!"

"But it's lover boy's fault too. That great dumbo should never have let the idea into his head, even as a joke, that he could get on a ship."

"I know. But now he's gone and we don't know where he is and we don't know what to do, and I miss him, Willie, I miss him so much!"

I started crying. Willie let me cry for a bit and then she said, "Phone Dumbo."

"What? No!"

"Yes, you should. He's in the navy. And he's a man. And he loves your mum and probably you two too. And you're right, it's partly his fault. Tell him."

"I don't know how to phone him!"

"Your mum has his number written down somewhere."

This idea, of phoning Hank, that I'd never have dreamt of doing, got into my head and pushed me to do it. I should have just suggested it to Mummy but I still didn't want her talking to him. Instead I looked up his number in Regina in her address book, and next time she went out shopping for food, I phoned him.

It took so long for him to be called to the phone I nearly hung up. But at last – just as I was going to – I heard his voice.

"Alex?" He sounded as if he knew already.

"No, it's Lindy."

"Lindy! What's happened? Why are you ringing?"

"Cameron's run away."

"*What are you telling me?*"

"He wants to try to get back to England. He thinks he can get on a ship somehow. You put that in his head."

There was a long silence. Then he said, "Did he take any money?"

"He didn't have any."

"Yes he did," Hank said. "I gave him a hundred dollars."

"What? Why?"

"I thought it would be to help your mom and you. The man of the house – you know. It – it was my way of helping you without – well – embarrassing your mother. Oh, Jesus. I shouldn't have. I'm sorry. Let me talk to Alex."

As soon as she got home, I confessed. I told her what Hank had said.

"Oh, that generous *idiot*! We must tell the police about this. He won't have had to hitchhike. He could have got a train straight to Montreal. Would they let him travel, three days, a boy of twelve alone? The police in Montreal must be told—"

"Will they find him? They must find him!"

She sat down and drew me close to her.

"Lindy, you love him, don't you?"

"More than anyone, except you and Daddy."

"Do you think – you could send him… thoughts – to make him get in touch with us? Make him come back?"

I shivered. Mummy had once told me she was psychic. But talk like that made me feel all spooky.

"But I love him more than he loves me," I said. "Wouldn't he have to love me more, for that to work?"

She let me go. "He does love you, he just doesn't know how to show it," she said. "But could you try it?"

I tried. I sat with my head pressed between my hands so hard I trembled, and I sent come-back thoughts with all my might. I didn't think it could do any more good than praying, but still, after that I did pray. I prayed to St Barnabas.

> *Oh, St Barnabas, be my speed*
> *And come to me in my hour of need!*
> *Cameron's gone, he's left his room,*
> *Him being missing is a doom.*
> *He's trying to get home to Cheltenham,*
> *To be in England with his mum.*
> *But that's impossible and dangerous, too,*
> *So find him and send him back, I beg of you!*

I stopped. This was all in my head, of course. I suddenly wanted Cameron more than I had until now. I wanted to tell him my prayer and have him say, "Yes, that's good, only that last line doesn't scan." Through the lump in my throat, I added, out loud:

"If you do this one great boon,
I'll ask no more neither late nor soon.
Oh, St Barnabas be my speed
And come to me in my hour of need!"

Then I cried my eyes out. How could he do this to us?
How could he?

Chapter Twenty-seven

Cameron's Adventure

Cameron was quite a secretive boy, and he's a secretive man right to this day. He never sat down and told us the full story of what happened while he was making his run for home. Just the bare bones, we got.

But across the years since then, little dribs and drabs of the story have come out. Auntie Millie told us some of it after the war. Someone else told us more. And as Cameron and I grew up, sometimes, just sometimes, when we were together (which wasn't all that often, till recently) I would ask him careless-sounding questions. Little questions, like "Didn't anyone try to stop you buying a ticket, that time?" or "Did you talk to anyone, on the train?" or, once, when he was a little bit drunk, "Did you feel me willing you to come back?"

And little by little I've pieced it together. Of course, I have to cheat a little, because I wasn't there, and some of it I've had to guess or imagine. It's Cameron's story. But when I asked him, the last time I saw him, "Do you want to write it? You should, you really should – it's your story," he said, "No. You write it. I give it to you. Just please don't make me sound like all kinds of a damn fool."

So. The day he ran away, he took with him only the bare necessities in a small suitcase. And Hank's hundred dollars. *And* fifty dollars it turned out he'd borrowed from Mr Gustin, and another twenty-five from Leo. How many of us there were who felt guilty about having helped, or encouraged, Cameron to make his run! I thought Mummy was the only one who didn't need to feel it was her fault, but she did anyway, because of the row she'd had with him at the lake. She thought maybe it was true that she didn't look after him properly.

He took a streetcar to the train station and went to the ticket office.

"One-way juvenile ticket to Montreal," he said in his best English accent.

"Are you travelling unaccompanied?" asked the man.

"Yes," he said, and then, using what he'd been practising, "I'm going to visit my grandmother."

"No school?" the man said suspiciously.

Cameron thought the whole thing was coming to an end right there. But he was inventive.

"She's ill and she's asked for me. I've got permission."

"So what's with the one-way? Ain't ya comin' back?"

"I've only enough money for one way. When I get there someone will give me the money to make the return journey."

On the train he prepared for the long, long journey. He'd cleared the first jump but his legs hadn't stopped shaking, and they didn't, for hours. He'd brought *England, Their England*, for company, but he couldn't read it. He told me how he stared at the lines of print (he knew whole chunks of it by heart) and they danced before his eyes and he couldn't take in a word.

There was an elderly man sitting opposite him who kept staring at him. Cameron felt like a criminal being watched by a policeman. He became more and more nervous. He began to fiddle in his suitcase. He brought out a pair of socks.

"Cold feet?" asked the man with a smile.

Cold feet was exactly what Cameron had. But he said, "Just wanted to make sure I'd packed them."

"Where are you bound for?"

"Montreal."

"That's a heck of a long way for a kid to be travelling on his own."

"I suppose so," said Cameron in his 'cool' voice. "I've done it before. I'm going to visit my grandmother."

The man didn't ask him any more questions, but passed a few remarks about the scenery and then they both went back to their reading.

The ticket collector came along as the sun was going down. He looked from Cameron's ticket to him and back again. Cameron tried to look calm and casual, but he was panicking inside. There was a long silence. Then suddenly the elderly man said, "It's all right, he's with me."

"Is that right, son?" said the man. He didn't sound too sure, but when Cameron nodded, he punched the ticket and left.

Cameron sat staring at his 'saviour'.

"Why did you say that?" he asked.

"I ran away from home myself, a long, long time ago," the man said.

Cameron waited for him to start asking him questions, but the only one he asked was, "D'you mind if I smoke?" Cameron shook his head. The man went back to his newspaper.

The next day, travelling through Manitoba, Cameron was the one asking questions.

The elderly man's name was Jacob Johnston. Oddly, he didn't ask Cameron's name. He said he was going to Montreal to meet someone. Someone coming from England.

"Someone a bit like you," he said.

"Like me?"

"Well, you're from England, aren't you. Probably an evacuee."

It wasn't a question so Cameron didn't answer it.

"And so is he."

"Is he a relation?"

"Yes."

After another two or three hours, loneliness made Cameron try again.

"Why did you run away?"

"It doesn't matter. But it matters why you are. No," he said, "please don't tell me. I don't want to know."

"But why did you help me?"

"I just thought I would. Someone helped me once. Not too much. Just enough."

After several hours more, Cameron said, "Aren't you going to tell me I ought to go back?"

"No."

"Why not?" Cameron asked, almost desperately. By

this time – nearly twenty-four hours since he'd left us, twenty-four lonely, frightened hours – he wanted to be told to go back. He wanted to be forced to. He didn't want to give up, but he wanted somebody to take him over.

But the man wouldn't interfere. What he said was, "You look like a smart boy. There's only one person who can tell you to go back."

Cameron's ticket didn't give him proper meals or a proper bed. He couldn't help hoping that Jacob Johnston would be another Hank, and might offer to pay for a meal for him, but he didn't. At mealtimes he folded his newspaper and put out his cigarette and left the carriage, coming back to his seat after half an hour, looking well fed. Cameron went down to the observation car and bought peanuts and an occasional sandwich, and sat outside watching the countryside unroll. He found he could read now and that helped. He was rereading, for the dozenth time, *England, Their England*.

Back in their carriage, he had short conversations with Jacob Johnston.

"How old is your relative that's coming?"

"He's nearly nine."

"Is he coming alone?"

"Supervised, but basically, yes."

"I came with my aunt and my cousin."

"Did you? Lucky for you."

Cameron thought this kid didn't know what was ahead of him. No auntie or cousin to keep him company. Just this strange, hard-to-talk-to old man.

Poor little beggar, he thought. *I'm glad I'm not him, anyway.*

By the time he reached Montreal he was dirty, hungry and very tired. Cameron was a very clean boy and he liked things to be regular and so he was thoroughly uncomfortable in about five different ways. One was fear. What would he do now?

He said goodbye to Jacob Johnston as they were leaving the train. The man put out his hand and Cameron shook it.

"Good luck, son," he said. And then, just as he was going, he suddenly seemed to remember something. He put down his case and felt in his breast pocket for his wallet. He took a card out of it.

"This is my hotel in Montreal," he said, and gave it to Cameron. "I'll be there for three nights." Then he left.

Cameron picked up his own case and left the station. He followed close behind Mr Johnston. He didn't want to part from him. He was scared and very unhappy. I'd like to think that was partly because he'd been receiving my come-back thought-messages and blanking them. But when I asked him about that, sixty years later, he said, "All I remember thinking was that the police would be looking for me."

He knew how worried Mummy would be. Not to mention me. So I don't care what he remembers now. I'm *sure* his conscience must've been beating him up. But one of his favourite expressions was, "The die is cast," meaning that it was too late to change anything. He kept saying it to himself over and over, as he found the right transport to take him to the docks.

He did tell me about that.

Docks – any big docks – are scary places for a child alone. The ships looming up beside the quays, vehicles driving about where there are no real roads, big cranes loading, loudspeaker messages booming out, great sheds alongside the quays – and, although there were lots of hurrying people, nobody to ask.

Cameron was so hungry after three days of eating from the observation car buffet that he blew three of his precious dollars on a hamburger and fries. And a cup of coffee (his first – Mummy didn't think kids should drink coffee) to wake him up.

He'd made his plan. He knew troopships and liners

weren't carrying civilians back across the Atlantic, so big ships were hopeless. He had to find out where the smaller, merchant boats docked. But the sheer *size* of the place nearly beat him.

At last, after wandering about for hours, with his suitcase getting heavier and heavier, he found what he was looking for: small ships that didn't look so huge and forbidding. They looked, in fact, rather ramshackle and shabby, and the men on and around them were shabby to match. No smart naval uniforms for them! They just looked like men of the sea, working men. The sight of them did nothing to change Cameron's mind about joining the regular navy. But he needed these men now.

He stood beside one of the boats, staring. He was wishing he were six inches taller with a bit of a beard, willing the sailors to be very short-sighted. Useless… He knew he looked like what he was: a boy too young to go to sea.

It wasn't long before he caught the eye of one of the seamen.

"Hey, you − lad. What arta hanging round for?" this burly man shouted down at him from the foredeck.

Cameron had already seen the name of the boat and its home port painted on the back. It was a British ship out of Hull.

He knew that lies weren't going to help.

"Are you the captain?"

"Say I am."

"Do you need anyone? I want to get home," he heard himself say.

Just as he'd half expected, the man threw back his head and roared with laughter.

"Not on my ship, tha won't, tha soft tyke! Go suck thy mam's titty!"

Cameron didn't flinch. "I'm too old to do that. Couldn't I work my way? I'm strong and I know the parts of a ship. I won't eat much. I can sleep anywhere. Just take me with you. I can pay."

"Oh cansta? Eh, tha's a caution and no mistake! Right. Two hundred pounds. Cash in hand!" And he sprinted down the gangway and held out a horny hand as if to take the money.

"I've only got fifty-one dollars," Cameron said. "But you can have that."

"Byyyy… Didsta think I meant it? Doosta know what's going on out there?" He pointed east, towards the ocean. "I heard there were a lad only fifteen drowned with his ship last month. Reginald his name was… At my age I take my chances, but I'm not goin' down knowing I took a lad wi' me no older than my youngest." He straightened up. "Any road, tha'd be no manner of use at home. Stay here and make t'best on it till war's over. Now move off, I've work to do."

Cameron didn't give up. He tried three or four ships. Once he was invited on board and allowed to look round. They were sorry for him. Said they understood. He walked about looking and thinking – how could he give them the slip? How could he stow away and stay on board? With the ship and the seamen all around him, the seagulls crying overhead, the smell of the sea in his nose, he felt so near to his goal! He peered down into the open hold and thought of jumping into the deep darkness.

But it was no use. When he'd finished 'the ship's tour' they gave him a couple of biscuits and a cup of cocoa and shooed him back on shore.

By nightfall he was exhausted, disappointed, and desperate for somewhere to sleep.

He drifted back to the main part of the port. He didn't mean to give up yet. He kept thinking of his mother all alone in that big house where he'd grown up, with Bubbles probably dying and his father gone. No servants any more – they'd all gone too. How would she manage, how must she be feeling? (Well, that's what I'd have been thinking.)

As he was passing the first boat, the one where the

captain had teased him and told him he'd be no use at home anyway, something happened.

As he dragged himself past the ship from Hull, someone called down to him. The docks were quieter now and he didn't have to shout. He called quite softly.

"Hey, lad."

Cameron looked up. The same Yorkshireman was standing at the rail of his ship, smoking a short pipe.

"Didst' have any luck?"

Cameron shook his head.

"Tell thee what. Gi' uz the fifty dollars, come back tomorrow afore we sail, and I'll sneak thee aboard."

"But you – you said—"

"Aye. I know. A man can change his mind. Tha'rt a plucky young whelp as'll make a good seaman."

Cameron, as he remembered it, stood stock-still in the shadow of the ship. He put down his case and reached into his inside jacket pocket. With his hand on the money, he hesitated.

"I'll come. I'll pay you then."

"Nay, tha'll pay me now, or never."

"And you'll take me home?"

"Aye."

There was very little light, and Cameron was light-headed from weariness. It seemed like a dream. He didn't believe the man. He'd already decided it couldn't happen.

But maybe it could! Maybe he could get home after all! Just the same, he wasn't going to hand over the money now.

"I'll come back tomorrow!" Cameron called. He picked up his case and with the last of his strength, he ran.

Chapter Twenty-eight

Benjy

Sleeping sitting up in the train was comfortable compared to curling up on a pile of filthy sacks in one of the warehouses. He dropped asleep breathing dust, thinking, *I've done it. I'm going home –* and fell into a dream of being at sea and the long longing, like stretched elastic, getting slacker. But in the middle of the night, someone bent over him and shook him awake. His head reeled with shock.

The night watchman took him by the arm and marched him to the port police post. He said he was a vagrant, a homeless person. This was too much for Cameron.

"I'm not! I just got tired. Look, here's a card. Phone

this hotel and ask for Jacob Johnston. He'll tell you I'm not a vagrant!" he said furiously.

Was Jacob Johnston expecting the call? I think so. I think in his strange, roundabout way, he'd planned it.

It was four o'clock in the morning, but he got dressed and took a taxi and arrived at the police post in half an hour.

"Hi," he said to Cameron. Then he told the lone policeman on duty that he was a friend of "this young man's" and that he would take responsibility for him. If it had been a proper, city police station, they'd probably have had Cameron's name on some list as a missing person, but this was just a little port-post and the man on duty only wanted to be shot of him. When Cameron said he knew Mr Johnston, the policeman let him take him off their hands.

There was a spare bed in Mr Johnston's hotel room. Cameron had his first bath in three days, crawled, clean and full of a room-service hot dog, between cool sheets, and slept as if he'd never wake up.

Early in the morning Mr Johnston brought him a cup of coffee (his second ever, and his first black) and said, "Get up now. We've got things to do."

They ate an enormous breakfast in the hotel dining room. Cameron still had his money, and he tried to pay for himself, but Mr Johnston said, "No. I've watched you go hungry long enough. This is on me."

"Why didn't you offer before?" Cameron asked curiously.

"Was I supposed to help you run away? You had some lessons to learn."

"Did you go hungry, when you ran away?"

"I ran away without a penny in my pocket."

"Well, I still have fifty-one dollars, and a captain told me he'd take me home for that."

Mr Johnston stared at him.

"Do you believe him?"

"I don't know. I need to go back to the docks."

"Good, because that's where I'm going."

Then Cameron remembered.

"Are you going to meet your relative?"

"Yes. His ship will have docked by now."

"What's his name?"

"Benjy. I want you two to meet. And for that, I'd better break down and ask what your name is."

Cameron told him. He was going to ask why Mr Johnston hadn't asked before. But he had a sort of idea of the answer. He couldn't put it into words, though.

The cab left them at the quay where a huge liner, as big as the *Duchess of Atholl* that we'd sailed in on our trip to Canada, was tied up. The gangway was let down and people started leaving the ship. There were a lot of children. Mr Johnston and Cameron stood together, watching. Suddenly Mr Johnston, who'd always seemed so distant, did a funny thing. He put his arm around Cameron's shoulders.

"Be nice to him," he said. Then he squeezed and let go.

After a long time of waiting, with the sun beating down, Mr Johnston stiffened, rose on tiptoe, and jerked his arm up in a wave.

"There he is!" he said in a voice Cameron hardly recognised, it was so excited.

At the top of the gangway Cameron saw a small boy wearing school shorts and a blazer. There was a woman behind him with her hand on his shoulder, guiding him, or pushing him down ahead of her. He was looking all around, over the rail, which he was only just tall enough to see over.

Suddenly he spotted Mr Johnston. He stopped still, half blocking the gangway, and waved both arms. He looked wildly happy – and relieved, Cameron thought. And, watching Mr Johnston waving just as wildly, he had an intuition.

"He's your grandson, isn't he?"

"Yes! Yes!" Mr Johnston started forward, through the crowd. "Come on! You must meet him! Benjy! Hallo! Hallo!"

They met at the bottom of the gangway. The woman smiled. She looked relieved too.

"Here's your grandpa, Benjamin." But Benjy was already throwing his arms around Mr Johnston's waist. "He's been no trouble at all. And no seasickness, eh, Ben? Such a good little sailor!" Then she bent forward over the boy's head, and whispered, "A bit of homesickness of course. As you'd expect."

Cameron was looking down at the boy's head. His face was buried in his grandfather's stomach. His shoulders were trembling.

"A bit of homesickness." Yes. You would expect that. That, and more – and worse.

Of course Cameron would never admit it, but *I* believe – I'm sure – that a wave of sympathy for this boy washed over him. No, not sympathy – *empathy,* sharing his feelings. He'd left *everyone* behind. He didn't know why or for how long or anything. 'Poor little beggar' was too weak for what he was.

In this whole story, how often has Cameron cried? Only a few times – not like me. But I think his throat filled up when he felt for Benjy. Because he did something

I wouldn't have expected, and I know this because we learnt it from Benjy himself, years later. He came out of his shell.

He stooped down beside the boy and said to him, "Hallo, Benjy, I'm Cameron. I'm English too. I'm an evacuee too."

Mr Johnston gently unfastened Benjy's arms from around his waist and turned Benjy towards Cameron. He didn't bother introducing them.

"Come on, boys," he said. "Let's go get something to eat while we wait for the luggage."

Of course, food's wonderful. While they tucked into toasted ham sandwiches and chocolate milkshakes, Mr Johnston kept very quiet. He just leant back in his chair, sipped a coffee, and let Cameron do the talking.

First he found out that Benjy came from the East End of London. Cameron knew there'd been a lot of bombing there, and he asked Benjy a bit about it, but when he could see he didn't want to talk about the bombs, Cameron talked about himself.

"When I first arrived I felt as if I'd left everything important behind," he said, man to man to Benjy across the café table. "And I had, in a way. But you know what – however difficult it is here, it's a kind of war work, when you think about it. Your mum and dad won't have to be worried about you, especially if you write to them regularly and tell them you're OK."

"But what if I'm not?" asked Benjy in a muffled voice.

"You will be. Your granddad's here and he'll look after you, won't you?"

Mr Johnston was nodding steadily. "I will."

"And if you're a bit miserable sometimes, which you will be because of being homesick, you must think of *positive* things to tell them. I write to my mother every week and in between I make notes of funny things to tell her, to cheer her up. Because our mothers miss us as much as we miss them. Sorry. Don't blub. Look. I'm going to give you something." He opened his suitcase which was on the floor beside him. "Here's my favourite book. It's all about England, and it's very funny. I've had it since I was nine, and I still love it. It's yours now. It'll remind you of England, but in a good way. You do read?"

Benjy wiped his nose on his sleeve and nodded.

"Good. I'm going to write in it."

Mr Johnston produced a pen as if by magic.

"I'm going to write, *To Benjy from Cameron, a fellow evacuee. Good luck and keep your chin up.*" He wrote the message and closed the book. He held it for a moment as if saying goodbye to it and then handed it solemnly to Benjy, who took it and looked at it, his head bent.

"Thanks," he said. "You're ever so kind."

"And so say all of us," murmured Mr Johnston.

After the meal, Cameron stood up, closed his suitcase and put on his jacket. Then he said, "Can we telephone my aunt now?"

"What?" said Mr Johnston. "But you're getting on a boat and going back home, aren't you?"

"No," said Cameron. "I've changed my mind."

They found a phone box in the docks. Mr Johnston gave Cameron some change, and that's when our ordeal-by-Cameron ended. The phone rang in our flat and I answered it, and it was him, and he said, "Hallo, Lind, it's your stupid cuzz. Please tell Auntie Alex I'm very sorry and I'm on my way back." Then he handed the phone to Mr Johnston while I screamed for Mummy, and they had a short conversation mainly about money. (When she hung up, Mummy said, "Another angelic Canadian. Did the original settlers *fly here*, do you think?" Then she burst into tears, went downstairs, and asked Mr Lynch if he had any brandy.)

Meanwhile Cameron was having a last, short talk with Mr Johnston.

"You said I was a smart boy, but I think you're a very clever man."

"Me? Nonsense. I've been practically an idiot all my life."

"Since you ran away, you mean. Did you go back?"

"No. I couldn't. I had nothing worth going back to."

"Well, I have. I thought I was a deserter from England but I won't desert again. Thank you."

"You'd have got there without me."

Cameron said quietly, "Maybe. But not without Benjy."

Postscript

S o Cameron came back to us.

There was a big blazing row and then we forgave him because we were so happy and relieved. Since you couldn't do telephone calls or telegrams to England in the war, and since running away was not one of the funny things he wanted to put in his letters, Auntie Millie never got wind of it until he told her when he got home. Of course she forgave him too, because he'd done it mostly for her.

Benjy kept in touch with him and that was a friendship that lasted for life.

And meanwhile, we three went on with our war work.

We somehow lived through the four more years (two of them without O'F) we had to go before the war in Europe ended in 1945, and we sailed back home to Daddy. We never had much money (and I never got my saddle shoes) but we managed.

Hank stayed on the edge of our lives and stopped worrying the wits out of me because I could see he knew his love was a hopeless passion (as Willie said).

We had some good times and some bad times, and Cameron and I shared them, and became teenagers together. After his adventure he was not so shut in and we got close (sometimes) because, after all, we were the nearest to a brother or sister that we each had. And that's still true.

The day in December when I was woken up by the newsboy running down Eleventh Street shouting that the Americans had joined the war, was the day I stopped for good and all, not being interested in the news.

We had more wonderful summers at Emma Lake.

Cameron kept up with his music and Mummy did more plays and more pageants and I won an acting prize playing another mother. Mummy made my hair look white with greasepaint and then we had to use kerosene to get it off, and we both passed out from the fumes, and that was just one little, funny thing out of all the big and small things that I remember.

And I can still sing the Canadian national anthem, and I do, when I'm remembering (and nobody's listening):

"O Canada!
Our home and native land!
True patriot love
In all thy sons command!
With glowing hearts we see thee rise,
The true north, strong and free,
And stand on guard, O Canada!
We stand on guard for thee!
O Canada!
Glorious and free!
O Canada, we stand on guard for thee!
O Canada, we stand on guard for thee!"

And it always, always makes me cry.

The End

Post Postscript

Bubbles was still alive when we got home.